"Look," Kayla started, choosing her words carefully, *"I won't press charges if you take me back...."*

Jase gave no reply, just a slow shake of his head.

"You can't expect to get away with this. You have to take me back right now!"

"Trust me, Kayla. You're not leaving here and neither am I—for two weeks."

She fought the tears. "Please don't hurt me," she pleaded. "Please."

Hurt her? She really didn't know who he was! "Kayla, that's the last thing I would ever do. You're in danger. I'm here to protect you...."

Dear Reader,

You enjoyed new author Kimberly Raye's first foray
into the shadows, *'Til We Meet Again,* and now she's
back with *Now and Forever.* It's another spooky but
sensuous novel, featuring a hero and heroine who were
promised to each other as husband and wife—but who
may also be each other's destruction. Read it with the
lights on.

And next month return for the exciting final volume of
Evelyn Vaughn's four-book miniseries, THE CIRCLE.
I think you'll find *Forest of the Night* a conclusion well
worth waiting for.

Enjoy!

Leslie Wainger
Senior Editor and Editorial Coordinator

Please address questions and book requests to:
Silhouette Reader Service
U.S.: 3010 Walden Ave., P.O. Box 1325, Buffalo, NY 14269
Canadian: P.O. Box 609, Fort Erie, Ont. L2A 5X3

KIMBERLY RAYE

Now and Forever

Published by Silhouette Books
America's Publisher of Contemporary Romance

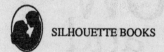 **SILHOUETTE BOOKS**

ISBN 0-373-27065-8

NOW AND FOREVER

Books by Kimberly Raye

Silhouette Shadows

'Til We Meet Again #60
Now and Forever #65

KIMBERLY RAYE

has always been fascinated by the supernatural, including ghosts, vampires, demons and other creatures of the night. She loves writing a story that frightens, yet thrills. Likewise, she enjoys creating a hero so dark and dangerous that the heroine doesn't know whether to fall in love with him or run for her life.

Kimberly lives in Pasadena, Texas, with her own dark hero and husband of five years, Joe. She loves to hear from readers and invites you to write her at: P.O. Box 1584, Pasadena, Texas, 77501-1584.

For my sister, Denise,
whose unfaltering love led me through the darkness
many, many times when I couldn't find my own way.
All my thanks and love.

And, as always, for Joe,
who shows me the miracle of life and love firsthand.

PROLOGUE

And beneath the full moon,
The night creatures dance.
They move to an ancient rhythm,
Their voices joining in tempo.
As they summon one of their own,
Home, lost one. Home...

The low chant filled the night, echoing the secrets of evil in a ritual as old as Time itself. The black-robed figures gathered around the blaze, caged the fire and worshiped the power before them. In response, the flames crackled, licking the surrounding blackness, tasting it.

The chanting continued. Louder. Louder.

One figure broke from the circle to step forward. The flames cast flickering shadows on the folds of his robe, the light catching the medallion that dangled from his neck. He threw back his hood, revealing hair as silvery white as the moon above. His eyes gleamed, intense and brilliant like the blaze itself.

"*Ashtaroth*, we call you...your power..." The name echoed around him.

Ashtaroth.

Ashtaroth.

He yanked the medallion from his neck, placed a kiss on the silver moonstar and dropped it into the ceremonial chalice.

"The blood is the power," he said. Next, he dipped his hand into the chalice. Liquid heat enveloped his fingers, the smell of sacrificial blood pungent in the air. "She must return to us."

Withdrawing his hand, he stared at his fingers, which glistened crimson in the firelight. With a flick of his wrist, he sprinkled several drops into the flames. "It's time, Kayla," he whispered to the night. "Time to come home."

The fire hissed and popped, devouring the lifeblood. The flames surged higher, begged for more sustenance, promised life in return for another sweet taste.

Twice more he answered the greedy call, making a call of his own. "Home, Kayla. The darkness awaits. You must come."

And in turn, the blaze grew hotter, the flames more frenzied. Sparks showered against the night sky. The fire breathed the air, surged with a life and power all its own.

The chanting resumed, rising to a deafening pitch.

He tilted his head back, his aging body rigid, arms wide, hands outstretched. Fiery fingers reached from the blaze and embraced him.

You shall have the power, my faithful servant, the night whispered. *Power to sustain your craving, feed your soul... My power.*

An invisible hand swooped down and the flames died. The ashes stirred and scattered with a furious gust of wind. Then darkness closed in. He felt the power surge through his body and bring his rapidly fading life back to him for a precious few moments. Soon, he would cease to feel altogether. Death would come. But not yet. He still had two weeks.

Hurry! his mind cried. *Hurry, Kayla.*

The darkness would bring her back to them. They'd already found her, eliminated the obstacles keeping her from them. At the blackest moments, they taught her their ways. Soon, once she understood her destiny, she would accept them.

Kayla... one of their own... a Keeper.

CHAPTER ONE

"It's midnight on a Friday night, and I'll be keeping you company until dawn. You're tuned into KCSS, home of Houston's classic rock favorites. I'm the night child and here's one off the request line going out to Janie from Tim."

Kayla slid the lever on the mixing board and a haunting rock ballad filled the control room. Only a single lamp burned above the console where she sat, the hallway outside the studio a gathering of inky black shadows now that the cleaning people had gone home. Moonlight streamed through the twentieth-floor windows surrounding her. Pinpoints of colored lights pulsed with the music, giving the sound equipment a vitality all its own.

Kayla felt the room breathe around her, alive with sound, with the beat that thrummed through her and forced her heart to pound faster. There was a time when she would have relished the feeling. Thrived on it, in fact. But no more.

Now, she sipped a cup of black coffee and turned the lamp a notch brighter, eager to dispel the darkness. A shiver eased up her spine and a cold fist settled in her chest. Loneliness. Grief. She felt them both now.

And fear...

Fear of being alone. Fear of the darkness she felt drawn to, tied to in some inexplicable way that haunted the farthest corners of her mind. And fear of the blackouts that she'd been having all too frequently lately.

She gulped down the bitter black coffee and poured herself another cup. Tears brimmed in her eyes, but she fought them back as hard as she could. She'd cried too much already over the past two weeks. Way too much.

Thumbing through the night's format, she tried to swallow the lump in her throat. No tears, she told herself again. They came, anyway, squeezing past her lashes, weaving hot trails down her cheeks. She popped a digital cartridge into the player and cued the next song.

"...fly with me to another time and place," she tried to sing the slow tune, to get her mind off Gramps, how much she missed him, how betrayed she felt, tried to simply keep her mind focused. She couldn't have a blackout on the air.

The words of the song seemed to muffle, and she reached for the volume adjustment on her headset. Kayla turned the knob higher, but the music still faded.

Static hummed in her ears and she froze. She knew what came next, even before she heard the familiar masculine voice.

"Don't cry, Kayla." The words were a soft, unnerving rumble.

"Who are you?" she demanded, snatching the plug from the console. Still, his voice stole through her ears, drifted through her thoughts.

"Someone who doesn't like to hear you cry. Someone who fears for you, and feels you, Kayla."

"This is impossible," she whispered, staring at the disconnected plug. But it *was* possible. She'd ripped out the plug last night when his voice had first come to her. Still, she'd heard him loud and clear over her headset, like tonight.

"Nothing is impossible, Kayla. Believe in me and what I have to tell you."

"Listen here, buddy," she said, a rush of fear feeding her courage. "I don't know how you've managed to tune in to this station's frequency, but you'd better stop. You're breaking major FCC regulations. I'll report you—''

''You won't,'' he said, his voice low, self-assured. And he was right. The entire station would think she'd gone loco, and, at the moment, she was half tempted to agree. Nobody was breaking into her transmission. Only into her headset. Her *unplugged* headset.

A delusion, she thought. Maybe the voice was a sick, crazed delusion brought on by her grief and the desperate need to communicate with someone the way she had with her father and Gramps. A real person couldn't tap into her headset.

Kayla gave herself a mental shake. The voice *was* real, and she wasn't going crazy. Somehow he'd tapped into her headset. Maybe he'd used a transmitting device implanted in the earphones.

She'd seen such things before, like the time back in college when some guy from one of the dorms had broken into the campus station's frequency with a homemade radio and antennae.

''I'm very real, Kayla,'' he said, confirming her thoughts. ''Don't be afraid of me.''

''I—I'm not,'' she replied, though her lips quivered with each word.

''You can't hide your fear from me. I feel it, like I feel you, and I can feel the loneliness, too. But they feel you, too, Kayla. And they're coming.''

They're coming. Her blood ran cold. Her hands trembled.

''Who's coming?'' she managed to say, all the while wondering why she was humoring this obvious nut case. Maybe because he didn't sound like a nut case, or *feel* like one. And Kayla had always been one to trust her feelings, the way her father and Gramps had taught her.

He paused, the steady sound of his breathing her only indication that he was still there. Then he spoke, his voice taking on a desperate note. "Be careful, Kayla. They'll swallow you alive, and you won't even know it until it's too late. That's what they do. They feed on your soul until there's nothing left. But you're strong. You can resist them if you want to."

"Tell me your name," she urged, the torment in his voice sparking a pang of sympathy. He sounded so lost, so lonely. And Kayla knew loneliness all too well. "I'll call someone and get you some help—"

"*Listen!*" he suddenly growled. "You have to *listen* to me. Be warned, Kayla. Be strong. Go away from here— far, far away. The distance will strengthen you." His words rang with a conviction that was unnerving.

"Who are you and why are you telling me this?" she asked. If she could find out something about him, hear his thoughts, see his demons, she might be able to help him. She'd never been one to turn her back on someone in trouble, and she'd dealt with overzealous fans before. Most were merely looking for someone to talk to.

"I'm your greatest hope," he replied, his words sending a shudder through her and scattering her good intentions. "And the darkest part of you, Kayla. I'm locked inside your thoughts, lost in your memories . . . a *real* part of you. I feel your fear getting stronger every day. I can feel them, too. They're getting closer."

"*Who?*" she demanded. The headset fell silent and she wondered if he would answer. Oddly enough, she wanted him to answer. As much as she tried to believe he was some psychotic creep, something about his voice, his words, the way he seemed conscious of her every thought, hinted that he was sincere. "*Please . . .* tell me who is coming."

"I want to tell you. I wish I could." He paused. "But I can't. Trust me, Kayla. Believe," came his reply. Then silence, and he was gone.

"Blast it!" she cursed, yanking off the headset. She flung it at the control panel and clasped her hands together to stifle the shaking. The music blared from the studio speakers, vibrated the console and sent the headset sliding to the floor.

"Maybe I am losing my mind," she mumbled, burying her face in her hands. Why else would she hear voices? No, not voices, just one voice. The same voice she'd heard last night when she'd put on the headset.

"Gramps," she whispered. But she knew there would be no answer. No familiar warmth spreading through her insides, letting her know she wasn't alone. No soothing voice in her head. She couldn't talk to him in their special way, using her mind, her feelings.

Her father had called it *connecting*—a way of feeling someone so strongly, sensing their every emotion as deeply as your own, until their thoughts became yours. All she felt now was cold. Gramps was gone.

"I haven't got much time left, Kaylie," he'd told her. "You remember your Gramps. Remember how much I love you. My old heart's wearing out fast, but my spirit will always be here, the same as your daddy's, even when my body's turned to dust."

"But I can't feel Daddy anymore, Gramps. When he died, the feeling stopped. He's too far away now."

"No," he'd said, shaking his head. "You try hard enough, and you can feel him. He wouldn't leave you, Kaylie. You were his baby girl. Suffered through a lot for you, he did."

"But I can't, Gramps." And she'd been telling him the truth. When her father had died, she'd tried desperately to connect with him—her efforts wasted. She'd known it would be the same with Gramps, no matter that he'd insisted otherwise.

"I won't ever leave you, Kaylie, and that's a promise." A promise that had been broken.

She'd watched them lower him into the ground, never feeling more lost in her entire twenty-seven years. Now she was alone. Desperately, miserably alone, and betrayed. Gramps hadn't only left her. He'd lied to her, as well.

An image flashed in her mind—fiery red hair, pale skin, a warm smile—the mother she'd never known, who had *supposedly* passed away while giving birth to Kayla. But Kayla had seen the pictures of the beautiful woman and the bright-eyed toddler—her and her mother. Kayla couldn't have been more than four years old, and her mother had been very much alive. Maybe she still was.

Her father and Gramps had lied to her about her mother's death. For some reason, they had kept her past from her—a past she intended to uncover. She'd made an appointment with the clerk at city hall. Her first order of business was to find some record of her birth, not the forged documents she'd found in Gramps's safe-deposit box. If she could uncover the woman's name, maybe she could find out what had happened to her. In the process, Kayla intended to discover herself, reclaim the first five years of her life and know the truth once and for all. The light on the switchboard blinked. She wiped the tears from her cheeks. Clearing her throat, she hit the speaker button. "KCSS," she mumbled, then grabbed her pen to write down the caller's request.

Minutes later, she took a deep breath and turned toward the control panel. With shaky fingers, she cued the next song. The topaz ring on her right hand glittered as the stone caught the EQ lights. The ring was one of the few mementos of Gramps she had left. One of his last gifts to her. The ring meant protection, he'd said without any further explanation. Only it didn't look as if the topaz was doing its job. It hadn't protected her from the voice in her headset.

More tears trailed down her cheeks and splashed onto the console. Maybe she needed to take her boss's advice and see a psychiatrist. What if the voice wasn't real?

No, she reassured herself, the voice was real. A sick individual was crying out for help. *Her* help, and tomorrow night if he contacted her again, she would give it. She would find out his name, no matter how much talking she had to do, no matter how upsetting his words were, and persuade him to seek medical attention.

But she needed help, as well. The blackouts were becoming more frequent. She hadn't had one on the air yet, but she knew it was only a matter of time. Even the gallon or so of coffee she consumed each night wouldn't keep them away.

Already, she was losing consciousness more often, for longer periods of time. She would feel the tingling in her hands, then her arms. Her vision would blur, blacken, then the numbness would set in. After that, she could only guess what happened.

She would wake up minutes, even hours later with no memory of what she'd done or where she'd been. She would find herself in the oddest places—sometimes in her car on a street she didn't recognize or in a store she'd never been to before. One time she even came to in an abandoned church.

A shiver ripped through her. The doors to the church had been locked...*padlocked* from the *outside*. She still hadn't figured out how she'd managed to get inside the sanctuary.

A professional might be able to help her cope with her loss rather than shutting her mind off from it. That's what the blackouts were—an escape mechanism, or so she'd convinced herself. She'd hoped they would stop on their own. But it seemed no matter how she steeled herself against the tingling when it first started, she couldn't shake it. The blackouts always followed, and day by day, her fear of being alone grew stronger.

The voice replayed in her mind, the warning an ominous echo.

They're getting closer. And somewhere, in the back of her mind, a vision of moonsilver eyes flashed. Then darkness came. Cold, frightening darkness and Kayla shuddered.

Jase Terrell leaned over and turned the stereo volume higher. Kayla's silky smooth voice drifted through the living room of his modest apartment near downtown. Near her.

"... clear skies for tonight with a low of forty-six. It's a cold one, folks, but the music's hot on KCSS. I'm Kayla Darland, and here's a little Bob Seger to heat up your night."

He could sense the unease in her voice. She was upset. He could feel her fear reaching out to him, begging for help, for comfort. The feelings were strong tonight. Much stronger than they'd ever been before.

Jase stifled a pang of guilt. Part of Kayla's fear was caused by him, but dammit, he'd had no choice. A phone call might have been easier, less frightening for her, but he was sure she would have hung up on him, dismissing his call as a prank. And she needed to take what he said seriously. That's why he'd contacted her using his mind, his spirit, to warn her and urge her to leave before it was too late.

Still, it was no wonder she didn't believe him. He couldn't even tell her exactly *why* she had to leave, and he certainly couldn't go to her as he wanted—to sit down, take her hands in his and explain. He couldn't reveal the past to her, and seeing her and touching her was much too great a risk to take. No part of the promise could be fulfilled.

The promise... A chill ripped through him, making his flesh tingle.

If only Kayla would heed his warning. She was too close to them ... they were too close to her, and he was all that stood in the middle. And damned, if that wasn't just as dangerous for her.

He stretched out on the black leather sofa and stared up at the ceiling. The dancing pulse from his equalizer flashed red and green patterns on the white sheetrock, dispelling the darkness that surrounded him.

As he always did, Jase touched the silver charm that hung from a matching chain around his neck. He traced the lines of the charm—a circle enclosing a crescent moon and a star. The moon and star overlapped, *connected,* drawn together by the magic circle that made them almost one. The same circle that drew him to her.

He pushed the thought to the farthest corner of his mind. The charm no longer represented their bond. Rather, it protected them from it. The magic of the silver...the tears of the moon...fighting the darkness to give safe refuge to two of its lost children. There was no more circle, no more moon or star. They were free. *Free!*

He almost laughed at the last thought. Freedom was a crazy notion that had never materialized for Jase, though he'd broken all ties to his past. His soul was still prisoner, still linked to another world where darkness ruled. Jase embodied that darkness.

She was his.

He was hers.

He belonged to her, shared her thoughts, felt her as intensely as he felt his own heart pound in his chest, the blood surge through his veins. They'd taken the vows...

But it shouldn't be. Her father and the Old One had sacrificed to see that she knew freedom, that she never realized the death and destruction waiting for her in the darkness with Jase, *if* she should ever remember.

Another had stepped into Jase's rightful place as her consort. Another more evil and more powerful...and now Kayla was to be his. The Keepers needed Kayla. Desperately.

"This song goes out to all of you keeping the night alive," her voice purred. "A fast tune to keep your blood hot and your body warm." A guitar exploded. The equalizer lights danced, and he remembered...

Betrayal. Jase had managed to escape the Keepers, leaving willingly, eager to forsake the darkness. Kayla, however, had been taken away, raised with no memory of the evil that stirred once the sun set.

That's why the Keepers sought her. She had not denied them, as Jase had. And she was the last of her line. Now Kayla had to embrace the darkness and the lover meant for her, to see the dark power live on.

And once a long, long time ago, Jase had been destined to be that lover.

Only the bond had been broken when he'd denounced the darkness. *Broken!*

Damn, but he shouldn't feel such a pull toward her. He wasn't the one... He should turn down the volume, roll over and get some sleep. He had an early shoot in the morning and elite magazines didn't publish mediocre pictures because the photographer hadn't had enough winks the night before.

Jase had learned perfection the hard way, trying to please the endless number of foster parents he'd had while circulating through the child welfare system. He'd never been good enough for any of them. Either too old or too young. His hair too dark. His eyes the wrong color. A boy instead of a girl.

And no one had really wanted a withdrawn twelve-year-old who woke up screaming every night, his sleep plagued by nightmares—memories. Not that he could blame any of those people. Everyone feared the darkness in some way or another, and he'd been a child born and bred in darkness, branded with the blood of innocents and fueled with a demon's power he'd never wanted. A child haunted by his past and frightened by the future.

He'd stopped hoping for a home at fifteen when he'd set out on his own, taking the first job he could find—carrying camera equipment for a hard-nosed photographer who'd paid barely enough for Jase to exist. But he'd learned from the man and had found something he was good at.

Jase had matured and the lessons in perfection had continued. He'd scraped and clawed for every two-bit photography assignment, never using his power to get ahead, afraid that should he allow himself a little taste, he might crave more until he was as tormented as those he'd left behind. Instead, he'd made a name through honest, hard work, and gained his freedom and a means to sustain himself. To stay close to Kayla.

Now, he could no more turn her off than he could stop thinking about her, though he could never, ever have her. Jase wouldn't allow any part of the promise to be fulfilled. The evil had to be contained and extinguished, and soon.

Still, he needed her voice filling his head . . . her image dancing in front of him, warming him when he felt the cold so deep in his soul that a blowtorch couldn't thaw him out.

And how clearly he could see her. Long, silky hair as bright as the most vivid flame, flawless skin like fresh cream, eyes like brilliant topaz. Hell, he could even smell her—a faint hint of perfume and sultry female.

If only that was enough.

If only the darkness inside of him wasn't still so strong, keeping the fires burning for a young child now turned woman. A woman he wanted so badly his entire body ached at the thought. Only lust wasn't the driving force. He might have denounced the darkness long ago at the young age of twelve, but the evil of past centuries still flowed through his veins. An evil that compelled him to take what was his. Each day was a struggle to keep from giving in to the darkness that slowly consumed him.

Kayla had been spared any knowledge of who and what she was. She knew only her fear—of the unknown, of what stalked her in the darkest moments when she blacked out. Jase knew her fear, as well.

However, he also knew the answers. They were buried within him, in his memory, in that soiled part of him masquerading as his soul.

The time had come.

He'd been waiting for it. The years had brought them to the threshold. The Old One's death had opened the door.

Jase glanced at the folded sheet of paper on the edge of the coffee table. The letter had arrived exactly two weeks ago—the day of the Old One's funeral. He'd read the man's familiar scrawl, over and over. He eyed the two keys that sat on top of the envelope next to the letter. In case Jase needed them, the Old One had said. But the keys represented a double-edged sword. Whether he used them or not, blood would surely flow.

With an angry motion, Jase scattered the stack of pictures he'd placed on the table earlier. Several fell over the edge, sailing to the carpet. He snatched up one that landed near him and stared into Kayla's eyes. Then his gaze went to the figures surrounding her . . . drawing closer.

The pictures—tangible proof that the Keepers were near. Vivid reminders they would stop at nothing until they had Kayla.

Jase closed his eyes and rested the snapshot on his chest. She'd been alone when he'd taken the picture, yet when he'd developed it, he'd seen the other faces. The Keepers . . .

And the closer they came, the stronger the connection between Jase and Kayla. He felt her fear, beckoning to him, tearing at his resolve. During the blackouts, the feelings escalated. That's when she was the most frightened, though she remembered nothing afterward. Jase remembered. He lived those darkest moments with her.

Now it wasn't enough for him to simply listen to her at night. He needed more. To see her, touch her. She was his—

No! The word exploded inside his head.

He wasn't the one. No matter how desperate the need for her burned within him or how the darkness whispered otherwise. Despite the damned pictures. He wasn't the one. Not anymore.

He was merely her protector now. A voice to warn her of things to come and hope that she listened and left. Otherwise, she would know the darkness firsthand, become a part of it, just as she was always meant to.

The shadows closed in and the whispers began, as they always did. But tonight, the dreams came, too, reliving Jase's past, feeding the dark hunger for Kayla that already devoured his soul.

Their soul, for Jase and Kayla were one now, no matter that time and circumstance had pushed them apart. The blood had flowed too freely, the vows had been taken, the promise had been made.

Soft cries stirred in his memory. A child's cries.

A young boy materialized in the darkness. The clear moonlight reflected off his raven hair, pooled in his silver eyes. And before him stood the crying child.

He took her hand and knelt before her, oddly touched by her fear, though he would never admit such a thing to his father. That would have angered the man.

He wiped her fragile cheeks with the pads of his thumbs, stared into her eyes and willed her to be strong. When she sniffled and blinked back her tears, he knew she understood. Her small fingers clasped his and she never averted her gazed, as if looking at him could block out the figures drawing closer.

The blackness surrounded them. Then the chanting began.

The Keepers formed a circle, their thick black robes obscuring their identities, making them one with the darkness they worshiped with such devotion.

He felt her fear again, but she made no sound. She tightened her hold on his hand, seeking protection from the evil.

Little did she know that *he* was the evil, or at least a part of it already, for he knew what was about to happen. But still only a child himself, he could do nothing to stop it.

He was forced to bend to the will of an overbearing father intent on continuing the bloodline that made them what they were. A bloodline that gained strength with every generation. Jase and Kayla would prove the ultimate union. They were direct descendants...children of evil...Keepers of the darkness, like their ancestors, yet different, as well. For the Keepers hadn't always wielded a magic as black as the pit from which they drew their power. They had been healers, seers, shamans...but no more.

The glow of the full moon bathed Kayla's tear-streaked face. He got to his feet. At twelve, he towered over the fragile five-year-old who gazed up at him with trust in her eyes. Trust that divided his loyalties and ripped at his soul.

The chanting grew louder, the blackness thicker as the Keepers circled them, their shadows obliterating the moonlight.

Hoods were pulled back, faces revealed. A woman with flowing red hair stood directly behind Kayla.

Jase saw the fear flicker in the woman's dark eyes, but she wouldn't step forward. She was a powerful woman in her own right, but Jase's father wasn't one to be challenged. The black magic ritual was new to the Keepers; they feared it just as they feared Jase's father. Kayla's mother could no more stop what was about to happen than she could fight the demon *Ashtaroth* himself. She knew it. All of the Keepers knew it.

She stood silent, her gaze fixed on her daughter.

The circle split as another figure appeared. Jase watched as his father pulled a crimson-wrapped bundle from the folds of his robe. With long, elegant fingers, he peeled away the velvet to reveal the jeweled handle of a dagger, the blade resting in a gold-stitched sheath inlaid with rubies.

"The quest for power has brought us here." Alexander Terrell's deep voice sliced through the chanting. "To you, *Ashtaroth*. Accept these two souls we promise to you. Embrace them. Fuel them. Two children whose blood is pure and worthy of you. When the time comes, they shall join as lovers, share their dark knowledge and produce a child to house your power—*our* power—a lifetime more."

With one fluid motion, the *athame* was unsheathed, raised in the air. The double blade gleamed with the luster of the moon.

Kayla squeezed Jase's hand tighter, her eyes wide, fear surging through her small body in giant waves that crashed against his senses. This time, she couldn't hold the cry that sprang to her lips. Jase felt his heart wrenched from his chest at the sound. And the urge to keep her safe fired inside of him.

"No, Father!" He raised his free hand to block the descent of the knife.

"Obey!" a voice hissed from behind.

"You can't—" Jase started.

"It must be!" came another voice. Someone caught Jase's arm and twisted it to his back. Pain ripped through his shoulder.

He opened his mouth again. A hand clamped across his lips.

"The power must be secured," his father growled. "You cannot change what must be. You *will* not."

Jase struggled, the hold on his arm becoming more painful. He had only one choice if he wanted to try to stop his father—to let go of Kayla's hand.

She held tight, her only strength coming from him. He knew then that he couldn't let go of her. He couldn't stop the Keepers. There were too many. Yet, he was all that stood between them and Kayla, and he wouldn't let her face them alone. No more divided loyalties. His soul had chosen sides.

Helpless, he watched his father grab Kayla's other arm. Large hands held her steady as the blade sliced a star pattern on her pale skin. She screamed. His fingers tightened around hers while a chalice was held to the cuts.

Then the knife was being raised to him. He forced his eyes open, stifling his own screams as a blaze seared through him where the knife carved his skin in a similar pattern.

He stared at Kayla's face, at the horror in her eyes and not once did he break their silent contact. He willed her to be strong, and in turn found his own strength. Their gazes fused, never wavering, even when his own blood was spilled to join hers.

The promise was made, the blood mingled, the souls joined.

The hoods were replaced. The Keepers resumed their walk, following the Magic Circle with military precision, calling forth the power and paying homage to the demon from whence it came. The chanting rose to an ear-splitting tempo.

Ashtaroth.

Ashtaroth.

CHAPTER TWO

Jase shot straight up, a sofa pillow clenched in his fists, the voices ringing in his ears as if the shrouded figures surrounded him even now. His gaze swept the dark living room. Empty.

A cold sweat bathed his body. He loosened his hold on the pillow and ran a hand across his eyes. The voices grew fainter. Slowly, the stereo became audible again, the music pulling him back to reality.

Yet the dream had been reality...once. A long time ago.

A union of two souls. Denial couldn't erase that fact.

Control had to contain it or he'd never be able to save her. For the Keepers were coming. Two weeks had already passed. Only two more until the full moon and his father's birthday.

The Keepers already had a hold on Kayla through the blackouts. She remembered nothing, her past erased from her conscience long ago by her father and the Old One. Yet the dark creatures came to her when she lost consciousness. They sought control. She was theirs.

But she was still his also. That knowledge burned through him, crumbled the walls he'd erected to contain the beast within.

His...

"Okay, where's the man? Let Uncle Marcky have a look at him."

Kayla glanced up into the smiling face of Marc T. Miles,

friend and disc jockey extraordinaire. "I'm sorry, what did you say?"

"I said where's the man? I know you had one up here. You were stepping on songs all night." He eyed the headphones still sitting on the carpet where they'd fallen the night before. "Probably because those phones were on the floor instead of over your ears, and there's only one thing I take my headset off for." He grinned wickedly. "So where's the man, baby? I won't tell."

"I appreciate your silence, but there is no man. I've just got a headache," she replied, dragging a hand through her long tousled hair and wishing she had a couple of extra-strength aspirin.

"Ah, a headache . . . every woman's excuse."

Wearily, Kayla leaned back in her chair fingering the necklace she wore, hidden beneath the crew neck of her emerald green sweater. As always, her fingertip traced the moon and star medallion that had once belonged to her mother. Whether she imagined it or not, the silver, warmed from her skin, seemed to relieve some of the pressure in her skull. A small sense of calm settled over her, just as it always did when she touched the charm.

Marc came around the console, his short blond hair still damp from a shower, his face pale from sleep. He was actually no more than three years Kayla's senior, despite his insistence on being her "Uncle Marcky."

"It must be a helluva headache. You've had it all week." Marc rummaged inside the bakery bag he carried and handed her a chocolate-glazed doughnut. "Sweets for the sweet."

Kayla accepted the doughnut. "Thanks." Her stomach grumbled and she took a small bite. Only she didn't really feel like eating. She just wanted to sleep as peacefully as she used to, lost in pleasant dreams, to wake up rested and relaxed. The blackouts left her exhausted and frightened, too frightened to sleep.

As worn-out as she was, Kayla couldn't help smiling as Marc devoured half a glazed doughnut with one bite. To look at him, one would never know that he ate like a horse. At a little over six feet, he had a trim build and a minimal amount of muscles. He was an average-looking guy. What set Marc apart, however, was his smile. He had the most fabulous dimples. And he knew it.

He grinned down at her and handed her a disposable cup filled with steaming black coffee. "You're out of here, kiddo. Go home and get some sleep. I'll meet you at the Rock Garden tonight, about nine."

"Oh, no," Kayla groaned after taking a gulp of the bitter liquid. She massaged the aching muscles of her neck. "That's tonight? I was thinking it was next Friday."

"Darlin', you need to touch base with reality. I reminded you about this yesterday." Concern flashed in his blue eyes. "I definitely suggest you get some sleep." Then he grinned. "*Sleep,* mind you, sweetheart. No men." At Kayla's frown, his grin widened. "You wouldn't want me jealous now, would you?"

She ignored his question and voiced her own. "So what's on the agenda for tonight?"

"We're booked until eleven, which means you'll have just enough time to drive here by midnight and make your show."

"Who's doing promotions with us?"

"It's just you and me. Rickie has everybody spread out tonight. The Rock Garden's paying the most, so they get us and a live broadcast. A couple of the other jocks are making appearances around town, but this one's the biggie. Rickie wants us on our best behavior."

"*You're* telling *me?*" Kayla shook her head.

"I'm truly offended by your lack of faith." Marc feigned a hurt look, but his eyes held a mischievous light. "I'm always at my best. You just haven't given me a chance to prove it."

She didn't miss the meaning in his words, but she pretended otherwise. "Tonight you can impress me," she said, "by behaving yourself."

"Don't I always?"

"Sure you do, Marcus T. Miles," said the woman standing in the doorway, one hand planted firmly on her slender hip. Clad in a navy pin-striped suit, her dark hair pulled back in a tight chignon, her face nearly devoid of makeup, Rickie Renee Morgan looked every bit the conservative professional she was. Every bit the *angry* professional she was, if her frown was any indication.

"Ah, Rickie, speaking of the devil," Marc murmured, glancing at the program director of KCSS. "What brings you here so early?"

His comment drew a glare. "I'm here to give you a little hell, Mr. Miles."

"Seems fitting," Marc retorted.

"You would do well to listen to Kayla, Marc. I'm not sticking this station's neck out for any more of your stunts. Behave yourself tonight, or else."

"Or else what?" Rather than cower as most of the station's employees were smart enough to do, Marc simply smiled, folded his arms and stared her full in the face.

"Or else I'll come after you with my pitchfork," she replied, "to boot your butt out of here. There are dozens of jocks waiting for a morning spot."

"You would be miserable without me," he replied, flashing his dimples.

Rickie's eyes narrowed. "I won't have any more incidents like the one last week. This station's still trying to live down the bad press your little stunt caused. You just couldn't steer that football jock off the dirty jokes, could you?"

"I can't control what comes out of some sports celebrity's mouth while I'm interviewing him."

"Maybe not, but you didn't have to launch into one of your own jokes and try to top him. The mayor's office called me, for heaven's sake! And damned if we didn't get a written warning from the FCC."

Kayla shrunk back in her chair.

"Are you finished, Boss?"

"Not quite. Don't even think about screwing up tonight's broadcast. I'll transfer back to pretaped music if you push me, Marc. And tomorrow, you'll be doing the evening slot," she finished with a shake of her finger, the ruby ring she wore a brilliant glimmer of red.

As calm as always and used to ruffling feathers, especially Rickie's, Marc simply flashed those dimples again—those sweet, irresistible dimples—that melted anger like heat melts butter.

"I mean it, Marc. Don't keep pushing me."

"I wouldn't dream of it."

Rickie glared at Marc a full minute more, then turned to Kayla. "And you, Ms. Darland, better be at the Rock Garden on time. You've been late for every promotional event I've scheduled you for these past two weeks."

Kayla felt tears brimming and blinked them back.

Rickie's frown relaxed. A sympathetic note crept into her voice. "I know you're having a rough time, Kayla, but our sponsors are the ones who suffer when you don't show up as scheduled. If sponsors suffer, they take their business elsewhere and this radio station suffers. Please try to pull yourself together. I'm being as understanding as I can."

"I will," Kayla murmured, her eyes burning. She sniffled and busied herself cuing the next song, conscious of both pairs of eyes following her every move.

"Take it easy, Rickie," Marc said. "The kid's having a hard enough time without you riding her."

"Kayla, I don't mean to be unfeeling," Rickie started.

"No—no, you've been very understanding. I know you have to do your job, Rickie. I'm sorry about these past two weeks."

"You could always take a little vacation time, Kayla. You're due for a couple of weeks. I know just the place. Very secluded, calm, quiet—"

"No," Kayla cut in. "I would rather keep working." Work was all she had. The one and only thing to keep her from going completely crazy. She *had* to keep going, to find out what really happened to her mother and uncover the years of her life buried somewhere deep inside. "I won't be late tonight. Promise."

"Good." Rickie sounded relieved, then her voice took on a steely edge. "At least one person here is cooperative. And the other—" she cast a hard look at Marc "—had better reevaluate his position at this radio station and how much he'd like to keep it." On that note, she stormed from the control booth.

"So much for starting off the morning on a cheery note," Marc said.

"I told you she's got a temper, Marc. You've been lucky so far, but you've pushed her too much lately."

"Not far enough," he muttered. "Rickie pitches a fit, but she loves the publicity." He grasped Kayla by the hands, pulled her to her feet and into his arms for a loose embrace.

Kayla might have resisted, only she needed a friend right now, and Marc, though he might want more, had never pressed her to be anything other than his friend.

"Maybe," Kayla agreed after a thoughtful moment. A pleading note crept into her voice. "Promise you'll behave, Marc. I don't want to have to face Rickie if you get us into trouble."

"Word of honor. Now go home and dream of me, sweetie." He gave her a chaste kiss on the forehead, then plopped down in front of the control board and grabbed the headset.

Kayla said goodbye. Taking a deep breath, she stepped out into the shadows that still lurked in the hallway outside the control booth. Marc's voice drifted over the speakers as she walked through the darkened suite of offices that made up KCSS. The only light came from Rickie's doorway at the far end.

At the elevator, Kayla fed her access card into the slot, then punched the elevator button. Retrieving the card, she glanced from side to side down the hallway. Darkness settled into the corners. An Exit sign glowed at one end near the stairwell. And beyond, the darkness continued, bleaker and blacker, making her skin prickle.

She hated the night shift. It was always dark when she arrived, dark when she left and dark in between while she sat in the control booth with so few lights. At first, she'd welcomed the escape. After three years as the afternoon jock at a top-forty station barely a block away, the peace and quiet she'd found at KCSS had been a relief. No people in and out, disturbing her concentration or her thoughts. She had only the music.

Soul-filling music that made her laugh and cry. God, how she'd always loved music. All kinds of music. Each style, each melody touched her in a different way, stirred different emotions, and so the solitude had been her chance to really enjoy her job. To listen and feel . . .

The solitude should have been just what she needed. A chance to get her head together, to remember Gramps and how happy she'd been, how satisfied until she'd found the pictures. Only, happiness seemed a faraway emotion she couldn't quite remember, lost with part of her childhood that still remained a mystery.

She tried her damnedest to recall any piece of information to fill the empty years, but she couldn't. She had always believed what her father and Gramps had said about children often not remembering bits of their childhood. Only Kayla *had* to remember. She had memories of her mother lost somewhere inside and she needed to dig them up, to understand who she was and what had happened to make her father and Gramps tell such a horrendous lie. Her mother hadn't died in childbirth.

Unanswered questions swirled in her brain, haunted her. The damnable solitude that afforded her so much time to think was driving her crazy. That, and the blackouts.

Finally, the elevator doors swished open and blessed light flooded over her. She stepped inside and punched the button for the first floor, grateful to leave behind the shadows that always followed her when she left the station.

Marc's voice drifted over the elevator speaker. "...whether you're waking up or going to bed, we're cranking out your favorite tunes here at KCSS. And here's a little something for one of *my* favorites...sleep well, Kayla."

She smiled as one of her favorite songs drifted over the airwaves. Kayla could picture Rickie flying down the hallway, smoke streaming from her ears. Marc would get hell for that. Kayla hadn't seen the song on the format for this morning, and Rickie had warned him about deviating from the playlist. Then again, Rickie warned Marc about everything. He rarely listened.

The doors slid open and Kayla walked across the carpeted lobby, toward the lighted security desk near a set of sliding glass doors.

"How's Ernie and Fay?" Kayla asked as she neared the security guard, a middle-aged woman with a red beehive hairdo and matching lipstick.

"That boy of mine is getting downright jittery," Gracie McWilliams replied, a smile creasing her pale, wrinkled face. Barely in her mid-forties, Gracie hadn't aged well. But her smile was warm, like the morning sun that chased away the night's cold, and her eyes as vibrant as the first rays drifting over the horizon. "Fay's due any day and Ernie calls me all the time."

"This is their first, right?" Kayla asked.

The woman nodded. "And probably their last, as scared as they both are. I tried to tell them not to go for that natural childbirth." She shook her head and took a sip of coffee from a bright red thermos mug before adding, "There ain't nothing natural to me about pain. I was begging for Valium when Ernie was born." She let out a deep sigh. "And my husband, God rest his soul, turned so many shades of white in the delivery room, I thought I was going to have to whip out my pistol and put him out of his misery."

"I think you're pulling my leg."

"If it'll get a smile out of you, then it's worth fudging on my story a little," Gracie replied, a sincere note in her voice.

"Thanks, Gracie." Kayla swallowed at the lump in her throat. Longing swept through her, and her thoughts went to the woman in the pictures she'd found. She'd forgotten the one thing she'd spent her life yearning for... a mother's love.

"Men," Gracie went on with a shake of her head. "Not a one of 'em could live through the mildest labor pain."

"Tell Ernie I wish him the best of luck," Kayla said. "And let me know the minute the baby comes." Visions of plump babies danced in Kayla's head. What she wouldn't give for one of her own. A little piece of herself to ease the loneliness, to fill the void where her heart had been.

"Will do, honey. You go home and get some sleep." Gracie touched a worn hand to Kayla's cheek. "You've been looking awful tired lately. Maybe you should see a doctor?"

"I haven't been sleeping well. Insomnia," Kayla replied, averting her gaze. She'd been friends with Gracie for over a year, ever since she'd taken the night jock's spot at KCSS.

Gracie, as observant as a mother hen, could already read Kayla so well. "You been thinking about your grandpa, sweetie?" It was more of a question than a statement.

Kayla nodded, feeling the tears start to gather. "M-maybe I will see a doctor. He might be able to prescribe something to help me sleep." But she was more worried about the blackouts than lack of sleep. They kept her from sleeping, from thinking straight.

"That's the best idea I've heard yet. In the meantime, drink some warm milk and tuck yourself into bed. That'll do the trick until you can make an appointment."

"I'll try it," Kayla promised.

Gracie smiled, seeming satisfied with Kayla's response. "Good. And bring Dixie up here first chance you get. It's been nearly a month since I've seen that spitfire."

"It's been almost that long for me," Kayla admitted, picturing Dixie's pale blond ringlets and sea-green eyes. "I missed last Saturday with her." A pang of guilt shot through Kayla. The Big Sister program was sure to boot Kayla out if she missed any more of her scheduled weekends with Dixie. Not to mention that Wanda, Dixie's mother, always made plans to work every other Saturday when Kayla took Dixie. Last weekend Wanda had had to search for a baby-sitter.

The blackouts had forced Kayla to cancel their outing. A sliver of fear went down Kayla's spine. What if she lost consciousness when Dixie was with her? "I'm not sure if I'll see Dixie next weekend. The station is keeping me very busy. But if I do pick her up, I'll be sure to bring her by to see you."

"Good, and tell that little girl Gracie's got homemade cookies for her, like last time." She followed Kayla to the entrance, punched in a security code and the doors swung wide.

Kayla nodded and murmured, "See you tonight."

A gust of air whipped at her and she hugged her arms, pulling the cuffs of her sweater down over her hands. She crossed the street to the parking garage. Gold streaks already zigzagged across the gray horizon. Dawn was coming, but not quickly enough to relieve Kayla's unease.

She pushed her way through a set of heavy double doors and onto the first level of the parking garage, which proved nearly as dark as the office building. Shadows folded around her as she walked, her boots a steady thump against the pavement. The sound echoed, mingling with her breathing and the beat of her heart.

Kayla...

The whisper, no more than an echo of the wind, came from no specific direction, as if some invisible demon circled her, taunted her.

She felt the cool hand on her shoulder. She swung around. Nothing. Only shadows...the damning shadows.

Come, Kayla... Again, the wind.

Cold fingers flitted over her cheek. She slapped at thin air, feeling only the smarting of her skin as her palm made contact with her face. Then her hands began to tingle.

"No," she said, trying to resist what had become the inevitable. She stumbled past several cars, across two empty spaces to her black Mustang—a classic '69 model. The only thing left of her father. If only he were here now.

She reached the car just as the tingling worked its way up her arms. Her nerves came alive. Streaks of fire shot through her body. She curled her fingers, feeling the silver of her topaz ring cut into her palm. If she could only concentrate on the pain. But the tingling persisted mercilessly.

"No," she vowed to herself, her voice soft, barely audible, yet the word held a wealth of meaning. Desperation, determination and fear—all three fought a battle within Kayla.

Frantically she blinked, willing her eyes to focus. Still her vision blurred. She steeled herself against the numbness drifting up her arms. Think! her mind screamed. Keep thinking and the numbness will go away. It will. It will.

She heard only the drone of the wind whipping through the entrance to the garage. Frigid air swirled around her, but she felt no distinct touch as she had before. No icy fingers conjured from her imagination...

Only the solid metal of her car, its coldness seeping through her jeans, cooling the flesh of one hip as she sagged against the door. But the numbness continued to creep through her until she ceased to feel the cold altogether.

Then the floor tilted, the walls started to wave and everything went black....

Jase doubled over the bathroom sink as a cold, knife-like pain sliced through his middle. The disposable razor slipped from his hand and plopped into the soapy water. The overhead light flickered.

Gasping for a breath, he clutched the moon charm around his neck and stared into the mirror. The silver burned into his fingers. Pain veiled his eyes and he struggled to see.

In between flashes of light, he glimpsed long, flame-red hair, topaz eyes wide with fear. His body started to shake as the the darkness descended, and Kayla slipped unconscious to the floor of the parking garage.

"*Kayla!*" his mind called her back to reality. But she slipped deeper into the blackness.

Jase flung his back against the bathroom door, fingers clenched around the charm, eyes clamped shut, thoughts carrying him to the dim parking garage. To her...

Then he was beside her, kneeling, trying to touch her. But he couldn't, not physically. He was there mentally, feeling, seeing, but not touching. Never touching.

A figure materialized from the shadows, swept Kayla up and flung open the car door. She tried to resist, pushing, squirming, not fully unconscious, yet not awake. Lost somewhere between the darkness and the light. Wildly she clutched at her own charm for strength, for *their* strength.

Shoving her inside the car, the figure climbed in next to her and closed a withered hand around hers, prying her fingers from the moonstar.

Kayla stirred and moaned, arching her back convulsively. She clawed at the air, searching for the silver as the figure forced her hand away from her throat. The hand squeezed hers. Her fingers opened and turned a stark white. The hand squeezed tighter, trying to weaken her with the pain and urge her deeper into the blackness.

Be strong, Jase willed her. *Resist, Kayla. Resist!* But she couldn't. She quieted and slumped back against the seat.

The figure let go of her, gave an eerie chuckle and revved the engine. Tires squealed as the car roared from the parking lot. Then they were speeding down the streets of Houston.

Jase swayed with the motion of the car, his chest heaving, keeping tempo with Kayla's ragged breaths. He felt the cold that gripped her, knew the all-consuming black fright holding her mind and body frozen.

Soon, the road blurred. The city disappeared. The darkness swallowed them as they traveled along. Farther, farther...darker, darker...colder, colder.

Jase clasped his hands together around his moonstar, as if he could generate enough heat to warm Kayla, to fold around her, sink inside and obliterate the cold. But he couldn't physically touch her, only with his thoughts and she was beyond comprehension.

"Kayla," the figure spoke, the voice as cold as a grave in the dead of winter.

Then the chanting began—a union of faceless voices, beckoning to Kayla's subconscious, weakening her mentally, tearing down her resistance until, eventually, she would consciously accept them, or at least submit, too weary to fight anymore. That's all they waited for. That and the new moon.

Already, Kayla was exhausted. Her subconscious was being schooled in the darkness. She was learning, bending. It would be soon now. Days, maybe a week, given her strong will. But soon, nonetheless.

Without warning, the figure reached out and ripped the charm from around her neck. Jase plunged into the blackness, Kayla's terrified face, flaming hair above him, growing smaller, smaller, to a pinpoint. Then, *poof!* Nothing.

He opened his eyes to the vague outline of the bathroom mirror. The lights stopped blinking. Quickly, his vision cleared and he stared at his own reflection. He released the charm and let it drop to his bare chest. He couldn't see her anymore, but he still felt her. God, how he felt her, and he had no choice now.

Deep down, he'd known it would come to this. He'd steeled himself against it, thinking he could warn her with his thoughts. But thoughts weren't enough. The danger was too real, and though their connection was strong, it wasn't strong enough for him to stop what was happening to her. There was only one way he could do that.

Wiping the shaving cream from his face, he strode from the bathroom, shrugged into a shirt and a worn leather jacket. He shoved extra clothes and a few essentials into a duffel bag and snatched up his camera. Plucking the Old One's letter and the keys from the coffee table, Jase stuffed them into his pocket. He paused at the pictures scattered across the table.

Kayla and the Keepers... his only tangible proof the nightmare was real.

Grabbing several, he added them to his nearly overflowing bag, then tore out of his apartment.

Dammit, but he had no other choice, he told himself as he brought the motorcycle roaring to life. May God help him now that he knew what he had to do.

God help her...

CHAPTER THREE

"**W**here the hell have you been?" Marc demanded, snatching the headphones from his ears, his face a mask of worry. "You're a half hour late!"

"I—I overslept," Kayla murmured, stepping inside the carpet-lined sound booth. She pulled the door closed behind her, shutting out the blaring music that filled the Rock Garden. "Is Rickie here?" She glanced around the booth, at the stacks of sound equipment and compact discs, the wall-to-wall mixing board. She saw no one except a sound assistant who stood in the corner pulling CDs off a large shelf.

The young boy, probably a communications major from the local college, gave her a small nod, mumbled, "Justin's the name," then turned back to his chore.

"She isn't here yet, but the club's owner has been hanging over my shoulder, ranting and raving that he's paying for two DJs and not one."

"What did you tell him?" She dropped her black shoulder bag to a chair in one corner and shrugged out of her leather coat, hooking it on a peg near Marc's battered blue-jean jacket.

"That you had a flat tire, but I'd stay an extra half hour tonight to make up for it."

Kayla let out a relieved sigh. "Thanks, Marc. I owe you."

He studied her a full moment more before his face relaxed into a smile. "You certainly do, baby, and I'm sure I can think of a way for you to pay me back." The smile turned wicked and he winked before handing her a headset similar to his and turning back to the control board. "Let's get to work, sweetheart." He motioned to the wall-size window in front of him that overlooked the club's dance floor. "We've got a birthday bash to liven up."

The song that had been playing faded and Marc's voice blasted over the speakers. "You're partying the night away at Houston's hottest dance spot with KCSS. I'm Mad Marc Miles bringing you the best classic rock live and uncensored. With me is the night child herself, Miss Kayla Darland." He grabbed Kayla's hand and pulled her up next to him, giving the partygoers full view of their hosts. Shouts and cheers erupted and Kayla forced a smile.

"We've got some hot music lined up for tonight," Marc continued, "so let's get this birthday bash pumping."

He shoved the mixing level up and sound vibrated through the club. Kayla shrunk away from him toward the far edge of the window where she could study the scene before her without being in full view. She need not have bothered, however, for her presence seemed quickly forgotten as the upbeat song became everyone's focus.

Kayla stared out over the mass of bodies gyrating beneath the swirl and flash of multicolored lights. Strobe lights rotated, hypnotizing with their bright white intensity. Her heart hammered against her ribs to the rapid beat of the song, the pound of the drums, the sizzle of an electric guitar.

She closed her eyes as her stomach did an involuntary turn. Flattening her palm against the carpeted wall, she willed the room to a standstill. It didn't cooperate. Her vision clouded. Her head throbbed. The floor seemed to tilt.

"Baby, are you all right?" Marc gripped her elbow, his fingers warm through her sleeve. Yet the touch did little to dispel Kayla's chill. The cold came from within.

She blinked her eyes, forcing them to focus. "Fine. I'm still tired, that's all." And confused and scared and on the verge of a nervous breakdown, her mind added silently.

He touched his thumb to her cheek, near the dark circles she knew were evident. The silver of his ring brushed her skin, the ruby stone a fiery flash of red near the corner of her eye.

"Dammit, Kayla, you look ready to drop. Did you sleep the entire day like I told you?"

She nodded, knowing all the while that she lied. But she didn't want Marc to worry anymore.

If only she *had* slept. Instead, she'd been lost to the world. Another blackout—this one longer than any of the others. When she'd opened her eyes, she'd been in her car in the parking lot of a bookstore—*The Bookkeepers,* the sign had said. A store she'd never been to before in a suburb of Houston clear on the opposite side of town from where she lived and worked.

The blackout had lasted the entire day. She had come to that evening with tears on her face, her head feeling as if someone had been pounding away at it with a hammer, her body so cold she didn't feel the forty-degree temperature inside the car.

This blackout had been different. She'd known this the moment she glanced at the red neon sign of the bookstore. She always awoke to the fear, like an iron fist in her stomach. Today she'd felt a much deeper terror, as if she'd glimpsed hell itself while in the blackness, and then clawed her way back.

Kayla's hand went to her throat, her fingers searching for the comfort of the charm. She felt only her bare skin above the plunging V of her blouse.

Gone. She'd had the charm when she left the station that morning, but when she'd regained consciousness, it had been missing. She'd searched the car, but found only the black satin band it had been attached to. The band was ripped in two, as if she'd yanked it from her neck. But Kayla knew she would never have done that. Not in a million years. The charm was all she had left of her mother. No childhood memories. Nothing but the charm. Now she didn't even have that.

A shiver went through her.

"You're sure?" Marc's voice forced its way into her thoughts.

"I'm sorry. What were you saying?"

"I asked if you're sure you can make it through tonight." Already, a crowd hovered outside the sound-booth door. People peered through the window, waiting for autographs, to make requests or just to meet two of Houston's top disc jockeys. "I could phone Rickie and tell her you have the flu. She can find someone to fill in for you at the station. And if she can't," he added when Kayla started to protest, "I'll call it a night here early and get to the station in time to cover your shift."

"No, no," Kayla said, shaking her head. "I can't let you do that. I'll make it. It's almost ten already. I can last through two hours here and four hours at the station."

Marc looked uncertain for a moment. "You're sure?"

"Positive," she replied, hooking her headset on and heading toward the control board. Taking a deep breath, she forced all thought from her mind. The song faded to a close and Kayla flipped on the mike. "We're nonstop and live till midnight here at the Rock Garden," she said, her satiny voice drifting through the speakers. The music beat an insistent rhythm in the background as Kayla mixed in the next song. "You're heating up the night with me, Kayla Darland, and my partner in crime, Mad Marc Miles, from Houston's one and only KCSS. Let's keep things rolling with another classic."

"A true professional," Marc murmured, a grin splitting his face as he came up next to Kayla.

"Professional is a dirty word to you, isn't it?" She cocked one eyebrow at him.

"To me, yes. You know I pride myself on being unprofessional. But I love a stubborn woman with a beautiful voice."

"You just love women, period."

"True," he conceded. "And I love very well, I might add."

"I'll take your word for it."

"I was afraid you might," he replied, feigning a look of disappointment.

"What am I going to do with you, Uncle Marcky?" Kayla murmured, a smile tugging at her lips.

"That's exactly what I've been wondering myself."

She shook her head and reached for the clipboard that held the format sheet, while Marc grabbed the next stack of CDs on their playlist.

Focusing every ounce of energy she had, Kayla lost herself in her job for the next hour, in the music, the introductions, the airtime banter with Marc. She prayed that keeping busy would keep the blackouts away. If only she could rid herself of the god-awful chill that iced her blood and fed her fear.

"Slow down, baby," Marc told her a good while later as she busied herself pulling CDs for the next hour slot. "Those CDs aren't going anywhere. Why the hurry?"

"Don't give me a hard time, Marc. I'm just working," she replied, glancing at him as he leaned against the wall, arms folded, waiting for the next song to play down.

"Too damned hard, from where I'm standing. You paid your dues doing that stuff back in college. What do you think he's here for?" He motioned to the young man barely a foot from Kayla who stood with his hands in his pockets. "Isn't that right, Justin?"

Justin nodded and moved to take Kayla's place.

Reluctantly, she gave up the stack of CDs and the play-list. Standing, she breathed deeply and rubbed her hands together to warm them. No luck. She reached for her headset, only to have Marc hold it out of her reach.

"Take a breather, and that's an order." He flipped on the mike and launched into another song intro.

Kayla stared out the slightly tinted window of the sound booth, scanning the sea of faces, her eyes now adjusted to the lights.

The place was so full that she and Marc had been told to announce that the doors were closing and no one else would be allowed in. She'd be willing to bet the owner was sitting in his office right now, counting his proceeds from the enormous cover that had been charged. And for what? she thought. A glimpse at two disc jockeys? A chance to put the faces with the voices? She closed her eyes. She liked being a voice. She liked the solitude of the control booth, the comfort of the music.

Until now, an inner voice reminded her, her skin prickling from the cold, or something else . . .

Her eyes snapped open and she saw him.

Or rather he saw her. He stood off to the side of the dance floor. Just stood there, staring at her as if he could actually see through the tinted window from such a distance. He couldn't, not without the overhead light on in the sound booth, and certainly not with just a small spot lamp burning above the mixing board.

Of course he couldn't see her, reason argued. No matter that his gaze seemed to penetrate the thick glass and capture her with its intensity. His eyes flashed silver brilliance with the swirl of the strobe lights, like shimmering moonlit pools on the clearest night.

Warm, liquid silver, she thought, a strange sense of recollection niggling at her brain. Silver dispelling the dark, soothing her fear. Warm fingers touching her cheeks, chasing the tears away.

She gave herself a mental shake. There was nothing familiar about him. Nothing at all, she realized as she tore her gaze from his to sweep the length of him.

From a slightly wrinkled white button-down shirt that peeked from the folds of his leather jacket, to the snug jeans that confirmed his narrow waist and muscular thighs, his body, hard and lean, exuded strength. A strength that seemed to reach out to her, to comfort and quell her fears.

Impossible. He stood clear across the room, a stranger to her. Or was he?

She studied his face—the angled lines of his jaw shadowed with stubble, the dark eyebrows that slanted across those incredible eyes, a perfectly chiseled nose. A mane of ebony hair, slightly tousled, fell to his shoulders, the silky thickness gleaming beneath the flicker of lights.

She found her interest drawn once again to his magnetic gaze. A haunted moonsilver gaze that called out to her, reached inside of her—

"Sit down, and I'll send Justin to get you something to drink," Marc cut into her thoughts.

Kayla glanced at him. "No," she murmured, her gaze swinging back to the stranger. He was gone. She scanned the area nearby, but it was so crowded she couldn't find him. Gone.

Tilting her head a fraction, she stared at her own reflection near the top of the tinted window. Her image appeared a wild tangle of red hair and pale skin, even paler against the V of her black knit shirt. She touched her throat, a pang of regret for the lost silver charm. The lost silver gaze.

A tremor seized her hands. Her skin turned hot, then cold. A face materialized next to her reflection. Glittering eyes set in ghostly white features, surrounded by complete, absolute blackness.

She jerked around, her glance sweeping the space behind her. Nothing. Only Marc a few feet away and Justin hunkered down in front of a CD shelf. She glanced back at her reflection, then the apparition. The face was still there, the eyes firing brighter. Kayla's hands trembled more violently.

"Sure you don't want something to drink?"

She turned a startled gaze to Marc. "I—maybe so."

"Justin, you heard the lady."

"No, I'll go myself," she told him. "I could use a little air."

"I don't think you'll find much out there," he said, motioning to the overflowing dance floor and the thick cloud of smoke that hovered above everyone.

"The walk will give me a chance to stretch my legs," she added, desperate to escape the ghostly face. What was the matter with her? She clasped her visibly shaking hands behind her back.

"If you're sure," Marc said.

"Yes."

"You sound like you could use a drink, baby. Your voice is a little scratchy."

Kayla swallowed with considerable effort, her throat like sandpaper.

"Bring me a beer, will you?"

"Sure." She turned and grasped the doorknob, making a quick escape into the chaos of the Rock Garden. After scribbling her autograph for a few eager fans gathered outside the sound-booth door, she started the long trek to the bar.

The music pounded in her skull, in sync with the insistent beat of her heart. She inched her way through the throng. There were bodies, faces, everywhere she turned, and Kayla quickly found herself sandwiched between two enormous men who had obviously overindulged at the bar.

"You're that disc jockey," one of them shouted, his beefy arm dropping onto her shoulder. "Night something or other—woman, kid..."

"Night *child*," Kayla corrected.

"Yeah, yeah," the other man chimed in. "You got the sexiest voice I ever heard." He fingered a flame-red curl near her cheek. "And you're a real looker, too."

"Damn straight," his friend agreed. "What's your name again?"

"Kayla Darland," she said, not that he could hear her above the noise level. "If you'll both excuse me," she murmured. She smiled and ducked free of the man's arm, leaving both men staring after her as she maneuvered herself straight through a cluster of people, grateful when she could no longer feel the men's gazes.

Finally, she grasped the edge of the bar, amazed that she had found her way at all. After ordering a beer for Marc and a diet soda for herself, she turned and let her gaze sweep the faces surrounding her. They looked preoccupied, lost in the music and energy flowing through the place. For Kayla, it was a nervous sort of energy that set her on edge. She jumped when the bartender's voice sounded behind her.

"On the house," he said.

Kayla whirled in time to see him smile.

"You've got the greatest voice. When I leave work, I always listen to you."

"Thanks," she replied.

When she reached for the frosty beer bottle, her hand froze. Her fingers started to tingle. The sensation spread into her wrist, up her arm.

She jerked around as the tingling seized her other fingers, working its way up. Staring across the club toward the sound booth, she mouthed Marc's name. The blackness hovered over her like a vulture about to swoop down and devour its prey.

"Hey, lady, you all right?" the bartender shouted after her as she stumbled away from the bar.

Kayla shoved past people, toward the Exit sign that flashed neon green above one of the doors.

Outside. If she could only get outside to her car, she wouldn't lose it in front of all these people. A few more steps, she told herself. Just a few...

Her vision clouded. Blindly she staggered forward. Barely an arm's span from the door, the numbness started. She reached for the door handle, but her arm fell back, limp.

The room started to spin, the lights flashing quicker, brighter, blinding her and making her swoon. Her knees buckled and she felt herself sinking to the floor, into the blackness.

In the next instant, strong arms closed around her, hauled her upright. A broad chest pressed against her back and a deep male voice filled her ears.

"Kayla..."

And she didn't know whether to thank God or curse him. For she knew that voice. It replayed over and over in her mind those few seconds before the blackness consumed her.

They're coming.

They're coming.

"Say, buddy! You're blocking the exit," came the irritated shout.

Jase inched to the side, Kayla held tight in his arms as a brawny man and his date squeezed by.

He glanced around, his gaze thorough as he took in the nearby faces. All ordinary. No one too interested in him or the woman he held. Yet Jase could feel the presence. Kayla losing herself to the blackout proved someone watched, ready to pounce, to take her away for another lesson. Someone was close by.

"...KCSS and we're cruisin' into another tune. Let's fire this place up!" A cheer reverberated through the club.

Jase swept Kayla up into his arms and pushed through the door. Outside, he breathed in the crisp night air. Kayla clutched at his jacket, fighting the blackness as she always did.

Always fighting...and always losing in the end. But not this time. He would see to that.

He kept a cautious eye on his surroundings while he strode through the parking lot, toward a dark section where the street lamp had been knocked out. The chrome trim of his black Kawasaki gleamed in the moonlight like a beacon guiding a lost ship through a fierce storm.

Jase moved faster, never once breaking stride, even when he heard the footsteps behind him. A Keeper followed. Someone who had been close to Kayla while she'd been inside. Someone waiting for the right moment, when the blackness would claim her. Someone who would continue to teach her the ways of darkness, brainwash her, until she returned to the Keepers willingly. She had to be willing. That was the key...the only reason they hadn't already taken her physically. They were after her mind now. But she would get no lesson in evil tonight.

Jase increased his step, mindless of Kayla's struggles, the burn of her fingernails as they raked across his face.

Finally, he straddled the motorcycle. He brought Kayla down on the seat in front of him, his arms on either side, holding her as she slumped back and clawed at his jean-clad thighs. He brought his knees up behind hers to urge her feet off the ground.

The footsteps were steady, closer, and he revved the engine, kicked the motorcycle into gear and flew across the pavement.

When he'd covered several yards, he chanced a glance behind him. He saw rows of cars, a few people here and there walking to and from the club's entrance, but no one in particular. Not that he expected to see anyone, not with the darkness to cloak them.

Still, the Keepers watched. He could feel them.

He snaked an arm around Kayla's waist and pulled her flush against him. Her head rolled onto his shoulder and he bent down, his lips grazing her ear.

"They won't have you, moonchild," he promised. Strangely enough, her movements ceased. She went still, her soft form pressing into his hard length, as if she waited for him to say more. And she did...

Jase had joined his thoughts with hers. His power was sinking into her, fusing with hers, holding her back from complete oblivion. "I need your help, Kayla. You have to move with me, hold your balance and keep your feet up. We have a long way to go."

She nodded, her breathing even, calm.

"Touch me," he commanded. "Help me, moonchild."

She opened her hands, placed them on his thighs and held on to him. Sitting a little straighter, she put her feet on the footrests and moved with him as he controlled the powerful motion of the motorcycle.

They moved as one, breathed as one, as they were always meant to.

The startling thought sent desire flowing through Jase. He inhaled the rich scent of her, felt her hair against his neck, like warm satin, and he damned himself.

And he damned her. As surely as he held her, he damned her, for seeing him would stir her carefully hidden past. Soon, she would know what had been meant for her, no matter that Jase only wanted to keep her safe. In protecting her, Jase risked her life, her very soul. And for the first time, he wondered if it might not be better to let the Keepers have her.

No! his conscience screamed. There was always the hope that seeing him might not trigger any recollection. Then as long as he kept his distance, maintained his control over the darkness inside of him and told her absolutely nothing of the past, she would be safe. The promise unfulfilled.

He could hold her for the next two weeks, until after the new moon and his father's death. Then Kayla would be free to resume her life, the evil of her past still buried. And Jase would be free, as well, released from the black clutches that held him prisoner and governed his soul.

Their flight from the city was swift. Soon they glided down a nearly deserted stretch of highway, away from Houston and, Jase hoped, away from the danger.

The beam of the headlight cut through the thick layer of fog and illuminated the tarred pavement directly in front of him. Beyond the reach of the light, the road extended far into the blackness, endlessly, it seemed, as they rolled along. The wind chilled his face and he shivered. He held Kayla tighter, wrapping the edges of his jacket around her to keep her warm.

In turn, she grasped the muscles of his thighs, scooting back closer to him, her movements an answer to the mental command he issued. She lingered on the verge of unconsciousness, Jase's mind linked with hers, holding her back like strong hands controlling a puppet's strings.

The Keepers had sought to push her into the blackness, but Jase's power countered theirs. He could hold her back, enough to keep her safe, but not enough to wake her. He wasn't that powerful. She would come to of her own accord, in her own time. Jase could only wait, and hope like hell that he wasn't making the biggest mistake of his life.

But the moment he leaned forward and inhaled the glorious scent of her hair, a peace stole inside of him. Past demons were forgotten for those long moments as they rode. With her so near, Jase could almost believe he hadn't made a grave mistake.

Almost . . .

For he still felt the craving deep within himself. A craving that would roar to life, consume him if he wasn't careful. The beast was hungry, so very hungry, and Jase would die before he appeased that hunger.

Kayla blinked, slowly bringing her watery eyes into focus. Tranquil silence caressed her ears. She'd never felt so warm before.

A glow filled the small room, casting a soft light on the red and gold patchwork quilt that covered her legs. She turned her head and saw the candle on the nightstand, the flame flickering low, wax dribbling down the sides to pool in the base of the silver holder. A brass alarm clock sat beside the candle holder... barely 4:00 a.m.

At that moment, a gust of wind lashed at the window near the bed. The room shook with the force. The walls creaked, ending the silence. A full-blown panic seized Kayla and snatched her from the lethargy of sleep.

She shot straight up in the double bed, eyes wide, gaze flitting around the room, from the antique washbowl and stand in one corner, to the dust-covered rocking chair, then back to the wrought-iron footboard of the bed where she lay.

Kayla took a deep, ragged breath and caught a whiff of stale cigarette smoke. Lifting her arm, she sniffed at her sleeve then grabbed a handful of her tangled hair and sniffed again. Smoke.

She began to shake as visions of the Rock Garden washed over her with the fury of angry waves beating the shore.

The tingling in her hands as she'd raced for the exit.

The bartender's voice... *Hey, lady, you all right?*

Then the numbness.

Kayla searched her mind for what came next. Nothing. No memory. Only the blackness...

She glanced around again. My God, where was she?

Scrambling from the bed, she dropped her bare feet to the hardwood floor. A yelp burst from her lips as her soles met the cold. She leaned down and searched for her boots. Immediately, she spotted them standing at attention near the corner of the bed. Grasping the soft leather, she began jerking on the boots. She'd barely slipped her foot inside the second one, when she heard the noise.

The slow grate as a door opened somewhere in the house. Her gaze flew to the closed bedroom door. Footsteps sounded on the other side and Kayla lunged to her feet.

Her hands shook with the violence of the panic swirling within her. She was in somebody's house! She'd awakened from the blackouts in some strange places before—the church, the bookstore—but no one had been around. Until now.

The bedroom door opened. Kayla jerked around and found herself gazing into shimmering silver eyes. Time sucked her back to the club, to the man staring at her through the sound-booth window.

"Take it easy," he said, hands outstretched. "I'm not going to hurt you."

Lights flashed in Kayla's memory. Music roared in her ears. She saw him again...standing across the dance floor, gazing through the glass, straight at her, *into* her, it had seemed. But there was no music now, no swirl of strobes, only the soft glow radiating from the candle and the sound of faraway wind. Maybe she was dreaming. "Wh-where am I?" she croaked.

"Someplace safe," he replied, his voice as familiar as his eyes, and much more frightening.

They're coming. The phrase echoed in her head, sending icy rivulets of fear down her spine. Reality crashed around her.

"You!" she gasped, taking a step back and coming up hard against the sharp edge of the nightstand. "Oh, my

God! You're the one who's been tapping into my head-set—"

"Trying to warn you," he cut in, his voice calm, steady, crossing the distance between them to push into her thoughts and soothe her panic. But Kayla felt anything but soothed.

She grappled behind her, her fingers closing around the brass alarm clock. Waving it threateningly, she said on a sharp intake of breath, "Don't come near me."

If he heard, he gave no indication. He stared at her so intently, his gaze so penetrating, her skin prickled. "I tried, Kayla, but you wouldn't believe me. That's why you're here, and why you'll stay here for the next two weeks."

Stay calm, a voice whispered as the impact of his words hit her. But her heart was pounding too fast. "You're crazy," she murmured. "You can't keep me here!" Her gaze flew from the doorway, which he blocked, to the room's only window.

"Don't even try it, Kayla. It's shuttered so tight you would need a crowbar to pry the thing open."

She noted the dust covering the window ledge, the cob-webs at the corners, and her hopes plummeted. "Why are you doing this? I—I don't have any family. If you want money—"

"I have plenty of my own money," he broke in. "Try to understand that this is for your own good. I wish I could tell you what's going on, but I can't. You'll have to trust me." His words rang with a conviction that pierced the wall of fear encasing her. He sounded so sincere, the way he'd sounded when he'd first talked to her on her headset. That's why she hadn't been frightened of him then, only touched by the desperation in his voice. Then again, he hadn't abducted her before.

"How—why—what do you want from me?" She managed to voice the question through quivering lips.

He looked thoughtful for a moment, his eyes glowing pools reflecting the candlelight. "Nothing," he finally said. "I don't want anything, except to see that you're safe. I won't hurt you," he repeated his earlier words. "Promise."

The way he said the last word, as if he could cross his heart and hope to die and she would believe him, almost made her laugh. Almost...if fear didn't have such a stranglehold on her. As it was, she could only stare at him, her fingers clenched around the alarm clock, waiting for him to make a move toward her.

He studied her for a long, excruciating moment. Her grip on the clock turned her knuckles stark white.

"It's late." His voice finally broke the unbearable silence. "You look like you could use some sleep. The bed's pretty comfortable. Rest. I'll be in the other room if you need me." He turned to leave.

"It's that simple?" Kayla found herself asking. He stopped and faced her, his features solemn, eyes guarded. "You kidnap me, tell me it's for my own good with not a single word explaining *why,* and then send me to bed?"

"You'll have to trust me."

"Trust you?" she blazed, her fear giving way to anger. "Well, excuse me if I don't, but I haven't the faintest idea who the hell you are, and I'm not in the habit of trusting strangers who steal me away while I'm in the middle of working."

"Jase...Jase Terrell," he said.

"What?"

"My name is Jase."

The name tugged at her memory. She did know him. Somehow, from someplace, she knew him. If only her mind wasn't fogged with exhaustion. She couldn't think.

Kayla studied him a full moment longer, but his good looks—the lean lines of his jaw, liquid eyes fringed with thick black lashes, sensuous lips—didn't stir any clear memory, just an odd familiarity that wouldn't subside.

"I'm a photographer for *Texas Life,* on the ninth floor of the building you work in," he offered.

Recognition came like a rush of cool water easing her troubled thoughts. A name credited at the end of a picture layout featuring Texas-born musicians. A picture next to the byline. "So you work in my building," she breathed, a weird sort of relief filling her. She gave herself a silent scolding. So what? That only meant he was a crazy who could hold down a job. For heaven's sake, he'd kidnapped her!

"Now you know me," he said. He grinned then, only a slight tilt of his lips, but enough to send Kayla's heart slamming against her ribs. She stiffened, her fear magnifying at her response to this dangerous stranger. And he was dangerous. No matter that he had a name and a job. He'd crossed the line. He wasn't merely an overzealous fan who needed someone to talk to. He was more like a stalker...a kidnapper.

Still, maybe she could reason with him. "L-look," she started, choosing her words carefully, "I won't press charges if you take me back."

He gave no reply, just a slow shake of his head.

"Be reasonable. You can't expect to get away with this. I have commitments. There are people depending on me..." Another thought struck her and hysteria infused her voice. "Marc must be worried sick! You have to take me back right now! I'll lose my job—"

"You won't," he said. "Trust me, Kayla. Accept this situation. You're not leaving here and neither am I—for the next two weeks." His voice rang with a finality that forced her mouth shut and brought home the weight of his words.

And then came the tears. She fought them, swiping at her eyes, hating herself for being so weak. But her control, sapped from the blackouts and the grief over losing Gramps, simply snapped. Tears of fear, frustration and ultimately defeat squeezed past her eyelids, trailed down her cheeks. Her vision blurred.

Seconds later, she felt the undeniable warmth as strong fingers touched her arm, burning through the black knit of her blouse. "Don't cry," he said, his voice low, disconcerting.

"P-please don't hurt me," she pleaded, jerking away from him, stumbling back into the edge of the nightstand. "Please. Don't hurt me..." Her words were lost in the lump that filled her throat.

"That's the last thing I would ever do." He stepped closer. His fingers whispered across her cheeks, wiping away the tears and warming her. "You'll only be here a little while. I know you don't understand what's happening, but you *are* in danger. There are people who want to hurt you. This is the only safe place."

Safe? She was trapped with a man who had tapped into her headset, followed her to the Rock Garden, spirited her away to a strange house, and she was *safe?*

Yes! a voice inside of her screamed, despite all rational thought.

"Believe me," he added. "I know you're frightened. Damn, I wish I could explain..." His words trailed off as he continued to stroke her cheek. "They were too close to you, Kayla. I had to do something."

"Who? Who is it that's trying to hurt me?"

"People—dangerous people. They followed you to the club."

"*You* followed me to the club," she breathed, still unwilling to listen to that part of her that told her to believe him. Not while reason claimed he was a bona fide nut case. One that could only mean to harm her.

But what if he spoke the truth? What if she really was in danger? What if...?

"Be glad I followed you to the Garden," he replied. "Otherwise, you would have wound up sprawled on the floor near the rear exit, lost in another blackout."

The blackout. In her fear, she'd forgotten the blackout. She'd been falling, faster, deeper, when he'd caught her.

Another blackout. "How do you know about my blackouts?"

"I know they frighten you, and that you've been having them a lot lately. Too often."

"How do you know? Have you been following me around? Not just to the Garden but other places, as well?"

"In a way," he replied. "I've been keeping an eye on you, Kayla. But I'm no psycho. I'm not going to hurt you, and I won't let anyone else hurt you, either." There was that strange conviction in his voice again.

Kayla closed her eyes, feeling his breath heat her face, his fingertips smooth away her tears. Déjà vu washed over her, as if she'd stood in this very same spot with him before, and they'd had this same conversation. As if she'd felt his touch before—so calming and soothing, dispelling her fears. But that couldn't be, reason reminded her.

"Trust me," he whispered again, adding more weight to tip the scales in his favor and convince her of his sincerity.

Opening her eyes, Kayla realized that for some strange, unexplainable reason, she believed him, at least for the moment, logic be damned. Maybe because those silver eyes were warm, liquid, heating her face and her blood. Or maybe because he'd saved her from losing consciousness in the midst of a club full of strangers. If he meant to hurt her, surely he would have done so while she'd been unable to fight him. And the fingers drifting over her face were anything but threatening.

Possessive maybe.

Soothing, yes.

Reassuring, definitely. And Kayla needed reassurance. Her life had been turned upside down, her sanity slowly slipping away with each dreaded blackout. She'd come to wonder if reality even existed, or if she was meant to spend her life lost somewhere else, in an illusion, a nightmare. But the stranger who stood in front of her was very real.

More than anything, however, he didn't seem like a stranger at all. He *felt* familiar, and Kayla had always been one to trust her feelings. Even though she'd never *connected* with anyone but her father and Gramps, she still found herself attuned to people. She could sense things, sometimes very strongly, like now.

God, how she could sense the intensity of his feelings. Feelings that swirled inside of him, battled for control. But none of his inner turmoil showed in his easy stance. Jase Terrell appeared to be a man in complete control. Only Kayla knew differently. She *felt* him.

"You really do need some sleep." He traced the hollow beneath her bottom lashes. "You look so tired, and pale."

Suddenly self-conscious, she lifted her hand. "I—I'm always this color. I've never been much for the sun."

"A night child," he commented. "Like me." He looked straight into her eyes as if searching, as if he wanted to know her thoughts at that moment, her darkest fears.

She forced the notion away. Yet, his gaze remained steadfast, delving into her bleak, lonely heart, and for the briefest moment, the emptiness within her was filled.

Like a rush of electricity, Kayla felt the connection between them spark, the feelings stir, flow. In the next instant she saw his pain, lived it as her own, and the intensity of it nearly doubled her over.

Betrayal, denial and hunger flowed from him into her. And the hunger, in particular, was strong. So undeniably strong. Ravenous, deep-seated and so close to consuming him.

A hunger that called to her.

A voice that called to her.

Trust me, Kayla. Jase's voice drifted through her mind. *I'm here anytime you need me. Close...watching over you.*

She opened her mouth, but no words came.

"I'll be in the living room if you need me. Just call out." Reluctance and something else flickered in the depths of his eyes as he released her. Without a word, he turned and strode from the room, shutting the door behind him.

Stunned, Kayla sank to the bed. Clasping her upper arms, she realized she was shaking. *I'm here, Kayla. Close,* his voice sounded in her mind.

Suddenly, she knew why she shook. It wasn't that he'd kidnapped her. He believed in what he was doing—that it was for her own good—even if she didn't, and so far he hadn't hurt her. And it wasn't that his touch had seemed familiar. More than anything, and what troubled her most, was that she'd *felt* him. Really *connected* with him.

With that realization came the fear. For something didn't *feel* quite right about Jase Terrell. She sensed great inner turmoil, but there was something more—a part of him so black, so tormented and lost, that it ripped at her very soul.

She grabbed the quilt, draped it around her and pulled the edges tight. Crossing the room, she sank into the straight-backed rocker, her gaze riveted on the door. If he came back, she didn't want to be caught unawares.

Shivers gripped her—from the cold, from the strange man who fascinated and frightened her at the same time. She could still feel his hunger.

She tried to quiet the sudden ache in her middle. She shouldn't be *feeling* him at all. He was a stranger.

Yet he knew about her blackouts.

He knows you, Kayla, a child's voice whispered, unfamiliar and familiar all at once. *You're safe now. Safe.*

Maybe for the moment, but beyond that she didn't want to think. How could she trust someone she didn't even know? Gramps had always said to be wary. She *had* to be, she decided, steeling herself against the exhaustion that grabbed hold of her. She had to stay awake, alert, watchful. She touched the bare skin at her throat. If only she had her charm for comfort.

I'm close, Kayla. Watching over you. Here if you need me. Jase's deep voice rumbled in her ear. The shivers ceased and, oddly enough, for the first time in two weeks, Kayla didn't feel afraid when her eyes closed completely.

CHAPTER FOUR

"Time to eat."

Kayla's eyes snapped open at the sound of Jase's voice. Disoriented, she glanced around. Sunshine drifted through the bedroom doorway, silhouetting his broad shoulders and narrow waist. He appeared a large, mysterious shadow, part of the darkness left over from the past night—a night she'd been convinced had been merely a very realistic dream.

But when he moved from the doorway, daylight filled the room and he became more than a shadow. Ebony hair hung in damp tendrils to his shoulders. His white T-shirt, damp, as well, molded to his sinewy torso, revealing every bulge and curve. He wore jeans faded from too many washings. They seemed slightly shrunk, too, for they clung to his thighs, his muscles rippling as he stepped toward her. Last night had been all too real, and her mysterious savior, or maybe nemesis, she hadn't quite made up her mind, was real, too, and unnervingly close.

Kayla shrank back, snatching up the quilt, which had slipped to her lap. Though she still wore her knit top and jeans, even her boots, she might as well have been stark naked. His gaze seemed to strip away all barriers—until he looked inside of her and knew her every thought.

"You look much better," he commented as he placed a steaming plate of scrambled eggs on the lamp table next to her. "Not nearly as exhausted as last night."

Her stomach gave an involuntary grumble. "W-what time is it?" She wiped at her sleep-filled eyes.

"Nearly four in the afternoon."

"You're kidding?" Alarm swept through her. She grasped the rocker arms to push herself to her feet.

He placed a restraining hand over hers, his fingers large and tanned against her pale skin. "Calm down. You needed the sleep."

The warmth of his palm sent tremors of heat spiraling through her. She glanced into his eyes, lost herself in their silver depths. In those few seconds, she felt his restraint, the excruciating tension that filled him and held his emotions with such a tight leash, she could only guess what brewed below the surface... violence, lust, or something much more powerful.

Abruptly, Jase pulled his hand from hers. He broke their silent contact as if he knew she could feel his emotions and he wanted to shut her out.

"You needed the sleep," he repeated, averting his gaze.

"I—I haven't slept so hard in a long time," she admitted. He nodded, as if he knew all about the troubles that plagued her and robbed her of sleep. He probably did, she reminded herself. If she could *feel* him, undoubtedly, he could *feel* her. That had always been the way things worked with her father and Gramps. Then again, the connection she felt with Jase was much stronger, and very disconcerting.

"You don't seem to have slept very much," she said, noting the hollow circles beneath his eyes. In all honesty, he looked dead tired, in sore need of a shave, and, though she hated herself for thinking it, dangerously attractive with his haunted moonsilver eyes.

"Yeah, well, I don't sleep well these days, either." He busied himself with the napkin he was tucking beneath the edge of her plate, never allowing his gaze to stray her way. He'd brought her here to save her, yet he seemed reluctant to look her in the face. Reluctant even to touch her, she realized when his elbow accidentally brushed her arm and he stiffened.

Kayla's heartbeat echoed in her ears as she watched and waited for him to say something, anything, to break the unnerving silence that had settled around them.

Jase finished his task and turned to leave, his boots a steady thud on the hardwood floor as he neared the doorway. "The well out back still has a good water supply. There's a bathroom down the hall. No bath or shower, though. I managed to get the water pump in the kitchen working. You can freshen up in there when you feel up to it. If not today, maybe tomorrow. It'll be dark soon and time for bed."

Panic streaked up her spine. "You can't really mean to keep me here," she blurted out, springing to the edge of the rocker. Her arm bumped the plate. The fork clattered to the floor.

He stopped, every muscle in his back drawn tight. "Yes," he said with cool authority, the word hanging in the air between them. "I told you that last night."

"I know but—"

"No buts." He pivoted, pinning her with his steely gaze, as if the expanse of the room provided a safe enough distance for him to face her now. Impatience and something else, maybe regret, laced his next words. "There's no other way, Kayla. You're in danger, whether you believe it or not. There are people who want to see you hurt. Two weeks and the danger will pass. You'll be free to leave then."

"*Two weeks!* But my job—"

"Can wait," he cut in, his voice low and steady, no matter that Kayla's sanity dangled by a single thread.

"I picked up those eggs from a roadside vendor we passed on the way here," he went on. "But we're going to need a good stock of supplies if we're going to last two weeks. I'm going into town. I'll call the radio station and tell them you're sick. That you need some vacation time.''

"What makes you think they'll buy that? I *disappeared* last night in the middle of a promo event, for goodness' sake! That's not like me. They'll know you're lying.''

"They'll buy every word I tell them," he replied, a trace of coldness creeping into his voice. "You haven't been the most reliable employee over the past two weeks. Always late for promotions, not to mention your regular shift. Besides, what I tell them won't be a lie. You did collapse last night. Luckily, I was nearby.''

"My hero," she snapped, resisting the hysterical urge to laugh at the irony of her predicament. She'd had her headset tapped by the man standing before her, who could very well be a modern-day Jack the Ripper, for all she knew. Still, she couldn't forget he'd come to her rescue last night. And he'd hardly touched her. In fact, he seemed intent on not touching her.

He smiled, a sad, melancholy tilt to his mouth. "I've never been hero material, Kayla. Remember that—for your own good.''

"Rickie won't believe anything unless she talks to me.''

"She'll believe me, Kayla. You know she will.''

Damn him for being right, she thought. No one at the station, including Rickie, would question that she'd taken ill. Not after seeing her behave so strangely over the past couple of weeks. They'd all been waiting for her to have a complete breakdown. Now they would simply think she'd finally gone around the bend.

Helplessness gripped her and she nearly screamed. She couldn't just sit idly by and let a total stranger take control of her life. So far, he hadn't hurt her, but she couldn't be sure. Even if a small voice claimed otherwise. She remembered the strange trust she'd felt last night, and again a minute ago when he'd touched her, and dismissed the feelings as irrational. Last night she hadn't been thinking straight and things were still a little fuzzy.

She couldn't trust him. She wouldn't.

"It would be more convincing if they heard the story from me. Take me with you and I'll make the call," she pleaded. If she could get to a public place, she could get away from him, scream, do something.

"That's not a good idea. It's safer here." The stern set of his jaw, the hard flash of silver eyes, told her he wasn't about to change his mind.

"So you're just going to leave me here?"

"Yes. We need food and—"

"You didn't plan any of this? It's just my luck to get abducted by a kidnapper who doesn't plan ahead."

He regarded her a thoughtful second. "I prepared a little. Extra clothes, matches, stuff like that—in case. But I didn't bring even a fourth of what we'll need. Honestly, I had hoped I wouldn't have to step in. I didn't want any of this to happen. Then last night when I saw you..." He paused and shrugged. "I had to do something. I couldn't let them have you."

She closed her eyes, grappling for her last bit of control. "Who is 'them'?" she asked through tight lips. "*Who*, Jase?"

"The people who want to hurt you."

"Now that sheds some light on the subject," she snapped.

"Stop doubting, Kayla. Believe what I'm telling you, even if it's not as much as you want to hear. For your own good, just believe."

"Why didn't you go after supplies while I was asleep?"

"I didn't want you to wake up alone."

"Why not? Did you think I might be frightened? Confused? I suppose you wanted to explain things to me."

"As much as I can."

"Which isn't much."

"No..." He shrugged, massaging the back of his neck with one large hand and glancing toward the doorway. "I have to go, Kayla. It'll be dark soon and I want to be back before sunset. We're about thirty miles from town."

"Which town?"

"It doesn't matter. I'll be as quick as I can." He strode through the doorway, leaving the door wide open behind him, to her utter amazement.

Seconds later, he reappeared in the doorway. Kayla felt sure he meant to lock her in, but he didn't. He merely leaned into the bedroom and murmured, "Stay in the house and you'll be safe while I'm gone. I'll see you when I get back. And by the way," he added, his lips hinting at a grin, "no matter what you think, I'm no kidnapper. You're not a prisoner here."

"No? I don't think I came willingly."

"You'll stay willingly." A serious expression slid over his handsome features. "You have to, Kayla. I know I'm asking a lot—I mean, you don't know me from a lunatic on the street—but I need you to trust me. As I told you, there are people who want to hurt you. This is the only safe place for you. *Stay in the house.*"

Fat chance, she thought to herself. No matter how sincere he seemed, she wouldn't sit by and wait to see her instincts proven wrong. The moment he was gone, so was she.

If only Jase didn't seem to read her every thought. "This place is in the middle of nowhere," he added. "Try to leave and you'll end up lost in the woods. I might not find you before they do. And then..."

He left his sentence unfinished and a shiver worked its way down her spine. He wants you to be frightened, she told herself. "Then I'll be free of you," she whispered the thought aloud.

He gave her a stern look, his voice taking on a hard edge as he said tightly, "Stay put, Kayla. You'll be free of me, and find yourself in a worse situation, or have you forgotten the blackouts? If you leave the vicinity of the house, you're sure to have one. Who knows where you'll end up then."

Determined not to cry, Kayla clamped down on her bottom lip to stop its quivering. With blurry eyes, she watched him shrug and rake a restless hand through his hair.

"Dammit, I know this is all hard for you to accept, but I'm telling you the truth. You're in danger. I wish I could tell you more—"

"Then tell me," she entreated. "Help me make some sense out of all this. *Please!*" She saw something flicker in the deep silver of his gaze and then it was gone. His expression closed, refusing her even a glimpse of his thoughts.

"I wish to hell that I could," he murmured. He regarded her a moment more then turned and disappeared.

She listened to his footsteps as he strode through the house, then outside. The door slammed in his wake.

The moment she heard the motorcycle roar to life, she was out of the rocker, flying through the doorway, down the small hallway to the living room. Escape! reason screamed and she had to listen. It didn't matter that she had trusted Jase for a crazed moment last night or this morning. She hadn't been thinking clearly and—

She came to a dead stop on the threshold of the living room, paralyzed by the musty smell of old newspapers and cigars, overwhelmed by the sight before her.

The curtains were pulled back. Afternoon sunshine filled the room, illuminating the small beige sofa covered with lime green throw pillows, the brick fireplace long since blackened with soot, the old-time radio in one corner, a magazine rack overflowing with yellowed newsprint—all strangely, inexplicably familiar, as if she viewed a rerun of a favorite old movie.

She gazed around. Drank in every nook and cranny of the room, from the cobwebs in the corners, to the dried husks of june bugs scattered across the windowsill. Her attention finally settled on a small ceramic vase that sat on a dust-covered end table next to a hurricane lamp and a box of matches. The hand-painted rose on the front of the vase had faded, the edges were chipped, old—like everything else in the room. A handful of paper violets filled the vase, the once-purple construction paper having faded to a pale bluish hue.

Drawn by an invisible force, Kayla crossed the room, her fingertips going to the faded petals, which nearly crumbled at her touch.

Here, Mommy, a child's voice whispered.

Startled, Kayla glanced behind her. The room was empty. Yet, she felt a distinct presence, and there was no denying the melodious voice.

For the best mommy in the world, the voice added, stirring something deeply buried and forgotten within Kayla. The same voice she'd heard last night just before she'd nodded off.

Her fear melted away and she closed her eyes. The sound of a child's bubbling laughter drifted through her head. A warmth enfolded her, like the strong arms of a parent comforting a child awakened by a nightmare.

No more nightmares, Mommy, the voice continued, soft and so very real. *Just like you said. I trust you.*

Trust me, Jase's words replayed in Kayla's mind, his deep voice so different from the soft whispers of the child. At the same time, his voice held a warmth, and a desperation that reached inside of Kayla and tied all logic and reason into knots.

I like Jase, Mommy. He's a good boy. He watches over me and chases the nightmares away. He even liked my flowers.

Kayla opened her eyes and the voice stopped. She quickly scanned the room again. Empty, except for the scent of fresh violets suddenly rich in the air.

Impossible. Kayla gave herself a mental shake, staring at the paper violets. *Paper.* "I'm definitely losing my mind," she declared, ignoring the urge to bend down and take a whiff.

Her hand went to her throat and she felt for the familiar charm. Skin contacted skin and a pang of loss shot through Kayla. No soothing silver...nothing. She curled her fingers into a fist and forced herself away from the vase and the warmth that had enfolded her for those few moments.

"I have to get out of here," she said, as if saying the words aloud could stifle the small voice inside of her begging for her to believe Jase—a stranger who had whisked her away without so much as an explanation, demanding "trust me," as if those two words could earn her belief.

Jase Terrell, photographer and possible lunatic, didn't know that Kayla trusted no one. There were only two people she'd ever put her faith in, and they were gone, leaving a legacy of lies.

The moment Kayla pulled open the front door and stepped up to the wood-framed screen, her hopes plunged. She quickly realized why Jase had dared to leave her alone, doors unlocked, with the assurance that she wouldn't flee.

No more than four or five yards from the house stood a solid wall of trees. Kayla pushed open the screen door and walked out into the yard, eyes wide as she gazed around.

The house sat in what appeared to be a circular clearing, the foliage so thick she could see nothing beyond the tangle of branches. Kayla walked the perimeter of the house. A small woodshed joined to the back of the house. A few feet away stood a small storage area, no more than a shack, really—the building old, boards rotted from years of neglect.

Kayla searched the surrounding trees for a trail Jase might have followed out. There was no break in the trees. Nothing, as if he'd disappeared into thin air.

Beyond the dense brown wall, Kayla could only guess what lurked. She'd never seen woods so thick, so impenetrable, anywhere near Houston. They probably weren't anywhere close to the city—any city. They could have traveled most of the night, for all she knew. It had been barely eleven o'clock when she'd left the sound booth at the club. When she'd opened her eyes in the bedroom of the old house, the clock had read nearly four in the morning. Had they been driving all that time or only a small portion? And in what direction?

Questions swirled in her brain, her stomach somersaulted and she stumbled back to the porch. She grabbed the wooden step-railing for support. Swallowing, she willed the sick feeling to pass. God, what was she going to do?

The forest seemed to whisper to her. *Strength, Kayla. You're safe here . . . always, child. Safe.*

The words fueled her courage. The moment the ground seemed to level again, she managed to climb the two steps onto the porch and stagger into the house, back to the bedroom.

The scent of fresh eggs hung in the air, not the least bit tempting. Her hunger had passed and a giant fist had settled in its place. Kayla slumped down on the corner of the bed and touched cool fingers to her temples.

Strength, the walls whispered, and she listened, gaining enough control to try to think through her situation rationally. Kayla had always prided herself on being sensible and clearheaded. Logic told her she couldn't wait around to find out if her instincts about Jase were right. That he was sincere. She couldn't chance that this one time, her *feeling* about someone might be wrong.

She glanced at the clock. He'd said he would be back in a little while. That meant that life existed past the trees, people, stores, telephones. If she could just reach a phone and call the police. She wouldn't turn Jase in. She'd given her word last night. She only wanted to go back to her job and try to piece her life together.

She snatched the quilt from the rocker and rushed back outside. Cold air swirled around her and she draped the quilt over her shoulders. She debated which direction to take, then threw caution to the wind and headed for the trees directly in front of her. She squeezed her way between two huge trunks, and left the sunshine behind for a bone-chilling darkness that quickly swallowed her.

The woods were much thicker and deeper than she had imagined. She moved as fast as she could, picking her way past limbs. There had to be civilization beyond the thicket.

The forest grew more dense, destroying her sense of direction. No shaft of light penetrated the overlay of branches. She squinted, limbs pulling and poking at her like long fingers.

"Dammit," she muttered, the word echoing in her head, like an ominous taunt reminding her of how alone she was. She took another step forward.

She heard the crunch of leaves, the rustle of a tree branch.

Stopping dead in her tracks, she waited, listening. The noise persisted and Kayla knew then that she wasn't alone.

She opened her mouth to call for help. Her voice failed as a rush of panic surged through her. Danger! her senses screamed.

Grasping a nearby limb, she inched back until she pressed against a thick tree trunk. She tried to discern the direction of the noise. It seemed to swirl around her. Louder. Louder.

Her hands started to tremble. The quilt slipped from her grasp, pooled at her feet. She searched for the moonstar at her neck, desperate for the warmth of the silver. She felt only the frantic beat of her own pulse.

The tingling started in her fingertips first, spreading to her palms, her arms. Her vision shifted, grayed.

"God, no!" she gasped, squeezing her eyes shut against the blurriness. She couldn't have a blackout. Not here. Not now. She couldn't.

Her knees buckled as the numbness started to creep through her. She slid down the length of the tree. The bark scraped her back. The sound of footsteps thundered in her ears.

With all of her strength, she grasped the tree and struggled to her feet. She staggered through the forest, but in what direction, she didn't know. Kayla knew only the burning desire to run.

The footsteps gained on her. She tried to move faster, arms flailing, shoving at branches and fighting the numbness.

Stay in the house. Why hadn't she listened to Jase?

She stumbled a few more steps and the toe of her boot caught on a protruding limb. She fell forward and slammed facedown into the ground. Air rushed from her lungs. She flung back her head and gulped for precious oxygen. Then she caught a glimpse of light through the fog surrounding her . . . the edge of the clearing.

Clawing at the ground, she pulled herself forward, toward the light. The footsteps moved closer. The numbness worked its way through her body, slowing her progress until she slumped, motionless.

As the blackness snaked around her, stealing into her mind, weaving its consuming spell, she found herself praying the footsteps belonged to Jase. That all he'd said about people wanting to hurt her wasn't true.

They're coming.

Trust me.

I like Jase . . . he watches over me, chases the nightmares away.

Kayla knew the moment the footsteps stopped beside her that Jase had told her the truth. She longed to open her eyes, to roll over and face the danger that stalked her. She couldn't. She was paralyzed, slipping into a pit as black as sin itself. Blood-thick silence pressed down on her, smothering her cries and feeding her fear.

When she felt the cold fingers drift down her spine, she managed to twist her head to the side. Her eyes opened a fraction and she glimpsed the pitch-black of a shadow.

"Jase," she said, sobbing. And with one last effort, she dug her fingers into the ground and heaved herself toward the light. Then oblivion claimed her.

Jase hooked several plastic bags of groceries on the handlebars of his motorcycle. Turning, he juggled a plastic bottle of soda to his other arm and reached to pop open the compartment beneath the seat. He would have to cram everything in to make it fit the small space—

Jase! the familiar voice called and he froze.

The soda bottle slipped from his grasp and splattered across the pavement outside the convenience store.

A gray-haired woman, wire-rimmed spectacles perched on her nose and a jug of milk clutched in her age-spotted hands, paused at her car door. She turned a curious gaze on him.

Jase put his back to her, ignoring her stare as Kayla's voice filled his head. *Jase!*

He knew in an instant that she'd left the safety of the house. The notion staggered him. He'd underestimated her power. Gravely underestimated it. He'd stressed her complacency when she'd been semiconscious, impressing his own will upon her. That should have made her obedient. When he gave her an explicit command, she should have listened. His will should have become hers—

Jase! she cried again, going deeper, deeper into the blackness.

His vision started to blur. The waning afternoon sunlight seemed to flicker. Flattening one palm against the black leather motorcycle seat, Jase concentrated on the clammy coldness and tried to hold on to reality. With the other hand, he grasped the moonstar hidden beneath his T-shirt, always hidden, lest Kayla get a look at it, and remember. The silver burned through the cotton and seared his palm. His fingers tightened.

He couldn't follow her into the blackout as he usually did. He needed to reach her physically, to get her back to the Old One's cabin—

"Jase."

Jase glanced at the pale, big-boned fingers that gripped his forearm. Then his gaze lifted to the man beside him. The real man whose image had filled Jase's nightmares for the past twenty-two years.

"You won't reach her in time, foolish boy. Don't even try." The man smiled, his dark mustache a direct contrast to the startling whiteness of his teeth. "You never should have interfered. Your father isn't pleased."

"Go to hell, Max," Jase snarled, shrugging away from the man's hand.

"With pleasure, my boy, and so will you. A lot sooner if you don't stay away from her."

Jase grasped Max Talbot by the throat and slammed him up against the thick window at the front of the convenience store. A dangerous inch away, Jase whispered, "He won't have her. Tell him that." To further his point, Jase clamped his fingers tighter, expecting to hear the man's gurgling, anticipating it after so many years of torturous memories. Max had been his father's most loyal follower. Jase's most ardent pursuer. He would have killed Jase long ago, but Jase's father had forbidden it. He still forbade it, though that fact didn't seem to quench Max's thirst for revenge.

His chilling laughter filled the air. "Look at you, Jase. So set on denying us, even though the bloodlust gleams in your eyes. Go ahead," he urged, his own eyes bright with anticipation. "Call forth the power. Send me to hell like you always wanted to. Here's your chance, my boy. Do it!"

Jase's blood rushed faster. His fingers ached to tighten and do exactly what Max said. The power was strong, tempting. So very tempting. Jase felt Max's pulse beneath his hands. A little pressure, and the flow would stop. The man's eyes would widen . . . lifeless, dead.

Resist! his mind cried, and his fingers loosened of their own accord. A shudder ripped through him as his body fought the ancient battle between good and evil.

"Jase," Max said with a shake of his head, a tsk-tsk sound on his lips. "You're a fool, and still as rebellious as ever. You could have had everything."

"At a price," Jase growled, still holding Max pinned to the window. "Much too high a price."

"No price is too high for eternal life."

"It's not life we're talking about. It's fire and brimstone."

"You've been listening to too many television preachers. Remember what you are, Jase. You can't change what is meant to be." Max placed one hand over Jase's and exerted a bone-crushing strength that forced Jase's fingers completely loose. "We're even more powerful now," he said at the stunned look on Jase's face. "We're stronger, and much more determined. We won't lose all that we've gained because you have it in your head to play guardian angel." He chuckled. "Imagine someone as jaded as you fancying himself an angel. You're as crazy as Kayla's father and the Old One put together."

"Maybe I am crazy—only because I left you breathing that night."

"That was rather foolish," Max agreed, grasping Jase's throat with his other hand. He squeezed, a merciless gleam in his cold blue eyes. "You never were a bloodthirsty child. That was the problem." He tightened his fingers. "I would snap your neck in two, but I'm sure your father wants that pleasure all for himself."

"And you wouldn't dare go against my father," Jase rasped.

"Your father showed us the true way, Jase. He taught us to leave behind the old magic and spells, to conjure a spirit that could make us all-powerful. Your father has the knowledge. That's why we won't lose him to death. His spirit must live on, and the only way is through a child of the purest blood. You and your brother are the last of your bloodline. Kayla is the last of hers."

"I won't let you get your hands on her," Jase said in a rush before struggling for another breath.

"You're too late, boy. Much too late," Max said, enunciating each word with frightening clarity. "You might want to rethink your position, Jase. You're as tied to the darkness as we are. More so, in fact. The blood runs through your veins pure and untainted, if you'll pardon the expression."

Jase shook his head, finding his voice despite the stranglehold on his neck. "Like hell I am," he croaked.

"You are," Max ground out. "And you know it. You're stupid to worry about us. You should worry about yourself. You're still one of us." He leaned closer until Jase felt the heat of the man's breath. "Touch her, Jase. Tell her our secrets. Fulfill the promise and return to us. She still feels a tie to you, she feels her destiny, just as you do. You aren't strong enough to deny us, Jase. Neither you nor Kayla. Come to us. Fulfill the promise and you shall have everything you've ever wanted."

"No," Jase growled.

Max tightened his fingers around Jase's throat, cutting off the oxygen for a long, threatening moment. "Such a fighter," Max mocked. Then he loosened his hold just enough for Jase to swallow and take a much-needed breath. "We know your thoughts," Max went on. "How much you still hunger for her. We know everything."

"I'll die before I let you take her," Jase vowed.

"If that's your intention, then beg mercy on your black soul, traitor, because you'll die soon. The only way to redeem yourself is to come back to us, Jase. For your sake, I hope you don't wait too long. You've already lost favor in your father's eyes and he isn't the forgiving sort. None of us are."

"He's a heartless bastard," Jase snapped. "Like the rest of you."

"He's much more, and no matter how you denounce him, you're a part of that 'heartless bastard.' The blackest part, I might add. He trusted you with his knowledge. He gave you to the darkness, to *Ashtaroth* himself, to us—"

"No!" Jase denied with his mouth while the truth cried out from his soul. And Max heard all too clearly.

He smiled. "Deny us all you want, but you're a part of the darkness, Jase. It's too bad you're so stubborn. We all had such hopes for you. The promise—"

"—was an abomination. A promise of death and destruction."

"No, dear boy, it was a promise of enduring power, your power joining with Kayla's to conceive a pure child to house your father's spirit. And it *will* be fulfilled, no matter what you do. A pity you betrayed us, but at least we have your brother ready to take your place. He's looking forward to it, I might add. Kayla is quite beautiful. She'll birth a fine son for him. *Ashtaroth* will be very pleased."

"She'll fight all of you."

"Don't be so sure. When she discovers all that she can have, she'll come to us willingly. She *has* to come to us willingly. She's only frightened right now."

"I won't let you force any more blackouts on her."

"You have no say, and the blackouts are necessary. What would really frighten her is to be confronted by all of us with no warning. The blackouts make her complacent and allow us to school her without any conscious doubts interfering. When the confrontation finally occurs, she'll understand her destiny and embrace it—with or without you, Jase. So make up your mind."

"When hell freezes—"

"Your father's spirit cannot die," Max raged, his eyes glittering with deadly intent. "His knowledge, his bond with the darkness cannot be lost. The Keepers will *not* lose him."

"So you'll see an innocent child possessed?"

"Not innocent. A child of darkness—young, healthy, trained in our ways. A new home for the power your father holds."

"You're sick!"

"Remember what I've told you," Max spat a second before he flung Jase away from him.

Jase slammed full force into the convenience store window. His head snapped back against the glass. He clamped his eyes shut as a blinding white pain shot through his skull.

"Stay away from her," Max warned, "or fulfill the promise yourself, Jase. You think you can resist, but you've already given in by interfering in the first place." The voice ended abruptly. Then silence.

Forcing his eyes open, Jase staggered forward, searching the parking lot for Max. There was no sign of him. Vanished... The Keepers had such powers. The evil cloaked them whenever they wished. Jase knew... That's what frightened him so much about himself. He knew way too much about the darkness and felt the pull too strongly. Max knew it. So did Jase's father. That's why they hadn't pursued him once he left the coven. They were confident he'd find his way back to the path chosen for him.

But Jase felt the pull toward Kayla, as well, heard her cries, sensed her fear.

He touched the back of his head and fingered the sticky wetness. Staggering the few steps to his bike, he managed to climb on. He fought a wave of dizziness and brought the engine to life. Moments later he was speeding down the nearly deserted highway.

Jase urged the motorcycle faster, desperate to reach Kayla before the first shadows of darkness fell. Damn Max for detaining him.

Dusk gave way to night, the air cooled and, try as he might, Jase couldn't suppress the craving that stirred to life.

The craving to feel her beneath him, to taste her, to savor every inch of the woman who'd been given to him. He'd been so condemning of the darkness, so set on denying what pulsed through his veins. Now he found himself wondering if it wouldn't be easier to give in. No, he found himself *wanting* to give in. He could have Kayla then, and the Keepers would have both of them, and the darkness would thrive a lifetime more.

"Dammit, no," he growled, his voice lost in the drone of the wind. As much as he wanted her, he steeled himself against the incredible force that drew them together. Their union would be an abomination like the ceremony forced on them as children.

Jase tightened his fingers around the motorcycle grips. Her protector—that's all he meant to be to her. Nothing more. He wouldn't sacrifice her to the darkness, and he wouldn't give up the life of his child to house the evil that filled his father.

As he neared the turnoff that led to the Old One's cabin, Jase slowed the motorcycle. His vision seemed sharper, his heartbeat calm. Something had happened.

Or rather, something hadn't happened, because the sense of fear he'd felt at the convenience store had vanished. Kayla wasn't fighting the blackout anymore.

Either the Keepers had left her alone or she'd finally given in to them completely, and Jase knew the Keepers would never give her up. That left only one answer.

Jase closed his eyes for a brief moment and prayed, and hoped with all his heart, no matter how shrouded in darkness, that for once He was listening.

CHAPTER FIVE

Kayla lifted her head and shoved a tangle of hair from her face. Forcing her eyes open, she blinked, letting her vision adjust to the gray shadows.

The sun had disappeared below the trees. Twilight filled the clearing where her upper body rested. She glanced at the snarl of branches that hid her calves. She'd managed to fight her way at least partway from the trees.

She forced herself to her knees. Dizziness swept over her. Seconds later, she managed to stand, legs wobbly, head reeling, the musty smell of earth and grass pungent in her nostrils.

Her gaze went to the wall of trees silhouetted against the last light of the sun. They appeared an army of dark skeletons standing at attention, bony arms outstretched to the gloomy sky, paying homage to some unseen entity.

Bits of memory flashed through Kayla's mind. The footsteps. The presence standing over her. Cold fingers along her spine.

She whirled, her stare sweeping the clearing, from the house to the trees and back, searching for someone . . . or *something*.

Kayla inched backward, her heart pummeling her ribs, her breaths coming in short gasps as fright swept through her. Jase had been right and she'd been too much of a fool to listen to him. To listen to her own instincts.

If you go outside, I might not find you before they do. And then . . .

Kayla jerked around and took off running, her gaze fixed on the refuge of the house. Her loneliness grew with each step. Her fear magnified.

Even when she reached the safety of the living room, the door shut tight and locked behind her, she felt little relief. She slumped against the chilled wood, took several deep breaths and tried to calm her frantic heartbeat. No luck.

She almost gave in to a hysterical laugh. Some night child, she thought. Her radio audience would be sorely disappointed if they could see her now—afraid of some unseen bogeyman.

No, she'd *seen* the bogeyman—the shadow in the woods. Jase had warned her about the danger. Danger she now sensed so keenly, the hair on her neck prickled.

She forced another calming breath, determined to pull herself together. Rather than sink to her knees and cry, she steeled herself and prayed for strength. Tears would solve nothing. She had to wise up and look out for herself. Jase had been right.

Funny, but that knowledge filled her with a strange sense of relief. At least her instincts about him were on target. She'd been so mixed up lately, she didn't dare trust herself, much less anyone else. Now she realized she wasn't losing her mind, not entirely, and that made her feel a little better. If only the inside of the cabin wasn't so blasted dark. The fire Jase had left burning in the hearth had died to a pile of glowing embers, giving off no heat and very little light.

Flicking the light switch near the door, she realized why Jase had put a candle in her room the night before. No electricity. She stumbled over to the end table and felt for the box of matches and the hurricane lamp she'd spotted earlier.

In seconds, she lit the lamp and turned the wick higher, letting the flame rise to a comforting glow. But there was no comfort. No warmth. Her nerves tingled, extraordinarily alive, tuned in to every creak of the house, every draft of cold air.

Quickly, Kayla pulled at the ties that held the drapes. They swished into place, shutting out any prying eyes. She picked up the lamp and made her way down the narrow hallway.

Her gaze swept the kitchen, from the wooden countertop and sink, a fresh bar of soap sitting on the sink ledge, to the wood-burning stove, ancient and rusted, a pile of kindling beside it. Obviously, Jase had been busy while she slept.

There were other signs of life in the small room. A plastic water pitcher and two drinking cups sat near the edge of the hand-carved oak table that graced the center of the room. Kayla trailed her fingers across the worn top marred with scratches from years of use. A twinge of regret shot through her, as if she'd touched this table, stood in this very room before.

She shook away the thought and turned to the counter. She was definitely teetering on the edge of a breakdown, but she wasn't going over without a fight.

Kayla placed the lamp on the countertop and opened a couple of drawers until she found a small, somewhat threadbare, towel. Tugging at the topaz ring Gramps had given her, she placed the piece of jewelry on the counter. Old habits died hard and she hated getting her jewelry wet. She leaned over the sink and grabbed the handle of the water pump.

After several cranks, water gushed into the basin. Kayla splashed several icy handfuls onto her face, eager to wash away the dirt, not to mention the fear that gripped her.

They're coming. The words played over and over in her mind.

She ducked her head beneath the spout, pumping the handle vigorously. Freezing water cascaded over her head, streamed down her neck to soak the collar of her blouse.

Her teeth chattered, goose bumps rose, but she didn't care. The water offered a much-needed distraction.

Shoving her sleeves up above her elbows, Kayla grabbed the bar of soap. She lathered her hands and washed her hair, scrubbing frantically, as if she could erase all traces of her blackout in the woods. Still, she saw the shadow at the fringes of her mind, waiting for her, calling to her.

She scrubbed harder, rubbing with a fierceness born of some primal need for survival. Survival of her sanity...

Seconds later, she rinsed the lather, wrung the excess water from her hair and began soaping her arms. The roar of a motorcycle stopped her cold.

The lock clicked, then the front door slammed open. Hinges creaked. The house trembled from the force. Jase's urgent voice reverberated through the small dwelling.

"Kayla!" Before she could reach for the towel, he burst through the kitchen door.

He stopped, his stare fixed on her, anguish flashing in his silver eyes. "My God, Kayla, I couldn't feel you and...what happened?" he demanded.

Her entire body shook, whether from the freezing water dripping from her hair or from her own fear, she didn't know. Tears sprang to her eyes. She opened her mouth, but no sound came out.

Then he was striding across the room. Strong hands reached for the towel and wiped the soap from her arms. "Tell me," he demanded, a strange tenderness in his husky voice.

He threw the towel on the counter. His fingers twined with hers, generating a compelling heat. A multitude of emotions rushed into Kayla, assaulted her—worry, relief, elation. More than anything else, however, she felt his fear and indecision—both emotions fierce, consuming, frightening in their intensity.

"I thought I might be too late," he said, his voice low, thick, weaving a spell Kayla found hard to resist.

"You are," she retorted, wrenching away from him. She rushed from the room, driven to put some distance between them. He filled her senses, fought for control of her mind, his thoughts as overwhelming as the blackouts. As terrifying.

More so because Kayla found herself wanting to succumb to him, to listen to his words, believe, to *feel* him, and that scared the daylights out of her.

"Kayla," he called after her.

She shoved open the wooden screen door and raced outside, into the moonlit yard. She stopped, looking for a place to run. There wasn't one, save the trees, and she wouldn't go back into the forest. Frantic, she glanced around, only to feel his hands on her shoulders, his voice, so deep and mesmerizing, in her ear.

"Kayla, I know you're frightened. Maybe if you tell me what happened—"

"*You* tell me, Jase." She whirled on him. "You have all the answers. Tell me what's going on because I still haven't a clue." Her voice rose a notch and she knew she sounded hysterical. But she'd passed caring. She wanted—no, *needed*—to understand what was happening. Her sanity depended on it.

"I wish I could—"

"You obviously don't wish hard enough," she snapped, anger a welcome relief to the terror that had seized her earlier. Anger provided distance, focus, and God how she needed both. "You tell me someone's after me, but you won't tell me who. You steal me away, albeit at a very helpful moment, but then you won't tell me your reasons. I wake up and find myself in this creepy old house with not a clue as to why. *Why*, Jase?"

"It's safe here."

"Right, I forgot. I can certainly understand the safety. There's not a break anywhere in this fortress of trees, yet you managed to ride a motorcycle through somewhere I still can't see." Her blurry gaze swept the wall of foliage. "I tried to find a trail, Jase. I *tried.*"

"I told you to stay in the house," he said, his tone accusing, fanning the angry flames that sparked inside of her.

"I know that, but you didn't tell me why. Who the hell are you and why is it that you appear out of nowhere, my knight in shining armor, rescuing me? I don't know you from Adam. Why is that, Jase? Who are you—really?"

He looked uncomfortable, as if he searched for the right words, yet hesitated to speak them. "I knew your father and Gramps," came the whisper-soft revelation.

The ground tilted and Kayla swayed. Jase's arms went around her, holding her steady.

"You knew them?" she breathed.

"From a long time ago, Kayla. I knew them well. They would've wanted me to help you."

"And my mother?" she pressed, leveling a stare at him. "Did you know her?" She waited, breath paused, but he remained silent.

"You did know her," she finally said, her voice laced with accusation. "You knew her like you knew my father and Gramps."

"Because of circumstance, our paths crossed a long time ago. I helped you because they once helped me." Quiet ensued for several long moments before he added, "Trust what I'm telling you, Kayla."

"No." She shook her head, her emotions fighting their own battle. Belief with disbelief, trust with mistrust. "You can't expect me to believe you without any shred of evidence that you're telling me the truth." But there was evidence, her conscience reminded her. The woods, the shadow, the strange familiarity she felt, as if she'd known Jase lifetimes ago.

"Isn't it enough to know that I care what happens to you? I stepped in because I couldn't see you hurt. Not only for your parents and Gramps, but for myself. There are evil people after you. I couldn't let them have you."

She glanced up and searched his eyes, which glowed liquid silver in the moonlight. Knowledge burned bright in their molten depths. He knew her, knew the memories just out of her reach, the answers that could fill the void of her childhood.

"I—I need to know more," she said.

"Why? Because all that's happened seems so unreal?"

Kayla nodded.

"It's very real." Jase placed gentle fingers under her chin and urged her gaze to meet his. "You can question me all you want, but deep down you know I'm telling the truth. You knew last night. You know now."

"I—you were right," she whispered, a shudder ripping through her, his gaze holding her captive with its moonsilver intensity, drawing her in, entrancing her.

He clasped her hand. "I was stupid to leave you here alone." A faint tremor fused his voice as though some emotion had touched him. "I should've known you would try to run."

Guilt churned within her, as if she'd betrayed his trust. But he was a stranger...

No! a voice screamed, and hot tears slipped from her eyes. "I—what else did you expect me to do? How could I have known you were telling the truth?" Her voice broke and she caught her bottom lip to stop its quivering. "I couldn't be sure."

"And now?"

Silence closed in for a long moment before she murmured, "I believe you."

Relief smoothed his features as he regarded her, then he lifted his hand to brush a few wet strands of hair from her cheek. "You should have trusted me, moonchild."

Moonchild. The name lingered in the black stillness of her mind. She tried to remember where she'd heard it be-

fore, but the effort made her head hurt. Instead, she closed
her eyes as rough fingertips brushed her tears away in a
gesture that seemed a lifetime old.

"I won't let anything happen to you," he said, the simple words tugging at some hidden recollection deep inside
of her. Warm fingers, moonsilver eyes . . .

And strength—a fierce, turbulent strength that radiated from his body, spinning and coiling through her, re-
storing her courage and filling her with a strange sense of
peace, as if she'd been meant to stand there in the moonlight with him. A stranger, yet not a stranger—touching,
feeling, *connecting*.

"I blacked out," she said.

"I felt it," he admitted. "Every dark moment."

She opened her eyes to find him studying her, a guarded
expression on his face. It was then that she noticed the red
trickle winding a path down the side of his neck.

"My God!" She reached out. "You're bleeding!"

"It's nothing." He shrugged away, swiping the blood
with an impatient hand.

"But you're *bleeding,* Jase!"

"It's nothing," he said again, his voice firm. "Go on
and tell me about the blackout."

She hesitated, staring at his neck where the crimson path
had been. When no more blood followed, she let relief sink
into her bones. Maybe it was just as he'd said . . . nothing.
But people didn't bleed for nothing.

"Tell me," Jase urged, drawing her from her thoughts.

"It wasn't like the others," she admitted, suddenly
compelled by those shimmering eyes to pour out her heart.
And though everything that was happening seemed unbelievable to her, to him it wasn't. He understood. He knew
the pieces of the puzzle that would make sense out of everything. "This one was like sleeping. I left the house and
tried to find my way through the woods. I got lost, and

then I heard footsteps.'' And I'd hoped it was you, she added silently.

He smiled then, a slight tilt of his lips that did crazy things to her heartbeat. She knew then he felt her thoughts as surely as if she'd spoken them aloud.

"I started to run," she went on. "Then came the tingling, the blackness, suffocating like always. But when I woke up, I didn't feel afraid. Just confused, like I'd been sleeping, or something. The blackouts have never felt like sleeping before. Never."

"It's the house," he said, glancing around him. "The clearing. It protects you."

Kayla closed her eyes, determined to break the trance he weaved. Her life had always been so normal. So safe. "This is all too weird," she whispered, urgency lacing her words. "None of this makes any sense."

"It doesn't have to make sense, Kayla."

"Yes, it does!" She clutched the edges of his jacket. "*You* have to make sense out of everything. Tell me what's happening. Help me understand!"

"I can't," he muttered. He pulled her hands from his jacket and put her away from him. "Dammit, why can't it be enough to know that you're in trouble and I want to help? Let me. Believe in me, Kayla, even though there are a lot of unanswered questions."

When he started to turn away, she clutched his arm. "Tell me what's going on," she begged. "Tell me why you took me, who's after me, what you know about my moth—"

He shrugged loose from her. "Don't touch me, and don't ask me what's going on. You wouldn't like my answers."

She stared at him, long and hard, noting the stern set of his jaw, the intensity of his eyes—eyes that had been so soft and liquid moments ago were now hard and steely. She yearned to reach out and touch him, to *feel* why he was so insistent on remaining silent. "Tell me, Jase. I have to know."

"Stay inside the house, Kayla," he growled. "You'll be safe there. If you do come outside, under no circumstances should you leave this clearing. Do it again and I'll lock you in," he vowed, the words low, threatening, leaving no doubt in her mind that he meant them. "I don't want to," he added, "but if you force me, I'll do it for your own good."

"Fine." Kayla swallowed the lump in her throat and wiped the wetness from her cheeks. "Do what you have to, but don't expect my gratitude or my cooperation, not without an explanation from you."

Blindly, she headed toward the house. Jase's footsteps thundered behind her. Rushing inside, she went into her bedroom and threw herself across the bed. Exhaustion and misery gripped her with a ruthlessness that drained the strength from her body.

"Gramps," she said on a sob, burying her face in a worn feather pillow, eager to drown out the sounds around her—the slam of the front door, the rustle of plastic bags, Jase's boots as he moved around the kitchen.

"Help me, Gramps. Please." If only he could hear. But he was gone and she was alone now.

No, a voice reminded her. Not completely alone.

Jase's footsteps came closer and she braced herself. Closer, closer... They stopped.

She held her breath and waited for him to come inside. She needed him to wrap her in his arms, comfort her, despite all common sense that screamed she *had* lost her mind. What kind of fool was she for wanting him near her? A stranger who'd walked into her life and taken control.

"Two weeks, Kayla," he said. "Give me two weeks. Trust me while we're here, do what I say, and then I'll tell you everything you want to know."

"About my mother?" she asked, her voice soft, wary.

"Everything...what I know of your mother, your past. *Everything.*"

Without lifting her head from the pillow, she nodded, a sob ripping through her. And what she wouldn't have given in that instant to turn into his embrace, all caution be damned, and feel his reassurance, his strength. If only he would cross the room, sit beside her...

She heard the slide of his boots as he turned, then the steady thump as he walked into the living room.

Disappointment welled up inside of her and for once, Kayla welcomed the tears. She cried for her mother, her father, Gramps, her lost childhood...and for a small boy with moonsilver eyes who haunted her dreams that night.

Help me.

The soft plea drew Kayla from a restless sleep. She glanced around. The bedroom was dim, with only the waning glow of a candle to dispel the darkness.

Kayla slid from bed, tugging on her boots. A child's cries drifted through the old house, calling out to her. She opened the bedroom door, peered down the empty hall, then made her way toward the living room.

A fire danced in the fireplace, casting flickering shadows across the empty room.

"Jase?" she called, her own voice strange as it echoed through the house. No answer.

The crying persisted and she turned toward the front door.

Outside...

Kayla reached for the door handle, then stopped. Fear ran in streaming rivulets down her spine.

"Jase?" she called again, this time louder. No answer.

Her fingers tightened around the doorknob. Her skin turned to gooseflesh as she remembered the shadow in the woods, the blackout. Maybe the crying was only her imagination, the wind...

Help me! The frightened voice shattered all indecision. She threw open the door and stepped out onto the porch.

The moon was nonexistent. Blackness devoured her. The wind played a haunting melody through the trees. Kayla hugged her arms, her eyes narrowed, searching.

"Jase, is that you? Are you all right?"

Help me! I'm afraid. Please! The trees seemed to voice the same frantic cry. Branches quivered. Ice-cold fingers clutched at Kayla, coaxing her out into the night.

And the voice coaxed her, as well. But she quickly realized that it didn't belong to Jase. It was a child's voice—hopeless, lost, begging for help.

Please!

The urgency of the word drove Kayla to the edge of the porch, propelled her down the first step despite the strange sense of foreboding that filled her. She shouldn't be outside. Jase had warned her. Yet, she couldn't resist a cry for help. She and Jase were in the middle of a deep forest. What if someone had been shot in a hunting accident or mauled by an animal? And it wasn't just any voice she heard. It was a *child's* voice.

She cringed at the thought of a child lying seriously hurt and helpless in the darkness.

"Where are you?" she called out, her words seeming to come from a long way off. Her voice disappeared in the rush of night wind that picked up as she stepped down into the yard.

Help me. Please, help me!

Kayla spotted the break in the trees immediately. Funny, but she hadn't seen it earlier. And she'd searched for it.

Her thoughts halted the moment she glimpsed the child. Just a pale white shadow, really, hand outstretched, voice filled with a terror that sliced through Kayla and drove her closer.

"What's wrong, honey?"

Help me!

"Are you hurt?" Only a few more steps, yet the child appeared farther away. Still a shadow. Only the voice grew stronger as Kayla moved closer.

She sensed the child's desperation, *felt* the child's terror, so all-consuming that it overrode her own fear of the forest and what lurked beyond.

Help! It's dark and I'm afraid!

Kayla reached for the pale white hands, visions of Dixie's cherublike face, sea-green eyes, dancing in front of her. She'd always loved children. Always thrived on helping them. She had to help the little girl who called to her now. She had to—

An arm snaked around her waist. A scream lodged in Kayla's throat as she found herself jerked backward. An angry voice boomed in her ears.

"What the hell are you doing?" Jase demanded. But he didn't wait for a reply. He hoisted her up over one shoulder and started to walk toward the house. "Didn't you listen to anything I said earlier? I told you to stay inside—"

"I was trying to help, Jase! Put me down! That little girl needs help!"

"What little girl?" He stopped in midstride and turned, his arm locked around Kayla's legs.

"Over there—" she motioned wildly "—at that break in the trees..." Kayla's voice failed her as she stared past Jase's thigh. The path she'd seen a moment ago was gone. Gone?

No, maybe her sense of direction was off. She strained her neck and scanned the wall of trees—solid, branches tight.

"But she was there. I heard her." Leaves rustled, the wind hummed. Nothing else. No crying. No calls for help.

"I told you about trying to leave," he growled, starting back to the house.

"I wasn't trying to leave, damn you!" She pounded his solid back. "Let me down. I wasn't trying to get away!"

But Jase didn't break stride. He carted her inside, slammed and locked the door behind them and then moved to her bedroom. Kayla found herself dumped none too gently on the bed. She rolled to the side and scrambled to her feet. "Damn you, Jase! I wasn't trying to escape—"

"I warned you, Kayla. You don't know what could've happened out there." His voice was rough with anxiety, his features as hard as stone.

"She was crying! I had to help—"

"There's no one out there. Go back to bed."

"There was," she insisted. "There was!"

"You're in danger, Kayla. They'll stop at nothing to get their hands on you. Remember that, *and listen to me next time!*"

He slammed the door before she could utter another word. The lock clicked. Next came the rattle of the doorknob as he tested it.

"You're not really going to lock me in?"

"For your own good," he murmured.

She opened her mouth, but he was already walking into the living room, the sound of his retreating footsteps reverberating through the house.

Shaken, Kayla paced the room several minutes before picking up the alarm clock and sending it smashing into the door.

"Damn you, Jase Terrell!" she shouted.

Balling her fists and ignoring the irrational urge to throw every godforsaken thing in the room until he returned, she flung herself onto the bed. A temper tantrum would do no good, of that she felt certain.

She had to be calm, patient. She willed her breathing to grow normal, and she waited for what seemed no less than an eternity. All the while she prayed that Jase would come back and unlock the door, but he didn't.

Finally, her anger subsided and exhaustion took hold. She tugged off her boots and crawled into bed. Shivers gripped her and she pulled the bedclothes tighter. She *had* heard the voice, seen the break in the trees, the child.

They'll stop at nothing. Jase's words followed her into her dreams just as his vision walked with her, talked with her, held and caressed her during the deepest moments of sleep.

No more loneliness, he whispered. *I'm here for you, Kayla. To help you, protect you.* Oddly enough, she believed him and no nightmares came to taunt her.

"You need to eat," Jase's deep voice cut through Kayla's thoughts several days later.

She glanced up from an old magazine she'd been mindlessly staring at, the edges yellowed and faded like those of the other magazines stacked beside the sofa. "I'm not hungry."

"We've been here three days and you've hardly eaten anything." He frowned, held out a mug of instant soup and muttered, "I brought you up here to keep you safe, not to watch you waste away. Eat or—"

"Or you'll be forced to feed me?" she challenged, glaring up at his towering form from where she sprawled on the sofa.

"Exactly." The one word was like a carefully aimed dart.

Kayla put the magazine aside and scooted to the edge of the sofa. She knew very little about Jase Terrell, other than he personified the tall, dark and silent man, and he rarely made threats. When he did, as Kayla had found the night she'd seen the child in the woods, he meant every word he said. Her bedroom door had stayed locked all night. Only when she'd pounded on the door the next morning, desperate to go to the bathroom, had he finally let her out.

"I'll eat," she conceded, "*if* you tell me something about my mother."

"You'll eat, anyway."

"Maybe," she admitted, fully aware of Jase's superior size and thus his advantage over her, physically. But matching wits was another matter. Fresh from college, Kayla had bargained her way into a top-forty station and gotten them to give her a shot at doing the morning show. During her career, she'd moved from station to station, battling male jocks for the top air spots, and winning. No matter how much Kayla had come to trust Jase Terrell, she wasn't about to roll over and bow to his every order. Not in this lifetime or any other.

"Wouldn't it be loads better if you didn't have to force me to eat?" She smiled sweetly despite the black scowl that slid over his features. "Just tell me something, Jase. *Anything* about my mother. I've been agreeable to your rules these past few days. The least you can do is keep your part of the deal."

"My part is to tell you at the end of the two weeks. We've only been here three days."

"So cheat a little." A pleading note crept into her voice. "Please."

"She was very beautiful."

"I already know what she looks like. Tell me something else."

"She was stubborn, too," he said tightly, his eyes narrowing to silver daggers. "Like her daughter. Now eat, and keep in mind that part of our deal is your cooperation."

Kayla glared up at him, noting the stern set of his jaw. She wanted to press him, to hurl herself across the room and demand he tell her everything, yet she knew that Jase wasn't about to budge from his decision. One more week and four days. Then she would know the truth.

"You're manipulative," she declared. "And arrogant, and as frustrating as hell." With a defiant lift of her chin and a cutting glance, she took the mug from his hand. "I would just as soon dump this over your head as eat it."

"Try it and I'll be force-feeding you." Laughter danced in his eyes, sparking her anger.

She would have railed at him had her stomach not given a traitorous grumble. The aroma of steaming chicken soup rose, tantalizing and tempting her. Actually, she was hungry. But when she had a lot on her mind, she always found eating difficult. With Jase watching her, the task wasn't any easier.

After managing several bites, she leveled a stare at him, her anger gone, desperation settling in its place. "I'm sick of staring at these walls, Jase. Why don't you sit down? Maybe we can talk, or something. I don't know very much about you." And I want to know all that you know about me, she added silently. Before her captivity was over, she would find out the secrets Jase knew... She had to remember her past. She *had* to.

He regarded her a thoughtful second, then murmured, "Eat," and disappeared down the hallway.

"So much for conversation," she whispered, wiping the tear that squeezed past her lashes. She would make him talk to her. Somehow, some way, she would.

If only he wasn't so aloof. He spoke little, looked at her even less and spent most of his time outside, fiddling with his motorcycle or the plumbing, snapping pictures with the most expensive camera Kayla had ever seen, chopping wood—whatever. Anything to keep him out of the house and away from her.

Kayla, in turn, spent her time reading old magazines—over twenty-year-old magazines, to be precise—sleeping and otherwise doing her damnedest not to go stir-crazy.

She glanced at the radio, which she'd tried unsuccessfully to turn on. It was old, and probably broken, like nearly everything else in the house. Again, she wondered how she could possibly endure even one more day, much less eleven, with only her thoughts and nightmares to keep her company.

Eat. The word echoed in her head. Dutifully, she spooned more of the creamy liquid into her mouth, her gaze unwillingly drawn to the doorway Jase had disappeared through. She heard the creak of wood as he moved around his matchbox-size bedroom next to hers. She considered the room his, though he spent little time there. He slept on the sofa where she sat.

When he slept, she reminded herself, thinking she'd never actually seen him close his eyes, other than the previous night when she'd gone to the kitchen for a drink of water.

Fully clothed, boots and all, he'd been stretched out on the sofa, one arm flung above his head, the other resting on his chest. The firelight had accented the deep hollows beneath his eyes. He'd looked exhausted, as if he hadn't slept in days.

She'd wanted so much to go to him. To smooth the exhaustion from his face, hold him and stop the trembling of his hands. To trace the tight outline of his mouth and see him relax. Thank God, she'd forced herself to turn away.

If only the nights weren't so frightening. That's when she found herself thinking about Jase, craving his strength and his warmth. But she couldn't let herself seek him out, no matter that the wind called to her, lashing at the outside of the cabin like a determined animal trying to get at its prey.

Kayla forced the thought away. She wouldn't think about Jase, or her sleepless nights—nothing but eating.

Surprisingly, by the time she gulped down the last mouthful of soup, a smile actually played at her lips. She was stuffed, and though she hated to admit it, feeling much better. Less edgy. Content, if that were possible, given her circumstances.

She placed the mug on the coffee table and leaned over the arm of the sofa to leaf through the stack of magazines for one she had yet to read. Picking one from the bottom, she leaned back against the sofa, only to see Jase framed in the doorway. With one shoulder resting against the doorjamb, he clasped a white bundle between his long fingers and watched her.

She knew he watched her only when he thought she wasn't looking. Out of suspicion, no doubt. He feared she would take off again, and she had to admit, the thought had crossed her mind. But one glance at the wall of trees surrounding the clearing kept any notion from taking root. Besides, she wasn't desperate to get away from Jase. She'd stopped fearing him that night in the moonlight. More than anything, she feared what waited for her outside the clearing.

Even though she wasn't afraid of him, however, she didn't feel at ease, either. He had the strangest effect on her. His presence never failed to make her heart pound faster. Like now.

"Have I sprouted two heads?" she asked, meeting his intense stare. She expected him to turn away, the way he always did when she locked gazes with him. He didn't. He continued to stare, to delve, to send her heart hammering against her ribs.

"Well?" she demanded, irritated that he should have such an effect on her. She slapped the magazine against the sofa cushion and grasped a throw pillow, irritation quickly giving way to nervousness. She clutched the pillow to her chest, eager to hide even a small part of herself from those penetrating eyes of his.

"Not two heads," he replied. "Thankfully. You're distracting enough with one head."

Before his words could register, he closed the distance to her, dropped the white bundle to the sofa and pulled the cushion from her hands. "Much too distracting," he murmured, more to himself, it seemed, than her. Taking her hand in his large one, he pulled her to her feet. Lean fingers trapped her palm, warmed her skin, sending delicious electric shocks up her arm.

"I believe this is yours," he murmured, opening his other hand to reveal the topaz ring she'd forgotten on the kitchen counter that first night. With the gentlest pressure, he slipped the ring onto her finger.

Instinctively, she curled her fingers, feeling the silver band against her tender palm. The ring brought no calm to her frenzied senses—not this time, or any time, it seemed, when Jase was near. A hairsbreadth from him, Kayla felt the heat of his body, the hunger whirling inside of him, shredding his resolve.

He touched her cheek with trembling fingers, his voice rough with emotion. "You've grown up, moonchild."

A part of her longed to slap his fingers away, to quiet the disturbing emotions he so easily stirred with one touch. Yet, she liked his nearness, the way his fingers drifted over her skin, traced her cheekbone to her temple. The way he threaded his fingers through her hair, almost reverently, his voice gruff, filled with awe. "The color is deeper than I remember. Deep, rich. I've never seen hair so beautiful, and I've never felt anything so soft, not since..." His words faded.

With his gaze, he followed the drift of his fingers through her hair. The gentle tugging provoked a delicate tingle in Kayla's scalp. His liquid gray eyes heated, smoldered, burned with a longing that pushed all thoughts from her mind.

If only you could remember, his voice whispered through her mind like a feather drifting on the breeze. *If only things were different for us.*

Kayla licked her lips, wanting his kiss more than she'd ever wanted anything before. Craving it the way her lungs craved oxygen, her stomach food, her spirit peace.

"I always knew your hair would feel this silky, your skin this soft." He touched her throat, the rough pads of his fingers drifting over her collarbone, hesitating at her pulse point. "I always knew... I've wanted to touch you for so long. I—" He broke off, clamping his lips together, as if a bucket of ice water had poured over him. Abruptly, his hand fell away and he averted his gaze, but not before she saw the flicker of regret, then pain. Pain so intense she felt it knife through her soul the moment before his hand released hers.

"Jase?" She touched his shoulder, but he shrugged away and backed up an inch to put some distance between them.

"Sorry," he grumbled. "I shouldn't have said those things."

"But you did," she said in a shaky voice. "You said—"

"A lot of nonsense I shouldn't have," he cut in sharply.

"It wasn't nonsense. You didn't just know my parents and Gramps. You knew me," she asserted. "You said you always wanted to touch me. That my hair was deeper than you remembered. *Remembered,* Jase." She reached out, only to have him turn and cross to the bay window, leaving a yawning chasm between them.

"I didn't know what I was saying. Lack of sleep, I guess." His T-shirt stretched taut over the muscled expanse of his back. Even a few feet away, Kayla could feel the banked tension in his body, almost as fierce as the anxiety pulsing through her own.

She knew, no matter what he said, lack of sleep hadn't made him speak those words to her. Something else had driven him.

"I found an old washtub in the storage shed. I'll wash our clothes. You can wear one of my shirts in the meantime." He motioned to the sofa and Kayla remembered the bundle he'd carried, the shirt he spoke of now a white heap on the throw pillow. "Get changed. There's only a few hours of daylight left and I want to be able to see what I'm doing." With those words, he opened the front door and disappeared outside.

Kayla blinked back a sudden swell of tears, immediately disgusted with herself for crying so much. Gramps would be disappointed if he could see her now. He'd always told her how strong she was. But then, he'd told her a lot of things that hadn't been true.

She sank to the edge of the sofa and snatched up Jase's T-shirt. Oddly enough, instead of tossing it across the room as her anger dictated, she found herself lifting the soft cotton to her cheek. She breathed deeply and Jase's scent—a mingling of fresh soap and pure male—filled her senses, weaving and winding through her body, touching every part of her, even her spirit.

A lone tear slipped from the corner of her eye as Kayla fought back a sudden wave of loss unlike any she'd ever experienced. Even when Gramps had died.

At that moment, her feelings crystallized. With a twinge of fear and a mountain of regret, Kayla realized she cried for a lost part of herself, a part intertwined with Jase. She didn't know exactly how or where their connection had come about. She only knew that it had, and she prayed he would reveal the truth to her and unlock the door to her childhood.

For Jase had been a part of that childhood. That's why they *connected* on such a deep level. She felt the connection more strongly than she felt her own heart pump in her chest. And even though he wouldn't admit it to her, Jase felt it, too, and he held all the answers.

CHAPTER SIX

The darkness whispered, pulling Jase back, reminding him of his past, who he was, *what* he was, carrying him through time and space to the place he'd fought so hard to escape.

Candles flickered in the hushed silence of the small room. Solid black walls formed the background for the red symbols marking the sanctuary where the damned came to worship and beg more power from the darkness.

A young boy with haunted silver eyes stood before an altar, the rough gray surface marred with deep red stains—testimony to the countless sacrifices offered in ritual. Secret rituals—the stuff nightmares are made of—wild, fantastic, violent acts too unbelievable to be believed. And had Jase not been there, the stone floor cold beneath his bare feet, the smell of musty earth and burning tallow and stagnant blood strong in his nostrils, he wouldn't have believed. He didn't want to believe. He longed to wake up, to find himself safe in his bed. But his childhood was an all too realistic nightmare. A nightmare that continued.

One by one, the Keepers filed inside the room, circling him, their voices a low, steady, hypnotic murmur.

"You shall have your first taste of power, my son." Jase's father rounded the altar and stared across the concrete slab, to his son who stood opposite him. Father and son—reflections of the same spirit, one older, wiser, more skilled in the evil, the other a novice with youthful features and a glimmer of innocence about to be snuffed out once and for all.

"The Keepers never knew what waited for them," his father's deep voice filled the room. "I brought the knowledge with me and taught the others." He caressed the worn cover of the black book he held. "I have carved a new path for us. One you will continue when the time comes. But first, you must understand what the Keepers hold ... You must learn the rituals, practice them. Then you shall take your rightful place, Jase. You and Kayla will be one. When your ages and power combine to equal mine, the time will be at hand. You must be ready."

The slow creak of a door sizzled across Jase's nerves. The circle parted and a girl appeared at the foot of the altar. She looked to be about fifteen, barely a few years older than Jase. She held a fragile innocence, mocked by the glaze of her eyes and the deep, exhausted circles beneath.

A nod from Jase's father and the girl stretched out on the stone slab, her eyes closed, a trance-induced peace holding her features passive.

"Such a good child," Jase's father murmured, touching porcelain-like hands to the girl's forehead. "A forgotten child, discarded by society. We took her off the streets, welcomed her and gave her refuge when she couldn't run anymore, like we do for so many others. Now she shall give herself to us. She shall be your first offering, my son." And with those words, Alexander Terrell pulled the *athame* from its sheath and held it out to his son. "Take it, Jase. Do your rightful duty."

Jase shook his head, his gaze darting from the knife to the girl. "N-No," he whispered, clutching at his moonstar, his grip tight, desperate. "It's not supposed to be this way, Father. The Old One said no real sacr—"

"Silence! Speak no more of that gray-haired fool. The old ways are no more. No more!" With his free hand, Alexander Terrell opened the black book. His fingers stroked the brittle, yellowed pages in silent reverence. "The power can only be obtained at a price. You must learn all there is to know. Then you shall teach our ways to Kayla. When the time comes, your powers will join, just as your bodies will. The moment the witching hour arrives, you shall plant the seed to assure my future. For me, Jase. Do this for me." His voice carried the same sting as a rattlesnake. "You *must* accept your destiny and learn." He slammed the book shut and thrust the knife at Jase.

Jase recoiled, gripping his moonstar so tight the chain snapped. The charm fell to the floor. Large hands came from behind to grip his upper arms, urge his hands out and force his fingers around the knife. "Do it, Jase," Max Talbot's voice filled his ears. "Do it!"

"Nooooooo!" Jase screamed, his voice quickly lost as the Keepers began an ancient chant that echoed through the cursed sanctuary like lost souls crying for salvation— a salvation that didn't exist for them. They knew only the darkness. Only death.

Max's strong hands held Jase's fingers around the *athame,* guiding the motion of the knife despite his struggles.

"No!" Jase cried. "Please, no!" The knife made a downward arc and Jase closed his eyes. . . .

"Jase," came the soft whisper, through the steady chant surrounding him.

He glanced down into the lifeless eyes of the girl. Empty. Vacant. *Dead. . .*

"Jase." His name sounded louder this time.

"Kayla?" Jase glanced at the black-shrouded figures caging him. "Kayla!" he cried, searching for her.

"Please . . . Jase," she pleaded. "It's just a night-mare—"

Jase's eyes snapped open to the feel of a warm hand against his bare chest. Wild-eyed, he shot straight up on the sofa, his gaze sweeping the dim living room.

"Jase?" Kayla's soft voice filled his head again. "It's okay," she crooned. "You were just having a nightmare."

"The voices," he murmured. He studied the room. The walls were a pale yellow. No glaring red symbols, no altar.

Jase stared at his hands, incredulous to find them unsoiled. There had been so much blood... He could still feel the warm heat ... smell it, even.

"The wind," she whispered.

"What?"

"You probably heard the wind." She glanced to the windows and shivered. "It makes everything creak at night."

"It wasn't the wind," he replied, his voice rough. Self-consciously he reached up, searching for the moonstar. Had she seen it? Panic and relief swirled inside of him when he felt only his bare skin, his pulse beat. In the nightmare, he'd pulled so fiercely on the charm, the chain had snapped.

His gaze flew to the crack of the sofa cushions. Silver winked at him. Quickly, he shifted, put one thigh over the charm and wedged it deeper between the cushions. He searched her face a full moment, but saw no recognition. Kayla hadn't seen it. Thankfully.

Breathing deep, he fell back onto the sofa, one hand going to his eyes to rub profusely. "No, it wasn't the wind. Damn him."

"Who?" she asked, her silky smooth tone soothing the tremors that still shook him. Her fingers stroked one muscled bicep, like licks of fire melting the cold that had slithered into his bones.

"No one." Yet Alexander Terrell's image remained in Jase's head, reminding him of what he'd done, the blood he'd spilled, the path he'd been forced to take. Disgusted, Jase wiped his hands on his jean-covered thighs, as if he could erase the past and force the memories away. He couldn't. God help him, he couldn't—

"It's all right, Jase," Kayla whispered, cutting into his thoughts and drawing his attention. "I have nightmares, too—about Gramps." She took a shaky breath, as if talking proved painful. "I never thought I could feel as bad as I felt when my father died. At least I had Gramps then."

Maybe it was the sight of her tears, her cheeks glistening in the firelight, her presence, or the way she traced tiny circles on his upper arm, that made him forget everything—his jaded past, his bleak future. He couldn't discern the cause, he only knew that for a few blessed moments, the darkness didn't hold him prisoner. Instead, he found himself a captive of the beautiful woman who knelt beside him.

"I always had such a nice, sane life," she went on. "It never really mattered that I couldn't remember certain things about my early childhood, like birthdays, Christmases—stuff like that. Gramps said it was normal, that people can't remember everything, especially things that happened at such an early age. But I didn't just forget a few things, I forgot *everything*. I draw a complete blank for the first five years of my life."

"Sometimes, it's better to forget," Jase muttered.

"Not for me," Kayla said. "I need to remember. I feel as if something's missing inside of me. I grew up and had a very typical life. I got good grades in school, had a fair share of friends. And I never had nightmares. In fact, when I was growing up, from six years on, I never even slept with a night-light. Gramps always told me I had a guardian angel looking out for me, but I know it wasn't any angel. It was him and my father. They always made me feel so wanted and safe. I used to think they tried extra hard because they felt guilty that I was raised without a mother. Now I know their guilt was because of the lies they told me about her."

"My own mother died when I was very young," Jase admitted, his voice low, pained. He didn't really know why he told her. He shouldn't say anything to her of his past. But he'd cried so many tears for a mother he'd never known, and a father he'd known all too well. So many silent tears that no one could begin to understand, except maybe her.

Kayla. This woman who had blossomed with all the beauty promised when he'd known her as a child. His chosen one. His destiny.

Jase shook his head against the surge of longing that swept through him. He placed his hand over hers to still her absentminded stroking that set him afire. She looked wistful, far away, caught up in her own reflections.

"I used to cry for my mother when I was little," she told him. "I don't really know why I cried. I never really knew her. Still, I felt this sort of loss. It hurts even more now because I know she really didn't die, not like my father and Gramps said. They lied to me." She turned pleading eyes on him. "Why?"

"I'm sure they had their reasons. Don't condemn them until you know what motivated their crime."

"Nothing could warrant stealing my mother from me. I *have* to remember her, Jase." Her voice was rich with desperation. "I feel this emptiness where my memories should be."

Tears trickled down her smooth cheeks, tearing at his control, stifling the voice that told him not to touch her, not to even talk to her. But in the soft light of the fire with the wind humming a faraway tune in the background, he felt compelled to reach out, to wipe away her tears and make her pain his own.

"My father died right after I graduated from high school," Kayla said, her words a steady outpouring like her tears. "A car accident. My life started to change then. I retreated from everyone, except for Gramps. He wouldn't let me pull away from him. He kept me going, told me what a fighter I was, how my father would have wanted me to get on with my life and be happy. My heart wasn't in it, but I tried. Then Gramps died . . .

"I used to think that's why I started having the black-outs," she went on. "I wasn't strong enough to deal with losing Gramps. The loneliness became nearly unbearable. Then I found out he and my father had lied. I felt so betrayed. I thought the blackouts were my way of escaping—"

"No," Jase interrupted. "The blackouts weren't an escape from the grief, Kayla. That's what They wanted you to think. They wanted you to doubt your own sanity, the bastards," he growled. "To make you weak. They wanted—"

"Stop it!" she raged, pushing his hand away. "Don't start telling me something you're not prepared to finish, Jase. I don't want partial truth. I want *all* of the truth. Until you're prepared to give it to me, don't say anything. I'm confused enough as it is. Please..." Her voice faltered, her anger dissolving as quickly as it had sparked.

"The truth," he echoed, his voice tinged with regret. "If only I could tell you now, Kayla. If only you would believe."

"But I will," she declared. "I'll believe what you tell me. You know what it is I can't remember, why my father and Gramps lied. Tell me, Jase!"

"Leave the past alone. It's better not to remember...easier. Having all the answers can be more of a curse than a blessing. Concentrate on the good things about your life, your father, Gramps—the stuff you already remember. I can't fill in the blanks."

"You mean you won't."

"No, I *can't*. I can only tell you you're here with me and I mean to keep you safe. You're a part of me, moonchild. The brightest part. The part I cling to when my own memories get so dark that I lose my way."

A strange quiet seemed to settle around them then. Jase watched her face, afraid to see her reaction to his words, yet desperate for it. She would undoubtedly turn away, tell him what a lunatic he was.

She did neither. She clasped his hand, the silver of her topaz ring warm against his palm. "Damn you, Jase Terrell," she whispered, but her words held no anger. "I want to hate you because you refuse to tell me what I need to know—what I have a *right* to know. I want to despise you, distrust you. Only I can't," she admitted, her voice suddenly small. "The two weeks following Gramps's death were the worst of my life, but then you came. You saved me from the blackouts." She leaned forward and touched her lips to his shoulder, her mouth moist, warm, sending a tremor winding through his body to settle in his groin.

He grappled for his last bit of restraint and managed to tell her, his voice low, hoarse, "You shouldn't be in here. Go back to bed, Kayla."

"That's not what you want," she replied, her palm flat against his shoulder where her lips had been. "I feel everything you do, Jase." Her hand trembled slightly from the raw emotions flowing from his body into hers. "You're afraid, but you feel more than fear. You're relieved that I'm here with you, that we're finally talking to each other."

He indulged the smile that played at his lips. "I know you feel me, moonchild. But you're wrong on one count. It's not relief that's making me shake." His expression grew serious, his voice husky. "Being close to you, knowing I can't touch you—*really* touch you—is ripping me in two, Kayla."

They stared at each other, the only sound that of their breathing, the crackle of an occasional log as the fire burned brightly. Fiery shadows danced across her profile.

God, how he longed to thread his fingers through the flame-red hair spilling over her shoulders, but he knew he wouldn't be satisfied with just that. She was too tempting, her soft curves barely concealed beneath his T-shirt, which dropped just below her hips. Long, supple legs curved under her, one smooth thigh completely exposed. He ached to reach down, to trail his fingers along the silky smoothness. He yearned to bury himself inside of her, feel her warm body convulse around him, draw him deeper, her hot juices blending with his.

Forbidden. The word thundered through his head.

"Talk to me, Jase. Tell me what you're thinking," Kayla whispered, seeming to watch his features as thoroughly as he watched hers.

"No," he said.

But he didn't need to say a word. Her fingers fluttered against his skin and he realized her hand still rested on his shoulder—feeling, *connecting.*

His muscles clenched and his breathing all but stopped.

Her gaze deepened, softened, pushing into his thoughts to see what tormented him—the incredible hunger for her that consumed his mind, his body, and slashed his control to shreds.

"My God!" she gasped.

She moved to pull her hand away, but Jase covered her fingers with his, driven to touch her though he knew it would prove his undoing. He didn't think of his father or the Keepers or the damned promise . . . only a lifetime of longing.

Raising her palm to his lips, he pressed a kiss to its center and murmured, "You've haunted my dreams, Kayla, for a lifetime. The connection between us is so strong."

"Yes," she breathed as his gaze captured hers. Her eyes were wide, sparkling with trust.

Invisible fingers clutched at his heart. A child's face flashed in the darkness of his mind . . . pale cheeks glistening in the moonlight, trusting eyes.

For a split second, a voice cried for him to resist the pull between them. But she was so close and he was so very weary of fighting what was meant to be.

Jase pressed her palm to his chest. His heart beat a frenzied tattoo against her warm skin. "You're here, Kayla," he whispered. "Here, inside of me. You always have been. That's why the connection is so strong. Why it's taking everything I have and then some to keep my hands off of you."

Her eyes deepened to a rich gold and Jase felt the longing sweep through her, like water through a sudden dam burst.

She took his other hand and pressed it to her bosom. Her heartbeat matched his. The warmth of her skin seared his palm as if the cotton T-shirt she wore didn't exist.

"I feel you, too, Jase." She took a deep breath. Her full breasts heaved with the effort, and desire knifed through him. "I've never felt a connection like I feel with you. I felt it that first time you touched me in the bedroom. It frightened me. It was so different from what I'd felt with my father and Gramps. It's stronger, more consuming, as if I'm not only drawn to you mentally, but physically, as well."

"Does it frighten you now?"

"I'm not sure. I've been a basket case since Gramps died. Then you showed up and made me feel . . . I don't know . . . just *feel*." Her eyes took on a strange light, the jewel-like depths filled with desire and desperation. "Jase, you make me feel anger, frustration, excitement—*real* feelings instead of the loneliness."

She took a deep breath. Jase's gaze went to her nipples, taut and aroused, straining against the thin cotton of her shirt. His mouth went dry. He needed to taste her . . . just one taste of those delicious peaks, one chance to feel them tighten, throb, extend against the velvety stroke of his tongue, and he could go to his grave a content man. Now, he was starving, aching, burning—anything but content.

With a slight tug, he drew her to him, fitting her upper body over his. Winding his fingers in the thick silkiness of her hair, he pulled her closer and took her mouth with a savage intensity. He swept his tongue along the fullness of her bottom lip and thrust deep to stroke and savor the soft interior of her mouth. Like a dying man, he drank from her, drawing life from the soul-saving fountain that bubbled inside of her. And dying he was, he realized, but the death was so sweet.

When she slipped her arms around his neck and her tongue tangled with his, control became a memory pushed to the farthest corner of Jase's mind. He needed to feel her heart beat against his own, her breath mingle with his, until they moved and existed as one. *One...*

He loosened his hold on her hair to filter his fingers through the long silken tresses. Moving his hands down the curve of her spine, he explored the hollows of her back until he found the soft swell of her buttocks. He cupped her bottom, moving her hips in a circular motion against his rock-hard arousal. A tiny moan slipped past her lips, into Jase's mouth, urging him on.

Her thighs were warm satin beneath his fingertips. He grasped the edge of the T-shirt and slid the material up over her hips, then higher until his hands found the throbbing fullness of her breasts. Her nipples hardened against his palms. Jase circled the distended peaks with the pads of his thumbs. Then he tore his lips from hers to slide her up the length of his body, dip his head and devour one luscious nipple.

She arched her back and thrust the ripe peak into his mouth. The softness of her thighs pressed flush against his pulsing flesh, and Jase knew a different kind of hell from the one he'd spent his lifetime in.

A hell where his body flamed red-hot, his manhood swelled to painful proportions, his hunger for her consumed all rational thought. Jase had never guessed that anything could be as wonderful, or as torturous, as their bodies touching, moving, *feeling*. In all his wildest dreams of her, his imagination had never come close to the sweet agony he felt.

Yet a small part of him, the part that had fought the darkness for so long, demanded he put a stop to what could only lead to destruction. He forced his mouth from her quivering nipple and took a ragged breath, closing his eyes when the damp peak seemed to beg his attention.

Control, his conscience whispered.

If only she didn't feel so warm and pliable in his arms.

And hungry. Her hunger raged as fierce and demanding as his own—frightening and thrilling him at the same time.

It was then that Jase admitted the truth to himself. He'd been waiting for this moment his entire life. This joining that would unite them forever. He'd tried to deny his destiny, but he couldn't any longer. He wanted her too much.

He turned and shifted, rolling her beneath him, his body moving to cover hers. Once again, he captured her mouth, his kiss savage, desperate, determined, and she returned it with a reckless abandon that sent raw flame shooting through his veins.

Jase slid impatient hands down her sides, her belly, to the wispy band of her panties. He pushed the silky lace past her hips, his movements swift. The delicate threads ripped and she cried out. Jase stifled the cry with his mouth, his hand going to his zipper. Seconds later, his manhood sprang free, swollen and eager to feel the wet heat of her body.

She struggled beneath him now, her mouth seeking escape from his, but Jase was beyond rational thought. He gripped both her wrists with one hand and pinned them above her head. With one sweep of his other hand, he parted her thighs and positioned himself just as she wrenched her mouth from his.

"Jase!" she cried out as he drove forward.

The sound of her voice stopped him cold. He pulled back, a fraction away from breaching the barrier that marked her innocence. Conscience flooded his senses.

"Please," she whimpered. "Not like this..."

Jase stared down into wide topaz eyes brimming with tears. Trusting eyes. She trusted him even though he'd been about to doom her to nothing short of hell itself.

Fury swept through him, as frightening as the liquid fire that pulsed through his veins. Angry and disgusted, Jase forced himself away from her. Climbing from the sofa, he fastened his jeans and paced to the window. He shoved the drapes aside and stared out into the moonlit yard, every nerve in his body wound so tight he thought he would surely explode. And it would have been a welcome relief from the guilt, and the god-awful craving clenching his insides.

"Jase?" Her voice reached across the room to him. But he didn't turn around. He couldn't face her... not after what he'd almost done.

"Go back to bed, Kayla," he said raggedly.

"But—"

"Go back to bed!"

He didn't need to see her tears. He heard them in her voice. "I'm sorry," she murmured a moment before he heard her scramble from the sofa.

I'm sorry.

He would have laughed, if his soul weren't already weeping. *She* was sorry, when it was he who had been about to sentence her to an eternity of darkness.

He slammed his fist into the wall near the window. Sheetrock crumbled and his knuckles throbbed—small penance for the vows he'd broken to himself. Beyond control, he'd almost ravaged her with no more mercy than a hungry animal devouring an evening meal. Ravaged her and sent her straight to hell, a voice chided. That's where they would both wind up should they come together and create a child to house his father's evil spirit.

Then again, there was always contraception. Jase closed his eyes for a brief, bittersweet moment. If only things were that simple. There were powerful forces at work. Evil forces demanding control, and though Jase was loathe to admit it, he felt himself growing weaker every time he looked at her, smelled her, longed for her.

No amount of protection was one hundred percent effective, and if they weakened by indulging their lust once, it would surely happen again and again. And then again, on that fateful night that had been predestined.

No, he had to abstain, just as he had to keep the past from her. Their bodies couldn't join, just as he could teach her nothing of the evil. For to fulfill even one small part of the promise would act as a catalyst and the rest would surely follow.

"Damn you, Alexander Terrell," Jase cursed. The tree branches whipped with a sudden gust of wind that caught the screen door. Wood and metal slammed together, hinges cracked—answer enough that his father had heard. Not that Jase had doubted for a minute that he wouldn't. Despite the protection of the house, the Keepers listened, and watched. They always watched.

Jase let the curtain swish into place. Turning, he faced the sofa where he and Kayla had been only minutes before. They had less than a week until the night of the full moon. Then their forced captivity would end. Maybe when all was said and done, and she was safe and the power extinguished, they could finish what they'd started tonight.

As he sprawled on the sofa, he felt between the cushions for his charm. Closing his fingers around the warm silver, he shut his eyes, pretending for the sweetest moment that Kayla was still there with him.

The Keepers ceased to exist as Jase allowed himself to join with Kayla in the quiet blackness of his mind, where he could touch and be touched, where their hearts could beat in perfect sync and he could make that final connection with her. The one their bodies could never make in reality. Not yet.

Tonight they'd come too close.

The Keepers knew. They watched.

At least they couldn't enter the house. The magic inside was too powerful. That was why Kayla didn't have any blackouts while she was inside. Still, the Keepers were close. Too close, and They knew everything.

Jase opened his eyes to stare into the fire. The flames danced higher, taunting, mocking, and he felt a shudder rip through him.

Damn them! They knew, and now they would wait for Jase to finish what he'd begun tonight. He wouldn't, he vowed. No matter how strong the pull, he wouldn't!

If only a vision of pale flesh and flame-red hair didn't fill Jase's thoughts, crumble his control and call to him. And in the back of his mind, he wondered if he could truly resist, and that uncertainty scared the hell out of him.

Shafts of sunlight filtered through the kitchen window early the next morning. Kayla paused in the doorway, her gaze fixed on Jase's back as he sat at the table, his camera and several lenses spread in front of him. He wore a black long-sleeved shirt, sleeves pushed up to reveal sinewy forearms. She watched the ripple of muscle and tendon as he picked up a soft cloth and stroked one lens.

Kayla balled the T-shirt she'd been wearing last night, her fingers opening and closing nervously. Clad once again in her own knit top and jeans, she felt safer, less vulnerable. Still, she couldn't quite seem to catch her breath.

"Jase," she said. His movements stopped. She watched the muscles of his back tense beneath the dark cotton. "We need to talk about last night."

"I think it's better if we put last night behind us," he said, his voice low, strained.

"I think it would be better if we discussed it."

"There's nothing to say." He flung the rag to the table-top. Reaching beside him, he picked up a leather case and began storing his equipment inside, each motion quick, almost angry despite the delicacy of the lenses.

"There is," she persisted. "You can't simply forget about what we…" Her voice faltered and his hand stopped in midair, his fingers white as he clutched one lens. Heat suffused her cheeks as she searched for her voice. "I mean, we … well, we nearly—"

"We nearly made a huge mistake," he said, dropping the last lens into the case. He turned on her, his eyes hard steel flecks.

"Mistake?" The one word stirred a rush of emotions within her—anger, disappointment, regret—and all because she'd stopped what she knew in her heart would have been the most wonderful experience of her life. "We almost made love," she replied, her voice a bare whisper.

"Love and lust are not the same thing," he retorted, his words stinging more than if he'd taken a switch to her. He shoved away from the table and stood, his presence dominating the small kitchen.

"But it wasn't just lust. There was something else. I know you felt it, Jase. I *know* you did."

"You might know what I feel, Kayla, but you don't *know* me. Not really. Don't fool yourself into thinking that you do. There are things about me you'd never guess in your wildest dreams—dark things better left alone."

Tension radiated from him in giant waves, smashing into her, pushing her farther away from him. Not that they'd ever been very close. Last night had been the first time they'd really talked or touched.

God, how they'd touched.

Her face flamed at the memory. She'd been so willing and eager in his arms, but when it came down to the actual deed, she'd chickened out. Not that she hadn't wanted him. She had, so much that it scared the wits out of her. She'd never wanted anyone the way she wanted Jase Terrell. The way she still wanted him. When she touched him, it was as if they'd known each other forever. She became attuned to his every fear, every desire, every regret. Their connection was so pure, so strong. And she'd never burned so hot from someone's touch before.

Nor had she ever been quite so frightened. "I'm sorry if I led you on. I wasn't ready. I mean, I was, but I've never—"

"Led me on?" He actually smiled then—a cold, bitter tilt to his sensuous lips that rattled her already shaky resolve. "I nearly raped you last night, Kayla, and you think you led me on?"

Rape. The word hung in the air between them. "You call last night rape?" Her voice was incredulous.

"Yes," he growled.

"I *wanted* you to touch me." With her words, he stiffened.

"Not like that, Kayla. You might have wanted me to touch you, kiss you, but you didn't want it to go as far as it did. Damn," he muttered, shaking his head. Anger slipped away and regret laced his next words. "I was too worked up even to realize what I was doing." He captured her face with his gaze, which had softened to a very unsettling liquid silver. "Don't you understand, Kayla? I lost control. I *lost* it."

Kayla stepped toward him, her heart twisting at the anguish in his voice.

"Don't," he said tightly, raking his fingers through his hair. "Stay away from me, Kayla. For your own good. I can't promise to stop next time. Dammit, there can't *be* a next time." Snatching up his camera case, he turned and stormed into the living room.

Kayla gripped the edge of the counter, her eyes stinging. With everything she had, she fought the urge to go after him and convince him how wrong he was.

She couldn't deny that she'd sensed a change in him last night. He'd gone from tender to brutal in the blink of an eye, his lovemaking an act of raw possession. But she hadn't been terrified of him. That's where he'd been wrong. More so, Kayla had been frightened of herself and the threshold she'd been about to cross.

At twenty-seven, she'd come close to losing her virginity more than once. But on all three occasions, something had held her back. Uncertainty or maybe anticipation of what lay ahead in the arms of someone special, someone she truly loved. She wanted the first time to really mean something.

She didn't want violence, second thoughts or guilt. She wanted... well, she wanted love. Plain and simple.

And she didn't love Jase Terrell. At least, she didn't think she did. How could she love someone she barely knew? A man with so many secrets he refused to share?

Those questions had raced through her mind last night, and so she'd fought what had felt so right. Now she regretted that decision. She and Jase held a special bond—a connection—and even though that didn't constitute love, it came closer than anything she'd experienced with any other man. Ever.

Kayla gathered her control and walked back to her room. The sound of Jase moving around in the living room followed her down the hall. She stretched out on the bed, Jase's T-shirt still warm in her hands. God, she was a fool—a lonely, desperate fool emotionally drawn to a man who wanted nothing to do with her.

A mistake. That's what he'd called last night. A mistake he had no intention of repeating.

Pulling the quilt up over her shoulders, Kayla bunched the T-shirt under her cheek and nuzzled the soft cotton. Exhaustion settled in and soon she drifted into hazy bliss. Sleep would occupy her thoughts and keep her from having to think about him.

But Jase came to her in her dreams, as he'd been last night—long ebony hair flowing to his shoulders, chest gleaming in the firelight, muscles contracting, rippling, mouth hot and determined, hands feverish. Kayla welcomed him instead of pushing him away, bold in her dreams and desperate for the one man who could ease her loneliness and make her feel again.

CHAPTER SEVEN

Late that afternoon, as the evening shadows started to settle, Kayla dragged herself from beneath the covers. She couldn't sleep forever, no matter how tempting the prospect. She had to do something—anything—to keep herself busy.

With a critical eye, she surveyed the bedroom. Cobwebs filled the corners. Thick layers of dust covered the furniture, the molding, the windowsill...everything. Running her hand along the edge of the nightstand, she frowned at the gray powder that covered her fingertips.

Not that Kayla had always been a stickler when it came to cleaning. She'd been known to leave a dirty dish in the sink overnight, but now she was desperate for a distraction. The room could certainly use a good going-over. For that matter, the whole house could. Suddenly, Kayla realized how she was going to live through the remaining week cooped up with Jase Terrell.

She headed down the hallway toward the kitchen, then paused in the living-room doorway.

Jase was perched on the arm of the sofa, his back to her as he leaned forward, his thighs framing the stand where the ancient radio sat. With every movement, the muscles of his back rippled beneath the simple cotton of his shirt. A memory of those sleek muscles moving beneath her hands made her fingertips burn.

Though she stood only a few feet away, she might as well have been on the other side of the moon. She felt no connection between them, no undercurrent of feelings bridging the distance. He was clear across the room, and she was by herself, alone with her thoughts just as she'd been from the start.

I'm here if you need me. Watching over you. His words played over in her mind, but they didn't ring true. Not now.

Kayla opened her mouth, eager to recapture those few moments last night when they'd talked and touched, and she hadn't felt so god-awful lonely. Sadly, she realized she couldn't.

He wanted the distance between them. He'd even told her to stay away from him.

That knowledge forced her lips together and propelled her to the kitchen, her eyes stinging with fresh tears. She rushed around the room and gathered the stuff she needed.

In minutes, she was back in her bedroom, her arms heavy with a panful of water, a bar of soap, several rags she'd found deep at the back of one of the kitchen drawers, and a renewed determination to get her mind off of Jase.

She shoved her shirtsleeves up past her elbows, climbed onto a chair and began fighting her way through a mass of stubborn cobwebs. She tried to push Jase to the most remote part of her thoughts, but he lingered, his moonsilver eyes lighting the darkness inside of her, haunting her memory.

A good hour later, Kayla wiped the last speck of dust from the nightstand. She stroked the gleaming cherry-wood with appreciative fingers. The sound of a hammer echoed through the house and Kayla whirled toward the bedroom door, her thigh slamming into the edge of the nightstand.

"Ouch!" she cried, rubbing her bruised skin. The china ballerina figurine she'd shined only seconds before crashed to the hardwood floor.

"Blast it," she mumbled, dropping to her knees to collect the shattered pieces. "I hope this isn't an antique..." Her words trailed off as the hand she'd shoved under the bed to retrieve one of the ballerina's arms, touched something solid. "What in the world...?" Kayla flung back the fringed hem of the bedspread and peered into the shadows beneath the bed. Her eyes lit on a cardboard box. Grasping the edge, she tugged. Stuck. Bracing one hand on the bed frame, she tried again.

This time, she managed to heave the box out. A thick cloud of dust stirred in its wake. Several sneezes later, she wrinkled her nose and waved a hand to clear the air.

When the dust settled, Kayla leaned back and studied the contents of the box. Toys—mostly ancient-looking dolls, hair matted, porcelain faces dirty, some even cracked—peered over the rim of the box. Curious, Kayla rummaged inside to find crayons, several coloring books, paper dolls, even some scribbled drawings.

She smiled, clasping the frail paper of one drawing to study it closer. Bold strokes of brown depicted a crude house, surrounded by several faded pink splotches— flowers. Kayla trailed her fingertips over the uneven lines. She had so many drawings just like this taped on her refrigerator at home. Dixie's drawings.

Every visit, the little girl would sit at Kayla's dining room table and create another masterpiece for her "Aunt Kaylie." As expected, Kayla would rave over the picture, even when she wasn't quite sure what she was looking at. The light in Dixie's sea-green eyes was worth every bit of carrying on.

Kayla's smile disappeared as another thought struck her. This weekend was her outing with Dixie. What would the child think when her Big Sister didn't show up for the second time in a row?

Closing her eyes, Kayla pictured the hurt on Dixie's face. She knew exactly what Dixie would think—that her Aunt Kaylie didn't want her anymore.

Well, Kayla would die before she would let Dixie think she'd been abandoned. She would go and demand, even *beg* Jase to take her to the nearest town, a neighbor, someplace, *anyplace,* to make a phone call. Just one call. Surely he couldn't deny her that. She couldn't live with herself if she hurt Dixie.

She placed the drawing back into the box, her fingers brushing against a velvety softness... Reaching deep, she grasped a handful of the soft material and pulled. Drawings and coloring books tumbled into her lap, followed by the most gorgeous doll Kayla had ever seen.

She stared into the exquisite, tiny porcelain face. The hand-painted features were delicate, intricate, with wide, hazel eyes that gleamed innocently, framed by a sweep of reddish-brown lashes the same color as the tumble of curls on the doll's head. A rosebud mouth highlighted apple cheeks. And the dress was as beautiful as the doll...a deep burgundy that accented the hair, with a lace collar emphasizing the china face.

Kayla simply stared at the doll, her stomach suddenly hollow, as if someone had landed a blow to her middle. Recollection stirred in the most remote corners of her mind. It was as though she were seeing an old friend after an endless separation.

I bet I can find you, Mrs. Moonfire, a child's voice sang through Kayla's head. *Betcha I can.*

Closing her eyes, Kayla gripped the doll, the voice holding her captive.

Betcha I can find you. Betcha I can.

Kayla touched a trembling hand to her numb face. She was finally having a nervous breakdown...a long-overdue one. First, she'd had the blackouts. Now she was imagining voices. No, only one voice. A child's voice...

The touch on her shoulder was whisper soft. Her eyes snapped open, but there was no one next to her. No one in the room. Not a single soul.

There you are, Mrs. Moonfire, the voice declared. *I told you I would find you.*

Kayla's startled gaze flew past the rocking chair, to the little girl who stood in the far corner of the room, a pale silhouette glowing in the shadows. The child stepped forward into the warm circle of candlelight.

"Oh, my God, I am losing it," Kayla murmured. Shaking her head, she glanced from the doll to the little girl...the same crown of red curls, the same sparkling eyes, porcelain-white features. The doll was an exact likeness of the child.

A *real* child?

Kayla did a double take. There was actually a child in the room. A little girl...a beautiful, smiling little girl.

Mrs. Moonfire, the little girl said again, though her lips didn't seem to move. She came around to stand in front of the rocker, her eyes riveted on the doll. *I've been looking all over for you. Daddy is coming, and we're going to play hide-and-seek. You missed last night, you bad girl. I couldn't find you, so me and Daddy played by ourselves, and I was the winner!* She climbed into the rocker. Hardwood creaked as the chair started to rock back and forth.

Kayla touched her palm to the floor where she knelt and felt the steady vibration as the rocker moved. Impossible!

She blinked, but the child didn't disappear nor did the rocker stop its motion.

"W-who are you and how did you get in here?" Kayla managed to whisper. The little girl held the arms of the chair and rocked faster, the heels of her white patent-leather shoes tapping the wooden legs with each sway of the rocker.

I love this chair, she said as if she hadn't heard Kayla's questions. *Daddy says I can sit and rock as much as I like,*

Mrs. Moonfire. Till him and Mommy come back, if I want. Then her smile vanished. Her bottom lip started to quiver. *I hope Mommy comes soon. I don't like rocking myself. My mommy always rocks me. Always.* A tear rolled down her pale cheek.

Clutching the doll, Kayla scrambled to her feet. Fingers clenched around her heart. "Don't cry, sweetheart. Please."

I want Mommy to come. The little girl sobbed. *She promised she wouldn't be gone long. Daddy said he would bring her back.* Her eyes were huge glistening pools. *I don't think they're ever coming back.* A rush of tears spilled past her long lashes, flooding down her face as she clutched the burgundy velvet of her skirt. *Ever, ever, ever!*

"Don't say that. I'm sure they'll come for you," Kayla said, taking a step toward the crying child. "Tell me their names and how you got here. Maybe I can help you find them—"

A loud blast of music reverberated through the house and Kayla nearly jumped out of her skin. Her head snapped in the direction of the doorway. The music blared louder, then silence. She heard Jase mutter a few curses that made her cheeks burn. Certainly not fit language in front of a child—

Her thoughts halted as she stared at the rocker which swayed back and forth.

Empty.

Kayla sank to the edge of the bed. Had she imagined the little girl? Was she *really* losing her marbles? Jase had made her believe in her sanity again, yet here she was seeing... seeing what? An empty rocker, which rocked on its own? But a minute ago, there had been a child doing the rocking. A child who'd talked, cried.

A jagged streak of fear worked its way down Kayla's spine and she stared at the porcelain doll she held in her arms.

Suddenly, a memory took shape—the outline of a shadow, pale skin catching the moonlight, a child's terror-filled voice. The same crying shadow-child who had called to her from the woods that first night.

But Kayla had dismissed the entire incident as a product of her overactive imagination. The wind howled so loud at night, the house creaked. The voice had been explained away easily enough. After all, she hadn't really *seen* much of anything that night. A silhouette, maybe. Barely.

Kayla glanced at the rocker. The motion had slowed little. It moved, back and forth, like the steady arm of a grandfather clock. Proof that the child had indeed been real this time.

Real, or maybe a ghost?

With a shake of her head, Kayla dismissed the thought. She didn't believe in ghosts or creatures that went bump in the night. As she'd told Jase, she'd never even slept with a night-light while growing up, at least during the part of her past she remembered. She'd never needed to because she'd never been afraid. Until now.

No! She wouldn't be afraid. A draft probably moved the rocker. The child had been a hallucination—a manifestation of the doll. She'd been thinking about Dixie. Struck by the beauty of the doll, she'd undoubtedly projected the features into a real child, a subconscious substitute for Dixie.

That was it. Leaving the doll on the bed, Kayla jumped to her feet and started across the room. When she neared the rocker, she reached out and halted the motion. As her fingers touched the wood, she noticed how warm it felt. The room was cold, as usual, but the rocker felt warm. *Warm*.

She turned away before she could contemplate the disturbing discovery. Her imagination, she told herself.

That's all. She was so lonely and bored, she'd started inventing things.

Music drifted through the house again, pulling Kayla from the room, down the hall.

Whether Jase meant to talk to her or not, she wasn't going to hide away. They could sit in stony silence if that's what he wanted, but at least she wouldn't be alone, and she had a question to ask him. A very important one.

"Jase..."

"Yeah?" He didn't spare her a glance.

"I need to get to a telephone."

"No," he stated, the one word intended to brook no argument.

"Yes," she countered. When he gave her a sharp look, she added, "It's very important. Just take me to a nearby phone—"

"That's out of the question."

"Please. I have to make a phone call."

"Stop worrying about your job, Kayla. I already called the station. Everything's squared with them. You're officially taking a well-needed vacation."

"It's not my job. It's Dixie," she said, her voice catching on the name.

He stopped what he was doing and leveled an intense stare at her. "Who's Dixie, and why this sudden need to call her?"

"I volunteer for a program that helps children of single parents. I was paired with a little girl named Dixie. I'm her Big Sister. I spend every other Saturday with her. I've been doing it for almost two years now. I had to miss our last visit because of the blackouts. If I don't call her about this Saturday, she'll think I don't care about her."

"I'm sorry," he said with a shake of his head. "She'll have to understand."

"She won't," Kayla said in a rush, never one to be swayed once she'd made up her mind. "I mean, not unless I call her. She's only five. She spends all day cooped up with a baby-sitter. I'm one of the few people she has. She depends on me. Her mother's always busy, what with working two jobs to make ends meet."

"There's too much at stake," Jase told her, his tone uncompromising yet oddly gentle. "We only have four days left. Surely you can make it till then without calling her."

"Please, Jase. I've been cooperative in every way." Doubt quirked his dark eyebrows and Kayla said, "Okay, so I tried to leave at first, but what did you expect? You kidnapped me and demanded my trust without any explanation. Only a vague story about someone coming after me."

"You still think it's a story?"

"So it's the truth," she conceded. "Still, I have to get to a phone. Dixie won't understand. *Please,*" she added, the word a low, desperate plea. "Grant me this one favor. Just this one."

Something flashed in his eyes, his eyebrows furrowed and Kayla knew he battled some internal force.

"Please," she said again, more determined than ever before. She wouldn't let him refuse her this. "If you don't, I'll find my own way out of here. And locking me in my room won't stop me. Nothing will. I'll find a way. You either help me, or I go it alone."

"I don't like ultimatums." Truly he didn't, if the edge in his voice was any indication. But Kayla wouldn't be swayed.

"Yet that's all you give me," she countered. "Fair's fair, Jase. Believe me, I don't find the idea of leaving here by myself very appealing, but I'll do it. You can help me or stay behind. The choice is yours."

Finally, after a tense moment, he nodded. "Tomorrow."

Relief rushed through Kayla and she smiled. "Thank you," she said, ignoring the crazy urge to rush over, wrap her arms around his neck and thank him properly. Instead, she took a tentative step in his direction.

He turned his attention back to the radio. Kayla's gaze followed his.

"You fixed it," she exclaimed, hearing the music, disrupted by an occasional crackle and pop, which drifted from the old-time radio. "I've messed with that blasted thing I don't know how many times trying to get it to work. What are you, some kind of miracle worker?"

"I thought it might help you pass the time," was all he said. He gathered up the screwdriver and wrench, then stood.

Kayla found herself backing up a few inches as he towered over her. She tilted her head to study his stonelike features—from guarded eyes to a strong jaw covered with dark stubble. He looked foreboding, dangerous. Certainly a man to be wary of, if she were thinking clearly.

But she couldn't think. She could only stare at him, mesmerized by his sensuous lips. Lips she knew were soft yet determined, tender yet purposeful. The urge to trail her fingertips over them nearly overwhelmed her.

No! her conscience screamed. He'd made it obvious that he didn't want her to touch him. That he didn't want to touch her.

"The reception's not very good," he murmured.

"No, it sounds fine. Thank you again." She couldn't resist her own impulses, or rather the unseen force that drove her to feel his skin against her own. She reached up.

He captured her wrist a fraction before her hand made contact with his mouth. "Kayla, don't." His grip was firm, his fingers clamped tight. "I don't want either of us to do something we'll regret."

"But I won't regret—"

"Dammit, *yes,* you will!" He thrust her hand away and shoved past her. Flinging open the front door, he added, his voice almost pained, "Please listen to what I'm telling you, Kayla. You don't know what you're getting yourself into. I'm not what you think. Listen and stay away from me. For your own good." The door slammed behind him, and Kayla caught her bottom lip. She wouldn't call him back, no matter how wrong he was.

Perching on the edge of the sofa, Kayla rested her hand on the radio, felt the sound vibrate through the speaker. Bless Jase. Music had always been her escape.

Kayla closed her eyes, picturing him as she swayed to the next tune that drifted from the speaker. "Only you..." And deep in Kayla's heart, the words rang with a frightening truth.

Suddenly, she needed to see Jase again. She moved to the living-room window and shoved the curtain aside. At the edge of the porch, he leaned against one wooden pillar, his arms folded, attention fixed on the surrounding forest. She knew he sensed her gaze. He stiffened, but didn't afford her a glance.

"There *is* something between us," she whispered. "I know there is and so do you."

A gust of wind blew across the clearing, stirring and scattering a layer of crinkled brown leaves. A frigid draft seeped around the edges of the windowsill. Kayla shivered. The night promised to be cold, like all the others.

Jase didn't seem the least bothered by the bitter cold. He didn't even shiver. He just stood there, like a finely chiseled statue that had weathered year after year, immune to the elements as he stared at something only he could see.

Dismissing the disturbing thought, Kayla forced her gaze from him and let the curtain fall into place. The music drew her to the sofa where she settled. She closed her eyes, to listen, and forget—her inexplicable attraction to Jase Terrell, the danger stalking her, the child her imagi-

nation had conjured up, the past just out of her reach—
everything, save the lyrics.

"When are we leaving?" Kayla asked the next day as she
stepped out onto the back porch, into the morning sunlight.

Jase paused in his chore, ax in hand, and wiped a few
beads of moisture from his forehead with the hemline of
his shirt.

Kayla found herself entranced by the rippled expanse of
his abdomen sprinkled with dark hair that funnelled to a
V and disappeared beneath the waistband of his jeans.
Silky smooth hair she had the sudden urge to touch.

"This evening," he mumbled, dropping the bottom of
the shirt and destroying her view. He raised his arms and
swung the ax downward. The log cracked in two where the
blade hit. Jase tossed the halves on the already monstrous
stack of kindling next to the woodshed.

"How long have you been out here?" She eyed the stack
of firewood, enough to last them a month rather than less
than a single week. Still, he kept chopping like a man possessed. Or rather, a man desperate to keep busy, Kayla
mused as she eyed the back of his shirt. Perspiration
darkened the fabric from his shoulder blades, down the
center of his back.

"A couple of hours," he said, turning to face her. "Are
you finished cleaning the living room?"

"A few minutes ago," she replied. She shivered and
rubbed her upper arms. "How can you stand there with no
jacket? It's freezing out here."

"Put my jacket on," he said, motioning to the worn
leather draped over the back porch railing. "You'll catch
pneumonia standing there like that." His gaze fixed on her
breasts. The fabric of her shirt molded to the outline of her
nipples puckered from the cold. A scowl slid over his fea-

tures and he turned back to his chore. "Put the jacket on," he repeated.

"What about you?" she managed to ask, despite the heat coiling inside of her.

"I'm used to the cold. Now put it on."

She swung the jacket around her shoulders and sat on the porch steps to watch him. "It's so isolated here." She fixed her attention on the lean, tanned fingers gripping the ax.

"That's the idea," he replied. His grip tightened, his fingers flexed.

Mesmerized, Kayla simply stared, remembering all too well how those fingers felt stroking the curve of her neck, the fullness of her breasts. She cleared her throat as the burning heat crept up her neck, into her cheeks.

"Are you catching a cold?" he demanded, dark eyes brooding over her, peering into her thoughts.

"Uh, no. Just a little dust in my throat, that's all." Kayla's face flamed even hotter beneath his scrutiny and she knew she turned every shade of red.

If Jase noticed, he made no comment. He gave her one last assessing look then returned his attention to log splitting.

She forced her thoughts to a dead halt, then steered them away from the unnerving path they'd been traveling. "How long have you known about this place?" she asked, her gaze sweeping the clearing.

"Long enough," he said rather sharply as he slammed the ax into the log with what seemed nothing short of murderous intent. Wood cracked and Kayla jumped. He threw the logs to the pile and turned to glare at her. "Did you come out here to stare at me, drill me with questions, or both?"

"None of the above," she retorted, pushing to her feet. "You're too damned touchy to talk to, and with that frown on your face, you're not much to look at, either." Liar! her conscience screamed—on one count at least.

She braced herself, waiting for him to reach out and grab her by the throat, the telltale gleam in his eyes showing her he'd like nothing more than to do just that.

Instead, he smiled, the first real smile she'd seen from him. "I wish I could say the same for you. You're quite an eyeful." His gaze held hers for the space of a heartbeat. Heat jolted through her body like an electric charge.

Startled, Kayla took an unsteady step backward, her anger quickly forgotten as she tried to understand what had just happened. "I—I was just trying to make conversation, since we're stuck here together." She pivoted and hurried into the house, not sure whether she ran from him, herself or maybe both. He made her feel things that were new, and so very extraordinary.

Even after she'd slammed the door, safely inside, her body still tingled from . . . from what?

He hadn't *really* touched her, not physically, anyway. But in that split second as the full power of his attention had burned into her, she'd felt him touch her, every inch of her, both inside and out. The feeling left her tied in knots and utterly confused.

A feeling that didn't subside, even when dusk settled and Jase called her outside, ready to take her to a phone, as promised.

"Where exactly are we going?" Kayla asked him, standing at the edge of the porch. She watched him stuff his black canvas bag beneath the motorcycle seat.

He paused and cast her a quick glance. "There's a place about twenty miles down the highway from here. They've got a phone."

"A neighbor?"

"No, it's a bar and grill, and the closest place to us. There are no neighbors out here, Kayla."

"Why are we going so late?" She shivered and glanced at the treetops silhouetted against the burnt-orange sunset. "It'll be night soon."

"Afraid of the dark?"

"Don't be silly," she replied, pulling his jacket, which she still wore, tighter around her. If only she could ignore the possibility that they might run into danger—the shadow in the woods, stalking her, looming over her. The shadow waited outside of the circle.

"You don't have to be frightened."

"I told you I'm not," she declared. She ignored the mocking smile that lifted his lips. "It just makes more sense for us to have gone during the day. You say I'm in so much danger. Wouldn't daylight afford us an advantage? At least we would be able to see someone coming."

He shook his head and stared at a dense patch of surrounding forest, as if he couldn't, or rather, didn't want to meet her eyes. "An advantage? There are no advantages, Kayla. The people after you thrive twenty-four hours a day—in the bright light of day, or the blackest night. They're powerful. The darkness fuels that power but..." His words trailed off and a haunted look touched his features. "But the darkness is a sort of protection, as well. It provides cover for us. That's our only advantage. Do you understand?" He drilled his gaze into her now. The skin at her nape prickled.

"No," she retorted, but she did. Somewhere in the back of her mind, his words made sense. They confirmed her strange fascination with the dark, for it wasn't the night that Kayla feared, rather the people Jase spoke of.

"Get on." He patted the seat behind him.

"It's freezing out here," she said. "You can't go without a jacket." She eyed the short-sleeved T-shirt he wore. The sleeves barely covered his smooth, muscled biceps. The wind whipped and goose bumps crept along her flesh. Jase sat, calm, undaunted by the bitter wind.

"The cold air will do me good." He gave her a smoldering look that said, if anything, he *needed* the cold air.

Her face heated. She felt the urge to simply shrug off the jacket herself and toss it to the porch. Being close to him would prove warm enough.

"Suit yourself," she mumbled instead. Resting her hands on his shoulders, she straddled the back of the motorcycle. "I still haven't figured out how we're going to get out of here. I know you rode out the other day, but I've looked everywhere for a trail and there isn't one."

"Do you really believe that?"

His question took her by surprise. "Well, yes, I mean, I've looked for a break in the trees and haven't found one."

"But you do believe there *is* one?"

"Well, yes. Yes, of course I do."

"Then there is," he replied, revving the engine. In a jolting second, they were moving. "Hold on."

Obediently, Kayla snaked her arms around his waist.

He circled the house and headed straight for the deep thicket behind the woodshed.

"Are you crazy?" she screamed over the bike's roar. The forest loomed in front of them, a solid brown wall, impenetrable.

"Believe, Kayla. Just because you can't see something, doesn't mean it isn't there." With those words, he sent the bike speeding forward, headed for what Kayla knew could only be disaster.

CHAPTER EIGHT

Kayla blinked, the scream dying in her throat as she stared at the break between two massive trees. The same opening she'd seen that first night when the child had called to her. Tree branches curved, forming a giant arch. The opening seemed to grow wider as they closed the distance to the forest, until a clear path stretched before them.

Jase sent the motorcycle roaring into the deepest, blackest thicket Kayla had ever seen. The headlight illuminated the path directly in front of them. Beyond, the darkness seemed fathomless. Not even a glimmer of dusk pierced the overlay of branches. It was as if she and Jase had been swallowed by some monstrous beast.

Kayla clung to him, her fingers digging into the muscles at his waist. The motorcycle's engine became a distant drone as the sound of the wind filled her ears. The forest seemed to reach out, the branches like giant hands poking and pulling at her. She held tighter to Jase and buried her face between his shoulder blades, suddenly more terrified than she'd ever been in her life, even when she'd slipped into the blackouts.

Finally, the trees thinned and parted. They emerged onto a gravel road. Jase slowed the motorcycle and brought them to a skidding halt. Cutting the engine, he pried her fingers from around his waist.

"Are you okay?" He held her hands and massaged the stiffness away.

"There wasn't any path, Jase," she breathed against his shoulder, her heart beating a frenzied tempo against her rib cage. "I searched everywhere the other day—after I saw the child. I thought maybe the child was real instead of something my imagination had conjured up. That would've meant the path was real, too. I looked everywhere, but I didn't see anything—not even a few inches of space between the tree trunks."

"A few minutes ago, you said there had to be a path," he softly reminded her, his long lean fingers tracing reassuring circles against her palms.

"But I didn't really think...I mean, I spent forever *looking* for one."

"Sometimes we look so hard for things, we can't see what's right in front of us. We can't tell the good from the bad, right from wrong. There's a fine line between real and unreal. Sometimes the two become confused."

"I'm the one confused."

"I know, and—"

"You're sorry, but it's for the best," she finished, forcing a deep breath and squaring her shoulders. She stared at the edge of the forest they'd come through. Once again, the trees formed a solid wall. No path, not even a dangling branch to prove they'd just ridden through.

"You're learning, moonchild," he replied, releasing her hands to grab the bars of the motorcycle. Flipping on the switch, he brought the bike to life. They took off down the road, dust and gravel billowing in their wake.

Kayla pushed all thoughts of the forest to the farthest edge of her mind. Trying to rationalize would only drive her crazy. She locked her hands around Jase's middle, feeling the hard ripples of stomach muscles beneath her fingertips.

Freezing wind rushed past her, but Jase's body provided a warm shield. She inched closer, her cheek resting on the curve of one shoulder, her breasts pressed to the sinewy wall of his back. Never in her life had Kayla felt so complete.

The blackouts, the desperation to discover the truth about her past, the danger closing in on her, all ceased to matter for those few moments. In her arms, she held a force more powerful and potent than anything she'd ever encountered. She held *him*—his strength, his secrets, his very soul, it seemed—and she realized in a startling moment, she never wanted to let him go.

A good half hour later, however, she had to. They slowed, veering off the highway. A stream of floodlights illuminated the gravel lot of Big Mick's Bar and Grill, the name written in blue neon on a peeling sign hanging in front of the enormous barnlike structure.

Jase weaved through the parking lot, past a row of motorcycles, several pickup trucks and an assortment of cars.

"The place is packed," she commented as he steered into a spare parking spot and flipped off the ignition.

"It's Friday night. This is the nearest wet establishment to town. Everybody heads out here to cut loose."

The doors swung open as several people pushed their way outside. A lively country song sailed into the night. The building's metal roof trembled as the doors slammed shut.

"This place has the nearest telephone?" she asked. "Don't you think we could find someplace quieter?"

"This is better," Jase replied. "More public." He stuffed his keys into his pocket and helped Kayla off the motorcycle. They strode across the parking lot and inside Big Mick's.

"What brings you to these parts, fella?" asked a giant of a man who stood behind the bar, or rather towered over it. Well over six foot five, he had long, unkempt brown hair and a thick mustache and beard. The red and blue lights above the dance floor cast colored shadows across his face and made his eyes seem darker, deeper and somewhat frightening.

Kayla inched closer to Jase.

"I know everyone around here," the man went on, "and I ain't never seen you." He stared suspiciously, probably a look reserved for tourists who dared to venture into a local haunt.

Jase didn't seem the least bit intimidated. "I'm not from around here," he replied, raking long fingers through his hair, a gesture Kayla had come to recognize as a warning that his temper was rising. "Are you always so friendly to new customers?"

Both men eyed one another for a long moment. Kayla itched to turn and leave before this Big Foot pounded both of them, but Jase tightened his hold on her hand and she found herself rooted to the spot. Her shoulder touched his, the connection alerting her to the anger roiling inside of him.

"Big Mick's the name," the man finally said, extending his hand. "Welcome to my place."

Jase shook the man's hand and Kayla breathed a sigh of relief.

"What'll you have, buddy?"

"A beer and..." Jase cast a questioning glance at Kayla.

"Iced tea," she croaked, still wary of the giant man who now studied her with open curiosity and a glimmer of lust in his dark eyes.

"Ain't got no tea, lady," he said, shaking his bushy head.

"A diet soda then."

Big Mick reached one beefy hand inside a cooler beneath the counter and pulled out a frosty beer bottle and a can of diet soda. He plopped both in front of Jase. "That'll be two-fifty."

Jase tossed a twenty-dollar bill on the scarred countertop. "I need to make a long-distance call. Can you give me change?"

"Ain't got enough in my register yet. The night's still young. But you're welcome to use my phone out back and just pay me directly for the charges. You can probably hear better back there, anyway, what with all the noise in here."

"We would appreciate that," Jase replied, taking a long swig of his beer, his movements stiff, controlled.

"You should. I don't usually let folks into my store-room. You seem like a decent enough fella, and the lady looks pretty decent, herself."

Kayla stared at Jase's shoulder, unwilling to meet Big Mick's eyes. There was no mistaking the meaning behind his words. She felt Jase's fingers tighten around hers.

"What will it cost me?"

"Smart man," Big Mick commented, a smile splitting his face. Then he grew serious. "Double that twenty you pulled out."

Big Mick's eyes took on a hungry light as Jase reached into his pocket and pulled out a wad of bills. He peeled off two twenties then stuffed the rest back into his pocket.

"Where's the phone?" Jase asked, his voice low, laced with a fury she felt flowing through his touch.

If Big Mick noticed Jase's tightly leashed anger, he made no comment. "I'll show you," he replied. He snatched the twenties from the counter and stuffed them into his pocket. Then he motioned to a skinny man standing at the end of the bar with a group of leather- and blue-jean-clad bikers. "Willie, get over here and keep an eye on things till I get back." He signaled Jase and Kayla. "You two follow me."

The storeroom of Big Mick's was a maze of cardboard liquor boxes, trash cans and spare tables and chairs. Against the far wall sat a battered brown desk littered with paper. Perched on one corner was an old-fashioned-looking black telephone—the kind with a round face and dial.

"Have at it," Big Mick said. "You got five minutes. Any longer and you'll be paying extra." Then he was gone, shutting the door behind him, muffling the music and noise of the bar.

Kayla rushed across the room, snatched up the receiver and dialed. "Wanda," she said when she heard the familiar voice come across the telephone line. "It's Kayla."

"Kayla? My God, girl, where have you been?" She rushed on before Kayla could reply. "One of the DJs at your station even called here looking for you. I think he said his name was Marc something or other. He was going out of his mind. Said you went on an unexpected vacation without telling him anything. Nobody else at the station was surprised, but he didn't think it was like you to up and leave at the spur of the moment, not in the middle of a promotion event. Said you just disappeared—"

"I wasn't feeling well," Kayla cut in. "I just needed to get away for a little while." She stole a glance at Jase who watched her with such intense eyes, she felt compelled to put her back to him. "That's why I'm calling. I won't be able to make this weekend. I wanted to tell Dixie myself."

"Hold on while I put her on the phone," Wanda murmured.

Kayla heard the door behind her open and close, and she knew Jase had left her alone. While she welcomed the privacy, a strange sense of loss crept through her. She couldn't deny the tangible bond between them. They *connected*. And at the same time, they became more estranged. The entire situation was maddening.

Maybe Jase was right. Maybe distance was better. She should steel herself against any attraction to him. At least then she wouldn't feel so torn—wanting him, yet fearing him, yearning for his touch, yet dreading it. Yes, maybe distance was better.

Funny, but it didn't feel better, or more comforting, or more soothing, than the protectiveness of his arms.

"Auntie Kaylie?" Dixie's familiar voice came over the line. Guilt knifed through Kayla and she sank to the edge of the desk.

"Dixie, honey, I've got something to tell you..."

By the time Kayla placed the receiver in its cradle, tears rolled down her cheeks. She sat staring at the phone. A fist settled in her chest, making each breath almost painful. Undoubtedly, Dixie felt just as bad. Worse, if the child's crying had been any indication. Then again, at least Jase had let Kayla make the phone call. The little girl would have been even more hurt if Kayla had stood her up.

Glancing around the cluttered storeroom, Kayla forced herself to her feet. When she opened the door, she expected to find Jase waiting for her. He wasn't. Thank God. Kayla made a beeline for the rest rooms near the end of the hallway. She had to pull herself together before she faced Jase.

After seeing to her first order of business, she draped Jase's jacket over the edge of the sink. Tugging off her topaz ring, she placed it on the soap dish and shoved her hands beneath the icy water gushing from the faucet.

When she reached for a paper towel, her hand froze, her gaze fixed on her own image staring back at her from the cracked mirror above the sink.

Frowning, Kayla noted her colorless complexion. Her hair, a windblown tangle of red, made a stark contrast to her pale skin. Skin almost as white as the shirt she wore.

"Is that your natural hair color?" The voice made Kayla jump.

She swung around, squinting into the darkness that hovered just beyond the dim glow of the flickering overhead light bulb.

"Over here, sugar," the woman's voice sounded again.

Kayla caught the slight movement in the far corner. She trained her eyes on the silhouette of a woman leaning against the graffiti of the opposite wall. Kayla couldn't

make out the woman's face, but she was able to discern her
petite frame, the long dark braid hanging over one of her
pale shoulders, the cigarette clasped between her fingers.
The butt glowed bright red in the shadowed obscurity of
the bathroom, like an evil eye come to jinx her.

Kayla felt rather than saw the woman's intense gaze.

"Sorry if I startled you, sugar," she added before taking a long drag on her cigarette. The tip flared, reflecting
the woman's dark eyes for a brief, startling moment before a cloud of shimmering smoke obliterated Kayla's view.

"That's all right." Kayla let out a deep, relieved breath
and quelled the shiver of anxiety that raced up her spine.
"I'm usually not so jumpy, but I didn't hear you come in."
She snatched several paper towels from the dispenser and
dried her hands, ignoring the odd twinge of familiarity that
rippled through her.

The woman smiled, her lips parting to reveal a straight
row of white teeth which gleamed in the dim light. "I'm as
quiet as a mouse. Actually, my husband doesn't like me to
smoke. He's ordering a couple of drinks, so I decided to
sneak away and get in a few puffs. Don't mind me—" she
motioned with a wave of one ghostly-white hand "—you
go on with what you were doing."

"I was almost finished." Kayla forced a smile and
dropped the paper towels into the wastebasket.

"I can't believe the bathroom isn't crawling with people," the woman commented. "Usually, there's a line
down the hall all the way to the men's room. But I guess
it's a little early. Wait till midnight rolls around."

Kayla glanced to the sole window, the glass spray-
painted black to keep prying eyes away, and suddenly, the
room seemed much smaller. She inched back against the
sink, but the woman seemed closer somehow, her face still
a mask of shadows, pierced by only the flicker of dark,
glasslike eyes. Then a sparkle of red flashed and Kayla's
attention riveted on the blood-red ring the woman wore.

"Red's my favorite color. Ruby red," the woman said, flexing her fingers. The carefully cut stone glittered like fiery ice. "That's why I couldn't help admiring your hair."

Kayla brushed a few curls back from her face, suddenly self-conscious beneath such open scrutiny.

"You're a true beauty," the woman murmured. Her face remained obscured by the shadows, but Kayla saw her gaze again. A strange glimmer lit her eyes. The same glimmer in a scientist's eyes when he observed a prized specimen, or a hunter's as he moved in for the kill.

Kayla gave herself a mental shake. The bad lighting was doing funny things to her senses. She reached for Jase's jacket, stuffed her arms inside the warm leather and moved toward the doorway. "Nice talking to you, but I have someone waiting for me."

"Have fun," the woman said and smiled, again flashing the dazzling white of her teeth. "I'll be seeing you."

The last words, like an ominous promise, followed Kayla through the doorway and urged her faster. Her insides knotted with fear. Fear she knew was irrational. After all, the woman had only been making small talk.

Kayla forced her breathing back to normal and headed down the hall. Brushing past several women on their way to the ladies' room, she moved toward the front of Big Mick's to look for Jase.

An image of him flashed in her mind and a hurting warmth fired her insides. She shook her head. She shouldn't let him affect her. Ignore him, reason advised. The attraction wasn't healthy, not when he refused to acknowledge the pull between them.

But her feelings for him had nothing to do with reason, she realized as she stood staring across the smoke-filled room, past the dance floor dotted with couples, to the bar.

Jase stood with his back to the counter, arms folded, his broad shoulders accented by the T-shirt he wore. His gaze was fixed on the dance floor, where several couples moved to a slow waltz. Ebony hair fell the length of his neck, framed the lean lines of his face and accented his high cheekbones. He was strikingly handsome with his dark good looks and haunted eyes, yet Jase's appeal went much deeper than his appearance.

Kayla had never met someone so intense, and though he frightened her at times, he also fired her blood. There was something primitive about him, something violent and threatening he kept locked inside himself. As if the dark chaos that existed before God had made the earth and heavens had been preserved. And it lived and thrived within Jase Terrell. He held the very essence of life and death beneath his controlled surface.

She sensed it.

She was drawn to it.

And she couldn't help wondering what it would be like to unleash all that Jase fought so hard to control. To find herself caught up in a savage maelstrom of emotion, as thrilling as a lightning storm at midnight, and as dangerous. She'd come close the other night. Close but not close enough.

"You sure are one fine-looking woman," the male drawl cut into her thoughts.

Dragging her gaze from Jase, Kayla found herself staring up into a pair of hungry brown eyes set in a face as weathered as rawhide. The scraggly beginnings of a beard covered the man's jaw, and a large scar streaked its way across his forehead. He looked predatory, an expression enhanced by the smile on his face, like that of a lion about to sink his teeth into a meaty dinner.

She inched backward and came up flat against the edge of a cigarette machine sitting just inside the doorway. The man planted one of his palms against the machine, the other on the doorjamb, and cornered her.

"I'd say you're about the prettiest woman I've ever seen," he said, leaning perilously close. The smell of liquor and stale cigarette smoke surrounded her. "I ain't never seen hair this color." He caught one red curl between his fingers. "And I ain't never felt anything this soft."

Calm down, she told herself. She'd handled flirty men before. Given her line of work, she'd spent many nights at area clubs doing radio promotions, and diverting unwanted attention. Nice and polite...those were the key words.

"Uh, thank you, Mr...." Kayla's voice trailed off as she tried to see past the man, to seek out Jase and silently beg his help. "I'm afraid I don't know your name."

"Travis," the man murmured, touching the curl to his lips. "My name's Travis, pretty lady." Travis loomed over her, a square head sitting on top of massive shoulders. He wore a black muscle-shirt at least two sizes too small, the skull-and-crossbones on the front stretched tight over his chest.

"Thanks, Travis. I appreciate the compliment. Now, if you'll excuse me—"

"Damn, you've got a sexy voice." His gaze riveted on her lips. "Sexy...like everything else about you." He trailed a rough fingertip across her cheek and Kayla flinched.

"Listen, Travis, I—"

"Come on, pretty lady," he bellowed, catching the hand she used to wave off his advances. "They're playing our song."

"I don't think so," she said, only to have him jerk her after him, onto the dance floor. "I'm with someone," she told him in a rush of words, trying to tug her hand loose.

"Doesn't look that way to me. Besides, it's only one dance, honey." He stopped and yanked her into his arms, bringing her up hard against him.

Kayla planted her palms against his chest and pushed. "Listen, Travis, I'm with someone. I promised him this dance. He's probably looking for me right now."

"Let him look," Travis replied. Undaunted by her struggles, he started to sway to the slow tune. "He shouldn't have left you by yourself."

"He's coming right back—"

"The man's a damn fool for leaving a looker like you alone. A single lady standing by herself is fair game. If you were my woman, I wouldn't let you out of my sight. You're with one stupid jerk, if you ask me."

"Nobody asked you," she snapped, forgetting the niceties. "Now, if you'll excuse me." She pushed harder and he pulled her closer.

"Not until after we're finished. Relax, sweetheart."

"*Let go,*" she said through gritted teeth. "I'm warning you, Travis..."

The man's only response was a hearty chuckle and a tightening of his arms.

"That's it, buddy." Kayla shoved one last time against his chest and managed to put a fraction of distance between them. Travis shot her a startled look, obviously surprised at her strength. She didn't stop to congratulate herself. She bent her knee and thrust it upward, turning his surprise to pain with one forceful motion.

He groaned, his breath coming out in one loud swoosh as he doubled over and Kayla found herself free.

"You bitch!" he bellowed.

"I warned you," Kayla said, then pivoted to make a quick exit before Travis recovered. She turned and ran straight into a hard male body.

Kayla jerked her head up and gazed into Jase's scowling face. His eyes glittered, the pupils lighting with a silver fire that sent a shiver down her spine.

"We ain't finished yet," Travis groaned, recovering enough to straighten. He grabbed Kayla's arm. "Not by a long shot, lady."

"Let go of her," Jase ordered.

"Like hell I will. Go crawl back under the rock you came from," Travis bellowed. A good foot taller than Jase, and at least fifty pounds heavier, he obviously didn't feel threatened. "She owes me now."

"She doesn't owe you a thing," Jase growled, his voice as steely as the glint in his eyes.

"Look," Kayla cut in, standing directly between the two men. "I appreciate your wanting to dance, Travis, but like I told you, I'm with someone. And as for you..." She turned on Jase and whispered, "I had the situation under control."

Travis snaked an arm around Kayla's waist. "You owe me a dance, and your friend can wait until we finish," Travis grumbled, eyeing Jase as he would a bothersome fly. "Can't you, fella?"

"You heard the lady," Jase said through clenched teeth. "She's with someone. Do yourself a favor and let her go."

Gazes clashed and fear rippled the length of Kayla's spine. The tension between the two men filtered out and snaked invisible fingers around her neck. Visions of Jase lying beaten and bloodied in a gravel parking lot flashed through her mind. Travis was so much bigger.

"What's the trouble here, Travis?" A man stepped up to them. He stood as tall and as broad as Kayla's dance partner. He was followed by another man, and she and Jase found themselves facing a trio of giants.

"I was having myself a little dance with this pretty lady, when this guy butted in," Travis drawled, motioning to Jase. Obviously, Travis didn't intend to tell his friends about the painful knee to his groin that had ended their dance before Jase had shown up.

"Listen, mister, if Travis wants to dance with her, it ain't none of your concern," one of the men said.

"She's with me," Jase replied, his voice low and dangerous.

"She wasn't with you when our friend asked her to dance."

"Damn straight," Travis chimed in. "You shouldna left her alone. Single women are public property around here, partner."

"I'm not single," Kayla blurted out. "We're married."

Travis frowned, suspicion gleaming in his eyes. "How come you ain't wearing no ring?" He inspected her bare hand.

"I—we just tied the knot a few days ago." She snatched her hand from his beefy fingers. "Now, if you boys don't mind, I would like to dance with my husband."

She turned into Jase's arms. Resting her hands on his upper arms, she ordered, "Dance."

He glanced sharply at her. "The hell I will—"

"Dance so they'll leave us alone," she entreated. "It's your fault for coming over in the first place. I had the situation under control without you. Now dance. Please, Jase." A pleading note crept into her voice. "I don't want any trouble. *Please.*" She felt the tightening of muscles beneath her palms, the surge of anger consuming him, and her fear escalated. "Please," she begged again. "No trouble, Jase." His bloodied face stayed rooted in her mind, feeding her anxiety. She tried to push him toward the middle of the dance floor.

He stared at her for an endless moment. Finally, the steely depths of his eyes softened. He dipped his hands beneath the edges of the leather jacket she wore. Locking his fingers around her waist, he let her urge him backward, through the cluster of couples, out onto the dance floor.

"They're watching us," she whispered.

"They can go straight to hell." Still, he pulled her closer and steered her even deeper into the dancing crowd until Kayla no longer felt the three pairs of eyes boring into her.

"You didn't have to make excuses to those guys," he said when they were a safe distance away, dozens of couples surrounding them.

"And have you end up beaten and dumped out back in the trash? No thanks. There were three of them, Jase. *Three.*"

"I could have handled them."

"I *had* handled them. One of them, at least, before you came along. I can take care of myself just fine."

"You wouldn't have made it three feet before that guy would have been all over you. He's not the type to let a woman get away with something like that."

"And you're so big and tough, you could have taken on all three of them, right?" Her voice rose a notch with her irritation.

"Not tough, Kayla. Furious, when I saw that guy with his hands on you."

"But there were *three* of them, Jase."

"Three that I could have handled," he repeated.

"Maybe..." One glance at the anger simmering in the depths of his eyes and she added, "Probably, but I didn't want to risk it." I didn't want to risk *you,* she screamed silently. She'd come to depend on him. To need him. To crave him.

And she felt something else for him... Something much deeper and much more disturbing.

The music closed in, the steady strum of a guitar, the soft play of a piano. The slow tune filled her ears, as thoroughly as Jase filled her senses.

"You still didn't have to make excuses," his deep voice echoed in her ears. "You didn't have to lie."

"I'm sorry," she murmured, guilt kneading her insides. "I didn't mean to tell them we were married. I just didn't want to see you in a fight." She swallowed, then added. "I'm sorry I forced you into dancing, Jase. I know you've made up your mind that you don't want anything to do with me, and you told me not to touch you..." Her words faded, every nerve in her body attuned to his proximity.

His fingers splayed across her spine, burning through her shirt. Her heart beat faster and she ached to feel him closer. If only he felt the same.

He tilted her chin and brought her gaze to meet his. "It's not that I don't want your touch. I want it—too much. That's the problem."

To her surprise, he pulled her flush against him, and for the briefest moment Kayla wondered if she wouldn't have been safer with Travis. The blaze in Jase's eyes frightened her, and at the same time sent an upswell of liquid fire through her body.

"*You're* my problem," he went on, his voice rough, unsteady. "One that I don't have any solution for. I know I should stay away from you, not look at you, block you completely from my mind. Hell, I try," he growled, frustration fueling his words. He hesitated, assessing her for a long, drawn-out moment that pushed her nerves to the limit. "You're a fever in my blood, Kayla. A fever that's driving me mad."

She opened her mouth, not quite sure what to say to such an admission. But before a syllable could form, he leaned down and captured her lips with his.

His tongue was velvet madness, stroking the interior of her mouth, plundering, claiming every sensitive curve and hollow, branding her his and leaving no doubt in her mind about his desire for her.

She wound her arms around his neck, leaning into his hard strength and reveling in the feel of muscle beneath her fingertips. Heat surged through her, *his* heat, chasing away the coldness that had crept inside of her such a long time ago.

The world around her ceased to exist. She felt only him, and he felt so very right. The moment felt so right.

Until the tingling in her hands started and she froze.

Jase pulled away, his eyes wild, sparkling with confusion. He said her name, but she saw only the movement of his lips. No sound . . .

Only the thunder of silence in her ears.

He seemed to move in slow motion, his head whipping left and right, eyes narrowed, searching the crowd.

"Jase," she formed his name, the blood pounding in her temples. She grasped at his shirt, the overhead lights now red and blue swirls in the darkness veiling her vision.

The black grew blacker.

The lights faded and the numbness started to creep through her body.

Kayla felt her legs swept out from under her a second before she plunged into oblivion, Jase's name still on her lips, his fear filling her heart. She knew then that the people he'd warned her about were near.

They're coming. Maybe they finally had.

Jase damned himself a thousand times as surely as the Keepers were damning him at that moment. He pulled Kayla closer, whispering for her to wrap her arms around his neck as he carried her across the yard.

She immediately complied, holding on to him as if he were her lifeline, and he was. He held her back from complete oblivion. His power kept her from teetering over the edge. Still, she was lost in another world, Jase's voice her only link to reality.

Hopefully, she would wake up soon. The ride back had been brutal, draining for him to keep her alert and cooperative enough for them to make the twenty-mile trip. At least now he could let her sleep.

Jase carried her up the porch steps, into the house.

The house...

It stood dark and ominous beneath the pitch-black sky. No longer did it serve as a sanctuary from what hunted them. Things had changed. He felt it, as intensely as he felt Kayla's warm body against his.

Something was different. Something had happened inside the club, in those few moments when he'd been absorbed in the feel of her, rather than conscious of his surroundings.

Still, she shouldn't have blacked out, not in his arms, not with their strength fusing into one potent force. Powerful beyond belief... yet not powerful enough.

That's what the Keepers wanted him to know, that they watched and waited, and they could crush him if they chose to. They could eliminate him from the picture and take her—if he didn't heed their warning and do their bidding.

He knew they were giving him a chance to do the deed himself. Undoubtedly, his father thought that the bond forged between Jase and Kayla as children would be strong enough to make them fall in love, and fulfill the promise. Oddly, it was the strength of their bond that gave Jase the will to resist. A resistance that was rapidly waning with each second that passed.

Jase thrust open the front door. Darkness enveloped them, blacker than tar, thicker, and very disconcerting. He moved to the bedroom and shoved open the door with the toe of his boot. After settling her on the bed, he turned and lit the single taper on the nightstand.

A soft glow bathed her pale features and a knife wrenched in his gut. Unable to tear his gaze from her face, he studied her, noting her cheeks, flushed from the wind, her hair a red tumble of curls across the feather pillow. Her eyes were open, but she didn't really see him. She was unconscious, in a sense, responding only to his voice, like a computer programmed to accept voice commands.

Innocent Kayla . . . breathtaking and so very forbidden.

Forbidden. Still, he found himself reaching out to touch the smooth satin of her cheek. Almost instantly, her skin warmed to his caress.

Pulling her into his arms, he eased her out of the leather jacket and tossed it to the rocker. Laying her back down, he touched his fingers to the T-shirt molding her full breasts.

No! The warning screamed in his head and he managed to move his hand away before he stroked the perfectly outlined crests.

He scooted down to pull her boots off and toss them to the floor. Then his fingers went to the button on her jeans. Breathless moments later, he stood near the foot of the bed and pulled the jeans free of her long, slender legs.

Clad only in the thin cotton shirt and lace panties, she presented the biggest temptation Jase had ever faced in his life. One that he wanted so much to surrender to. He grew harder, hotter, and a pain twisted his gut.

His gaze traveled from her calves, up her slender thighs, to the wispy lace barely covering the cluster of fiery red curls between her legs.

He swallowed, his mouth suddenly dry. With a sweep of his tongue, he licked his lips, the urge to taste her sending the blood jolting through his veins at an alarming rate.

Never had he wanted a woman so much . . .

His past was filled with nameless faces, warm bodies— all sought out for those few moments of blissful relief when he could forget the darkness, the promise. But no matter how many times he drove deep and hard into another, he couldn't escape the one woman who filled his soul.

The same woman stretched half-naked before him. So close, he could smell the sweet scent of her heat, almost taste the honey deep inside of her. So close. *Too close.*

He had only to whisper his thoughts to her and she would willingly do all that he wanted, all that he craved. Just a whisper and she would be his.

His hands started to tremble and he felt a driving force wrap around him, propel him toward her. He dropped to the bed beside her and touched his fingers to the velvet of one hip.

His hands seemed to move of their own accord, traveling the length of her body, exploring every curve, every dip, lingering at the lace covering her moist heat.

Jase grappled for his last bit of control. He moved his hand up over her flat belly, her skin satin and fire beneath his fingertips, to push her T-shirt up. Higher, until he bared one creamy breast.

With a gentle finger, he circled the dusky nipple, inhaling sharply when the already turgid peak ripened even more. Leaning over, he touched his lips to her navel, dipped his tongue inside, only to lick a path up her fragrant skin, to her breast. She tasted of innocence and light and virtue...a bittersweet feast to a man so filled with darkness that even the sunlight brought him little joy.

Closing his lips over her swollen nipple, he devoured her. He swept his hands downward, cupping her heat through the scanty lace of her panties. Wisps of silky hair brushed his palm like soft licks of fire.

Jase barely heard her sigh through the roar of blood in his ears. Then she squirmed and arched her hips, her body demanding as much as he yearned to give. But she didn't know what it was that she asked for.

She didn't know what his touch could do to her.

Reality crashed around him, like waves breaking over a weather-worn pier, the wobbly poles trembling, the foundation threatening to crumble.

He drew away and stared down at her flushed cheeks, her parted lips. She still moved her hips, as if searching for him.

Jase took a deep breath, closed his eyes and yanked the quilt up over her. Only when he had covered her completely did he dare open his eyes.

He shouldn't have.

No matter how many quilts covered her, it wouldn't have been enough. Her image had been burned into his memory, her breasts colored with wanting, her nipples full and ripe, her body rich cream against the flower-print sheets. He would never forget her. Never stop wanting her.

"Sleep," he said, the word a raw whisper. His body stiff, throbbing, he managed to walk to the door. He had to leave before he took her, conscious or not. Willing or not.

Seconds later, Jase grabbed his black duffel bag and dumped the contents on the kitchen table. He reached for one of the snapshots that were scattered across the wooden surface.

The Keepers surrounded her, closer it seemed, than any other time when he'd looked at the pictures. *Closer.*

Jase threw the reminder to the table and turned to the sink. He stripped off his shirt. With a shaky hand, he reached for the water pump. Cranking vigorously, he splashed handfuls of frigid water onto his face, his torso, but the cold did little to dispel the inferno raging inside.

Something had indeed happened tonight.

The Keepers had found a way inside. A way to manipulate him. To reach Kayla despite his protection. To weaken him.

He felt them at his back, laughing at his defeat.

Jase slumped over the sink, water dripping from his chin, the drip-drop echoing in his head like the steady tick of a clock. Time was running out. They had all of three days left.

For the first time, Jase allowed himself to think the unthinkable. To consider doing what he'd vowed never to do.

He could make her his lover.

Teach her the ways of darkness.

Mate with her during the witching hour and plant the seed for the child his father so desperately needed.

Better Jase do the deed than his brother. He couldn't, no he *wouldn't* let another touch her.

She was his...and maybe their destiny couldn't be altered. Maybe the only answer was to fulfill the promise. Once he took her, there would be no escape for either of them. The lure of the evil was too strong. To join with her would start a certain chain of events, like the first domino.

No escape. He'd always known freeing himself was impossible. He'd spent his life trying to do just that. All for naught.

There was only one solution. One answer. The truth roared in Jase's head and he sank to his knees.

The shadows of the kitchen joined and swirled around him. And the voices came together...a slow, steady chant surrounding him, beckoning him, and he knew he wasn't strong enough to shut them out. Not that he ever had been in the first place.

CHAPTER NINE

Five pinpoint flames glittered. Wax drizzled down the tapered candles like silent tears. Alexander Terrell swished into the black-walled sanctuary, his thick robes swaying. A draft of cold air followed him. The candle flames flickered, died, then flared again, as if an invisible hand held the life-sustaining fire to them.

The high priest knelt before the stained altar and splayed his fingers over the worn pages of the black book spread in the center. The book was flanked by the other tools he used to strengthen his power—the golden chalice, its once-engraved edges now smooth from use, the double-bladed *athame,* the silver pentacle, the blackened censer still smelling of herbs and blood, and the hand-carved ebony wand, the head that of a serpent, mouth open, fangs bared, fiery ruby eyes reflecting the twinkling flames.

Max Talbot broke the reverent silence. "It looks as if Jase might take her himself." Hands clasped in front of him, he stood at attention near Alexander's right. A woman, brunette braid peeking from beneath her hood, stood to his left. Her ruby ring, identical to the one on Max's hand, sparkled like fiery ice, casting reflections on the pitch walls, as glaring and obscene as the demonic symbols already depicted there.

"I knew he would," the high priest murmured. "Still, we must be sure that he will follow through." He opened his palm. "Have you a gift for me, Rickie?" he asked the woman.

"She knew who I was," the woman replied as she placed a brilliant topaz ring against the priest's parchmentlike palm. Veins traced blue crisscrosses just below his skin.

"No," he said, curling his fingers around the warm stone. "She didn't recognize you. Your face was hidden in the shadows. She sensed something familiar, but she couldn't place you. She can *feel* us, however. She'll remember... very soon."

"Jase knows we're close. That we'll take her if he doesn't," Max commented, a smile tugging the corners of his lips. "When I confronted him, I could tell he doubted our power. After tonight, he knows what we can truly do. His strength is nothing compared to ours. I believe he's even frightened."

"Don't underestimate him, Max. He is my son. My eldest. He has powers of his own."

"But he won't use them," Max added.

"He might. To save the girl," Alexander said, tightening his grip on the ring. The topaz cut into his palm and he relished the pain. Welcomed it, if only to feel *something*. He grew weaker with each day that passed. His life was slipping away. In two days he would turn sixty-one. Jase was thirty-four, Kayla twenty-seven.

When your years combine to equal mine, the time will be at hand. His own words echoed in his ears, as if he'd recited them only yesterday rather than twenty-two years ago.

Two days and he would be sixty-one.

The time was near. The witching hour...the moment of conception. The seed would be planted for a child—a child of the purest, magical blood—and Alexander's spirit would make the transfer, from an old withered body to a fresh young fetus. A chance to live and thrive a lifetime more.

Max touched a hand to Alexander's shoulder. "Let us bring her back now. She can join with Miles. Jase can't be trusted."

"No," Alexander growled. "You're still angry about what happened. You underestimated my son, even when he was a mere twelve years old, and you've spent a lifetime regretting it."

"I only regret that I didn't snap the bastard's neck when he came at me with that knife," Max retorted.

"Then I would have snapped yours," Alexander said, his voice cold and exact. "Like a bird's neck. You knew that then, as surely as you know it now. You're lucky I didn't gut you for wounding him with that gun."

"I was aiming for Darland."

"And you hit *my* son."

"Your son was a traitor. He still is."

"Enough!" Alexander commanded. "Mark my words, Max, Jase and Kayla will be lovers before the hour draws nigh. Already, the boy can barely control himself." His baritone voice filled the sacred room, resounding off the pitch-black walls. "He didn't even sense us tonight. She's weakening him. He saw only her. Felt only her. As it should be."

"But he betrayed us," Max persisted.

Alexander Terrell ignored the remark and touched his drawn lips to the topaz stone. Then he placed the ring on the altar, reached into a black-velvet drawstring sack and pulled out the silver moonstar he'd ripped from Kayla's neck over two weeks ago. Jase wore a matching talisman. The two charms had been made by Kayla's mother to protect the children. But all her efforts had been for naught. Now he would use the charm to draw his son deeper into the darkness.

He dropped the moonstar and topaz ring into the chalice. Taking up the *athame,* he pulled back the sleeve of his robe to slice a single line up the inside of his arm. He held the crimson drops to the goblet.

His lifeblood drained and a giddy excitement filled him.

Jase and Kayla were his. Children of the darkness. His eldest son's rebellious spirit wasn't enough to alter destiny.

"What if Jase doesn't do his part?" Max persisted. "He turned on us once before. What if he does so again?"

"We'll take her from him and she'll join with Miles. But Jase will have his chance first. It's that simple."

"I hope so."

Alexander gripped the knife and touched the razor-sharp tip to Max's hand that rested on his shoulder. Pricking the skin, he drew a single drop of blood. Max sucked in a deep, shocked breath through his teeth.

"Do not doubt the power," Alexander growled. To further his point, he drove the tip a fraction deeper and Max flinched.

"You have been a loyal follower, but doubts weaken us," Alexander went on. "I would just as soon slit your throat as let you destroy what we hold."

"Forgive me," Max implored, but his voice held no remorse, only bridled anger.

"There is no forgiveness," Alexander retorted. "No redemption and no forgiveness. Obey me and you shall live. Disobey me and I'll feed you to the rats."

"Yes, Alexander." Max withdrew his hand from Alexander's shoulder. "It will be as you wish," he said through clenched teeth. "*Whatever* you wish."

Alexander Terrell closed his eyes, his lips forming the desperate whisper. "Listen to what's inside of you, my son. Hear me, Jase. Answer me. Obey and you shall have everything. Ignore my voice and I will have no choice but to crush you."

He raised the chalice to his lips and drank, greedily, hungrily. Jase knew the same thirst for blood, for power. Alexander had instilled that in him long ago.

He fixed his eyes on the book of shadows spread before him and recited the ancient words.

Now it was only a matter of time. . . .

I'll be seeing you . . . seeing you . . . seeing . . .

Kayla bolted upright, eyes wide, heart hammering against her ribs as if it meant to burst from her chest. She stared at her surroundings through a crimson haze.

Red is my favorite color. The echo of the woman's strangely familiar voice lingered in Kayla's ears. The empty shadow of her face danced in Kayla's head. No real features, just a disconcerting blank mask. The red of a ruby ring flashed in the dim interior of Kayla's bedroom.

Kayla blinked, willing her vision back to normal. She clutched the edge of the quilt and stared at her lap. The red faded. The quilt took on its usual gold and orange hues. The T-shirt she wore, hem bunched in her lap, turned a soft white. The furniture gleamed brown in the candlelight.

A wave of dread swelled inside Kayla as she stared down at her bare hands. No comforting topaz. The ring, like her moonstar, was gone. Now she had nothing. No reminder of her mother. No mother. Nothing.

Cold air swirled around her and she tugged the quilt up over her bare arms. Goose bumps prickled her flesh, despite the sweat on her forehead. She lifted a shaky hand to wipe away the cold beads of moisture.

Frigid bed sheets swathed her bare legs. Kayla glanced at her jeans draped over the back of the rocker. Her boots had been tossed to the floor. Jase had undressed her . . . or maybe she'd never left the bed at all.

A nightmare?

She could have imagined everything. Big Mick's, the woman in the bathroom, the blissful kiss with Jase, the blackout.

She clutched her hands. No. Everything had been real, and she'd had her ring on before she'd left the house. Her mind traveled back to Big Mick's, to the dance she'd shared with Jase. She remembered her hand on his shoulder, her bare fingers resting against the sinewy curve of one muscled bicep. By the time they'd danced, she'd lost the ring.

I love to dance. The child's voice floated toward her, scattering her thoughts.

Kayla's gaze snapped to the far corner of the room. The soft glow of the candle didn't pierce the shadows. Still, the voice rang loud and clear, a child's delighted laughter filling the thick silence.

Jase danced with me, Mrs. Moonfire. He twirled me around. The little girl stepped from the blackness and pivoted. *He said I was the prettiest girl ever and I danced better than anyone.*

"You know Jase?" Kayla asked, her voice incredulous. She rubbed her eyes. Still, the child moved closer. She paused at the rocker to snatch up the look-alike porcelain doll, seeming oblivious to Kayla's presence.

Hello, Mrs. Moonfire, she said to the doll. *You should have seen me dancing. Jase held my hands and showed me how to turn. He's my friend, you know. Mommy and Daddy said so. They said for me to listen to Jase. He's good. Not like the others.* She shook her head, auburn ringlets brushing the white lace of her collar. *He really isn't like them. But I knew that the first time he held my hand. Mommy said to trust my feelings. If I felt Jase was good, then he was. Mommy was right.*

The child stepped toward the bed, her white patent-leather shoes clicking on the wooden floor. Climbing onto the foot of the bed, she smoothed her skirts around her and stared at the doll for a few thoughtful seconds.

When she glanced up, her eyes were bright with unshed tears. *Mommy didn't come back after the shadow took her, Mrs. Moonfire,* she told the doll. *I knew she wouldn't.* The tears started, like crystal drops trailing down her ivory cheeks.

"Please don't cry," Kayla pleaded. She threw the quilt aside and scooted toward the foot of the bed. "Who's your mother, sweetie? Who took her?"

The little girl inched backward, out of Kayla's reach. Fright held her eyes wide as she stared at her doll. *The Old One said I had to be careful. Not to listen to anyone. Only to him and my daddy and Jase. Only them.* She made a mad scramble off the opposite side of the bed as if the devil himself chased her.

He said not to listen to my mommy if she did come back, she went on. Said the people came and took her so they can make her bad like them.

She glanced around before adding, her voice a hushed whisper near the doll's ear, *Daddy didn't want to tell me they took her, but I saw, Mrs. Moonfire. I was watching under that crack in the door and I saw.* More tears spilled past her lashes. Her bottom lip trembled. *They took her. They wanted to take me, too, but Jase wouldn't let them.*

"Who are you?" Kayla said in a rush of breath, her heart accelerating to a frightening pace. Her mind searched for some memory. If only the past wasn't so stubborn.

The little girl smiled at the doll and wiped her eyes with one chubby fist. *Jase will protect us. He promised. Always, Mrs. Moonfire.*

Mrs. Moonfire. The name echoed, pushing and pulling at Kayla's memories, battering down her last bit of resolve. Hot tears spilled over her lashes. Her hands started to shake. Her heart seemed to pause, then pound even harder, more furiously than before. She knew the name... the doll...

Kayla's vision clouded, her tears like a newly opened spring, trailing down her face, splattering her hands. "Mrs. Moonfire," she whispered. "I know Mrs. Moonfire."

The little girl's shoes clicked as she walked around the footboard, the doll held tightly in her arms.

Kayla swiped at her tears, focusing her eyes just in time to see the little girl move toward the darkened corner.

"Don't go," Kayla begged. Her brain swirled with unanswered questions. Her chest ached with desperation. "Who are you? *What* are you?" she demanded. "Please, I have to know."

The child stopped. Still, she didn't face Kayla. Clutching the porcelain doll in front of her, she said, *Mommy isn't coming back, Mrs. Moonfire. Not for either of us.* She moved into the shadows.

"Wait!" Kayla called, bounding from the bed. "Tell me who you are and where you came from. Please!" She reached out.

Velvet brushed Kayla's hand. A warmth enveloped her fingers. She felt the sensations, yet her hand didn't make contact with anything solid. No living and breathing flesh, only air.

The little girl turned, as if she'd finally heard Kayla's desperate words. *I came to help you,* her voice drifted through Kayla's mind. *You wanted to remember.*

"I do want to," Kayla cried. "I do!"

The child seemed to shrink toward the shadows. *Try hard. Remember.*

"Wait!" Kayla pleaded, making a mad grab. The child disintegrated. The doll crashed to the floor and shattered.

Mrs. Moonfire! The little girl's wail pierced Kayla's ears.

"Oh, my God! I'm sorry," Kayla gasped, staring in horror at the shattered porcelain. "I'm so sorry," she cried. Kayla dropped to her knees and started gathering the broken pieces, as if her own life depended on the recovery of each and every bit of the doll. Frantic, she scooped up the razorlike shards, oblivious to the porcelain cutting into her fingers and palms.

"I'm sorry," she cried over and over. "Mrs. Moonfire, I'm so sorry." Tears streamed down her cheeks.

"Kayla," Jase's deep voice rumbled in her ears a second before she felt him beside her. He took her hands in his and pried her fingers loose from several large chunks of milk-white glass.

"Jase!" she cried, turning to him and clawing his bare chest, as if she were sinking into the floor, being swallowed by some unseen force and he was her only lifeline. Her only salvation.

He pulled her into the powerful circle of his arms and Kayla gave in to the convulsions which racked her body. She buried her head in the curve of his neck and wept...for the broken doll, for the lost child.

"My God, Jase!" She pulled away from him and stared up into his eyes. "I saw her again. The little girl. The one I saw that night in the woods. She was right over there..." Her voice died as she glanced to the now-empty corner.

Jase's gaze followed hers. "There's no one there, moonchild. Just the shadows. We're the only ones here. You and me," he crooned, his voice deep, steady and so very reassuring. He pushed back a wayward curl that had fallen into her eyes. "It's all right, Kayla. You must have dropped the doll. I'll help you pick up the pieces."

She twisted in his arms, her gaze darting around the room. "She was here, Jase. She really was. I saw her—" Her attention riveted on the broken doll scattered on the floor at her knees. "No!" she gasped. "I broke Mrs. Moonfire, Jase. I broke her." She reached for a fragment with one golden eye painted on it. Horrified, she held the broken piece up to him. "Look! I broke her. I *killed* her—"

"Kayla!" Her name was a sharp intake of breath.

She glanced up to find him staring at the scarlet drops that trickled from her fingertips. Then she noticed the red smears on his chest where she'd clutched at him with her bloodied hands.

Jase's eyes took on a wild light, darting from her hands, to the red smudges on his chest, then back again. "No," he whispered, gazing at his own hands, which were also streaked with her blood. He closed his eyes, his fingers grasping at the charm suspended around his neck. Anguish covered the lean lines of his face. "I don't want to feel this," he murmured. "Please...I don't. No more blood. *No more.*"

"Jase?"

He didn't answer. He clutched the charm tighter, his fingers turning white. Kayla reached out to touch the taut knuckles of his fist.

"Jase," she whispered again, her hysteria forgotten as she felt the fear and the hunger swirling inside of him, consuming him. "Look at me. Please."

He opened his eyes to reveal a brilliant gaze, his pupils like sharp steel blades glinting firelight.

But there was no firelight, only the small flame of a candle. His eyes glittered, drawing her in with their intensity, holding her captive. The air around them seemed alive, charged with an invisible vitality that heightened her senses.

His warm breath fanned her face. The frenzied tempo of his heart thundered in her ears. The pungent scent of her own blood filled her head.

Jase took a deep, ragged breath, chest heaving, nostrils flaring. His shoulders quaked and Kayla knew his senses were as alive as hers.

He dropped the charm as if it were red-hot and grabbed her hands, his grip bone-crushing. "I can't control it," he rasped a second before he let go of her. He held his hands up in front of him, his fingers flexed, his knuckles white from tension, his palms stained with her blood. "I can't."

"Jase, it's okay—" She stopped mid-sentence, her gaze suddenly riveted on the charm. She'd never seen him wear it before, yet it looked so familiar. Leaning closer, she drank in the detail, and shock bolted through her. The charm was identical to the one she'd lost! The crescent moon and star overlapped, making an unbreakable connection.

"Where did you get this?" She moved to touch the silver, needing its warmth, its comfort. She knew now without a doubt that she and Jase were meant to be together. That he held her past, and her future, and she his. "I had a charm just like this one." Her fingertip brushed the silver.

"No!" The cry seemed wrenched from his very soul, as if her caress brought an unbearable agony. "Don't touch me!" He thrust her from him. "Stay away!"

She landed against the footboard of the bed, the side of her head slamming into one sharp corner. Jase became a wavering silhouette . . . first one shadow, two, then three.

Kayla closed her eyes as a lightning-hot pain ripped through her skull. She gasped for air and grabbed at the bed rail for support.

"Jase." She struggled to open her eyes. When she finally managed the effort, he was gone, the room empty. There was no sign of him, or the child.

Only a crumbled Mrs. Moonfire, pieces scattered across the wooden floor, streaks of red where Kayla had tried to gather what was left of the beautiful doll.

Kayla heard the first of a series of crashes in the living room. Wood cracked, glass shattered, then the back door slammed. The entire house shook from the force.

Struggling to her feet, she swayed down the hall, her head reeling. She staggered to the kitchen window, only to see Jase, a black silhouette against the moonlight, the ax in his hand flashing silver as it descended.

He turned toward her then and she saw the feral gleam of his eyes. His gaze crossed the distance to her, to grip her with a jolting energy like a live electric wire.

Stay away from me, Kayla. Stay far away...I can't control it. The whisper drifted through her mind, bringing goose bumps to her bare arms and legs. *I don't want to control it, and God help you. God help us both.*

Icy fingers of fear seized her, propelled her from the window and down the hall to her bedroom. She ran for her very life, or so it seemed as she hurled herself inside the room, slammed the door and slumped back against it.

Safe...or was she? How could she be safe when she hadn't the slightest idea who or what she ran from?

She believed in the unseen now—in ghosts and bogeymen and strange knights who rescued damsels in distress.

Jase was her knight, her protector, only she couldn't shake the distinct feeling that now she needed protection from *him,* rather than from what stalked her outside the house.

Silver flashed in the pitch black of her mind and she closed her eyes, willing the image away. Snatching the quilt from the bed, she draped it around her shoulders before padding to the mess on the floor.

Minutes later, she'd gathered the fragments of her beloved doll. She knew it was hers, like a mother knows the cry of her child. What she didn't know was how it had come to be here. Had Jase brought it? Had he left it under the bed? Why hadn't she recognized it right away?

Kayla shook away the questions, wiped the tears from her face and placed the doll pieces in a trash can near the bed. Then she settled into the rocker, her gaze fixed on the door.

I came to help you. You wanted to remember. The child's words sounded over and over in her mind. *Remember.*

She wanted to remember, but she couldn't think through the pounding in her skull. Gingerly, she touched the lump at the back of her head.

She curled her legs under her, determined to stay awake and alert. The sun would rise and her fear would be forgotten. Hopefully. For if she found herself still frightened, and Jase the cause of that fear, she would face the ultimate challenge—finding her way from this place, back to civilization to face the shadows on her own.

Unwillingly, her eyelids drifted shut, her dreams haunted with visions of Jase, eyes catching the moonlight, a savage wildness about him that made her ache and burn and tremble all at the same time. Out of fear or desire, she couldn't discern, for the two seemed so closely twined together, each feeding the other until Kayla came awake, her body yearning for his.

The candle had died down and the blackness of the room had settled around her, thick and stifling in its absoluteness. She managed a deep breath, willing her heartbeat to normal. No luck. The air was frigid, yet every inch of her burned.

She put a hand to her chest where her heart beat rapidly. Her fingers seemed to melt through the thin material of her shirt, like a lover's touch rather than her own.

She closed her eyes and trailed her fingertips to where her nipple pressed eagerly against the fabric. Tracing the budding crest, she caught her breath. A ripple of heat danced through her to settle between her thighs. Her body cried out for him, as loudly, as desperately as her soul, issuing a call he had no inclination to answer.

She continued her exploration, pretending for a delicious moment that it was Jase's palm that massaged her, made her come alive...

In the next instant, her movements stilled and she turned ice-cold. She felt the presence, even before she heard the creak of floorboards.

The hair at her nape prickled. Kayla opened her eyes wide. Still she saw nothing. She felt only the faint stirring of air.

"Jase?" she whispered. No answer.

Kayla moved from the rocker, feeling her way along the dresser until she found the small box of matches. She fumbled and then flicked the match. The flame caught. She whirled.

She glimpsed the unmade bed, the nightstand, the empty corners of the room, before the match burned down. Heat blistered the tip of her finger and she sucked in a breath.

Turning, she fired another match and lit the candle on the dresser. Her imagination was definitely working overtime. There was no sign of Jase.

Regret welled up inside of her and Kayla chided herself for being such a gullible fool. She'd wanted Jase so badly, she'd let herself imagine him there.

Her thoughts skidded to a halt as the soft melody reached her ears and she realized the bedroom door stood wide open. She knew she'd closed it herself, but she didn't stop to wonder or worry over that fact.

She was too busy remembering.

A wave of sweet recollection swept over her and she closed her eyes. Kayla knew the song as well as she knew her own name—"Yesterday," by the Beatles. The lyrics had always touched her in a way she couldn't explain. Until now.

In a crystalline moment, Kayla realized the song had been her mother's favorite. She didn't know how she knew, only that she did, just as she knew Mrs. Moonfire was her own doll. Just as she knew with aching certainty that she and Jase were meant to be together.

Her eyes snapped open and her heart jammed into her throat. As if her thoughts had conjured him, he stood behind her, close enough that she felt the heat of his body sinking into hers. Afraid to move lest he disappear, she stood paralyzed, her attention riveted on his reflection in the mirror.

The small flame of the candle drove back the shadows just enough to reveal Jase's handsome face framed with thick black ebony waves that fell to his broad shoulders. His eyes caught fragments of the candle flame, their haunting depths drawing her in, holding her captive, and she could no more move than she could have plucked a star from the sky.

There was something unnerving about him, more so than usual. The uncompromising rigidity of his stance, the compelling light in his gaze, the purposeful set to his jaw—combined to send a tingle of fear up her spine. For a man who had raved at her to keep her distance, he seemed to have disregarded his own advice. Kayla couldn't help wondering what had brought about such an abrupt change.

"Jase." She managed to form his name. "What are you . . ." She didn't get a chance to finish.

His hands were at her waist, pulling her back against him. The breath rushed from her lungs. He was carved muscle and warm flesh, and heat flared in Kayla's stomach to snake through her.

Certainly hell itself could be no hotter, she thought, nor the devil as merciless as Jase, who pushed the hem of her T-shirt up to slide rough fingertips across her silken belly in a slow torturous motion that drew a shameless moan from her.

The bittersweet agony continued as he slipped his hands lower and dipped them inside the lace of her panties to cup her. He trailed his fingertips over her moist flesh, his eyes alight with a savage lust that took her breath away.

Kayla gasped, her lips parting, her eyes drifting closed at the intimate caress.

"Open your eyes," Jase demanded, his voice simmering with raw need.

Kayla obeyed and he caught her gaze in the mirror again, silver fusing with brilliant topaz.

"Your eyes are like windows, Kayla. I want to see what you feel—*everything* you feel." He slipped a finger inside of her. Then another.

Kayla's legs turned to liquid. She would have collapsed had Jase not held her, one hand at her waist, touching, stroking, the fingers of his other weaving their own magic deep inside of her for a blissful moment.

Then he stilled and the magic veered to a halt.

"Jase?" Her breath caught. He didn't withdraw from her. Worse, he didn't move at all. Tension coiled deep within, building, mounting. "Jase, please..."

Still, he didn't so much as flex a muscle.

"Dance for me, moonchild," he said, the words a rough caress against her ear. "Move for me."

"I...can't." Her voice was a weak and tremulous whisper. Just breathing proved difficult. Every gasp vibrated her upper body and her insides tightened around him, drawing him more fully into her.

"Move your hips," he said. "Listen to the music, stare into my eyes and move for me, love." His lips grazed her temple. "Move."

At that moment, she heard the familiar melody through the pounding of her own heart. His gaze called to her, urged her. She concentrated on the smoldering depths and shifted her weight the tiniest bit.

Jase stood still, solid, barely breathing, much less moving.

Kayla swayed, the movement of her own body driving him deeper. The more she moved, the deeper he went. The pleasure heightened.

"That's it, love," he coaxed. "You're getting closer."

She continued to move from side to side, creating the most delicious friction, her insides slick, sweltering from his invasion. She breathed in deep soul-drenching drafts, gasping from the nearly unbearable ecstasy, all the while rotating her hips to the melody singing through her head.

His manhood pressed against the soft swell of her buttocks, the rough material of his jeans chafing her. The steady friction added to her excitement until every nerve in her body screamed. She arched her back, drawing his lean fingers deeper until she could stand it no longer.

"Jase," she whimpered, her hands going to his muscled forearms which held her upright. Frightening expectancy filled her and she hesitated, her body going stiff. She'd never crossed the threshold, never responded to a man with the primal instincts that Jase aroused within her.

"Relax, love. I can feel you . . . so hot and wet, ready to explode around me. Let the hunger take control, Kayla." His lips touched her nape and she came unglued right there in his arms.

The song filled her head and Jase filled her body, his fingers now moving with her hips until the blackness of the room seemed to burst open with a thousand pinpoints of dazzling light, as vivid as the pair of silver eyes that held her captive.

She flung her head back, her lips parted, and a low moan came from deep in her throat. A moan he stifled as he withdrew his fingers and turned her in his arms, his lips smothering hers with demanding mastery. He thrust his tongue deep, mimicking the careful attention his hand had given her only seconds before.

Kayla wasn't even aware of being lifted until she felt the mattress at her back. The bedsprings protested as Jase eased her down and followed. Straddling her, his knees trapping her thighs, he leaned back to gaze down at her.

He was a black silhouette, a man made of shadows and secrets and an undeniable force that drew her like metal to a magnet.

He was the unknown . . . a demon lover come to claim her, his face a mask of darkness, his eyes gleaming moonsilver.

She blinked, thinking maybe she was imagining him. Maybe what she'd just felt had been her own wishful thinking . . . just a very erotic fantasy.

Yet the hands splayed over her rib cage were more than figments of a vivid imagination. They were real, warm and very purposeful as they slid the T-shirt up to bare both her breasts. Then his hands went to her hips to push her panties down, until he tugged them free and tossed them to the floor.

"I've dreamed of you like this," he said, his voice thick and unsteady. "Beneath me, aching for me . . . Your vision warmed me so many lonely nights, Kayla. I tried to forget you, tried to pretend that we haven't been meant for this all along. Now, I know it's the only way for us. I won't let someone else have you. Ever . . ."

She searched for her voice, to beg him for answers to the questions swirling in her mind. Then he lowered his head and drew her nipple into the moist heat of his mouth, and her thoughts fled. Kayla dug her fingers into the cotton sheets, falling victim to the warmth of him.

He suckled her breast as if he were a hungry child, his teeth grazing the soft globes, nipping and biting the crested peaks. The pressure intensified, became almost painful . . . but not quite. Instead, her breast swelled and throbbed with a need all its own.

Jase licked a path across her skin to coax the other breast in the same torturous manner. His moonstar dangled against her belly, the warm metal firing her already feverish flesh.

A decadent heat spiraled through her and she moved her pelvis against the muscled expanse of his chest. She wanted him, surrounding her, inside of her. Kayla unclenched her fingers from the bed sheets to twine her arms around Jase's shoulders. That's when he pulled away.

"Jase?"

His eyes glowed in the darkness, like two moons suspended in a pitch-black sky. A shiver worked its way up her spine when his deep, husky voice advised, "Don't touch me, moonchild. I'm trying to go slow, but I don't know if I can. Not if you touch me." He took both her hands and raised them above her head.

"But I want to touch you," she blurted out, scarcely aware of the begging note in her voice, and too inflamed to care. "I *need* to, Jase. Please!"

"No," he said, the word a painful groan as if wrung from his very soul. She sensed the emotion warring inside of him, as if he fought some invisible enemy for control.

"Just feel what I'm doing to you," he went on, his voice softer, the words an erotic caress. "Feel the gnawing in your belly." He trailed his fingers across her abdomen. "The heat between your legs," and his touch went lower, a fingertip stroking the drenched flesh he spoke of.

Her teeth sunk into her lower lip to stifle a whimper.

"Let me love you, Kayla," he added. "Every inch of you."

His words sent a deep, sensual ripple through her and she nodded, desperate for what he offered, despite the alarm bells sounding in her head. He held too many secrets, yet, with his body covering hers, she didn't really care. Fear fed her desire, like oil feeds a flame, and she burned all the brighter.

"Hold on here," he ordered. "Like this." He wrapped the fingers of one of her hands around the iron rail of the headboard. Obediently, she did the same with her other hand, the motion lifting her breasts in silent invitation.

Jase smiled, his teeth a startling break in the black shadow of his face. Then his smile disappeared as he studied her. "You're mine," he whispered, his voice low and fierce. "You've always been mine." As if to brand her with his touch as well as with his words, he slid his hands from her wrists to her shoulders. With tantalizing possessiveness, he continued their trek over her collarbone, down the creamy fullness of her breasts, to her sensitive nipples. A sharp breath caught in her throat.

"Your breasts are so beautiful. Like the rest of you," he murmured before leaning down, his mouth closing over her as he resumed his torment of one swollen peak.

She writhed beneath him, clutching the bed rail, crying his name and begging for something she didn't quite understand.

He slid down her body, now slick from the fever that raged inside of her, and left a blazing path with the velvet tip of his tongue. With a gentle pressure, he parted her thighs. Almost reverently, he stroked the quivering flesh between her legs.

Involuntary tremors seized her body when she felt his warm breath against the inside of one thigh. Then his lips danced across her skin, to the part of her that burned the fiercest.

She gasped as his tongue parted her. He eased his hands under her buttocks, holding her to him, his shoulders urging her legs farther apart until she lay completely open.

And then he devoured her, every thrust of his tongue, every caress of his lips, a raw act of possession that marked her undeniably and irrevocably his.

All too soon, she was bursting with the fury of a volcano that had stood bubbling for thousands of years. Waves of heat washed over her like molten lava until she thought she would surely disintegrate. But Jase was there, holding her, anchoring her until the heat subsided.

Only when she had calmed to a slight shudder, did he pull away from her. Moments later, he glided his body over hers and gathered her in his powerful arms. He had removed his jeans, she realized, as she felt his manhood burn against her bare skin.

"I've wanted that for so long," he murmured. "You're even more delicious than I imagined." He captured her mouth in a slow lingering kiss, his tongue delving deep inside to stroke and entice hers.

He tasted wild—like a ripe fruit both bitter and sweet at the same time. A spurt of hungry desire spiraled through her, driving her to meet his kiss with all that she was. All that he made her feel. All that she yearned to be.

She let go of the bed rail and wrapped her arms around his neck.

"No—" He broke off as she put her fingers to his lips to silence him.

"Yes," she whispered. "If I can give you even a fraction of what you've given me, I'm going to. Let me, Jase. Let me love *you*. I'm not afraid. Not this time."

His answer was an electrifying sweep of his tongue across her fingertips. He captured her hand in his and pressed a kiss to the center. "You've given me more than you could ever imagine. You've made my one and only dream into reality."

"But there's more," she added. "I don't think we're finished dreaming."

She didn't need to see his smile. She felt it, warming the air between them, stirring the heat in her breasts, her thighs.

"You're right. We're not finished—not yet." And with that, he began a thorough exploration of her body, his hands caressing pleasure points she never knew existed.

She stroked the small of his back, rubbed against him, both thrilled and frightened by his pulsing length, which pressed into her stomach. He was rock-hard and deliciously warm, and Kayla found herself wanting to feel his strength inside of her.

"Please," she breathed. "Please, Jase."

He growled, a low barbaric sound that spooked as much as it delighted. Still, she refused to be frightened.

When she felt the tip of his arousal probe the moist entrance to her womanhood, all of her fears and misgivings swirled together in a furious whirlwind of emotion. She wanted to run, yet she also wanted to stay.

Before Kayla permitted herself to weigh the two, she wrapped her legs around his waist, gripped the hard muscles of his buttocks and arched upward.

"No," Jase gasped. "Don't—"

White-hot pain fired through her as she impaled herself on his rigid length. She shrunk away immediately, a scream lodging in her throat.

"Stop!" she pleaded, sobbing, but it was too late. She sensed the change in him a moment before she felt it—the tensing of muscles, the savageness of his hands as he swept aside her attempts to fight him. He grasped her hips and she knew that whatever silent battles had been fought, the primitive side of him, the beast itself, had won.

Kayla flung her head to the side, tears spilling past her lashes. She'd made a mistake...a terrible mistake from which she had no escape. Clutching the bed sheets, she braced herself as he drove into her, sheathing himself with one full thrust.

A cry tore from Kayla's throat the moment Jase buried himself fully inside of her...the sound one of pure unadulterated joy, for the pain had subsided to a hungry, throbbing pressure. A pressure that increased when he withdrew and thrust into her again, and again.

Her fingers loosened from the sheets and she skimmed her hands over the sinewy flesh of his back, urging him with her as she raced toward some unknown precipice.

Through the thunder of her own heart, she heard the music, the same song that had been playing earlier. She didn't stop to think the song should have been over ages ago. In fact, she couldn't think at all. Not when Jase moved harder and faster, each thrust more powerful than the last.

He was dark perfection, like a wild tornado sucking her up, spinning her senses until she soared higher and higher, with no thought of ever touching ground again.

The music rose to deafening pitch—the drums pounded in her head, the violins reached an awesome crescendo— like a symphony of spirits choreographing their every movement. Then Jase drove into her one final, mind-shattering time. A burst of brilliant light split open the blackness surrounding them.

Eyes wide, Kayla glimpsed him poised above her, his arms braced on either side, muscles bulging, skin glistening with perspiration. He held his eyes clamped shut, lips parted, forehead furrowed. Most disconcerting of all, were the streaks of wetness on his face.

He shook with the violence of his release and she bucked against him, drawing him fully inside. Then blackness settled over them again, and she was left to wonder if she'd only imagined his tears.

In that instant, Kayla felt a drop of moisture fall softly on her breast. She reached up and trailed her fingertips over the lean lines of his face, the moisture burning her like scalding water. *Real* tears . . . as real as the man himself.

He wrapped his arms around her and rolled onto his back, bringing her to lie on top of him, their bodies still locked together.

Kayla caught one of his hands and twined her fingers with his. Resting her head against the curve of his neck, she felt the erratic beat of his pulse, which echoed her own.

They were one now.

Bodies and souls joined, the darkness embracing them. "Forgive me," he whispered, the desperate words following her into an all-consuming sleep.

Forgive me.

CHAPTER TEN

The darkness whispered and Jase found himself lured into
his past. Light cracked open the blackness. The familiar
faces materialized. The voices rang with an odd clarity as
if he didn't simply dream them, but heard them again and
lived the scene itself for the first time. A Beatles' tune
played softly in the background.

"She'll be safe here, won't she?" Worry etched Susan
Darland's face. She clasped her husband's hand with one
of hers and with the other held the moonstar suspended
around her neck. She stared across the room at the old
man, clad in a red flannel shirt and worn jeans. He leaned
against the mantel of the fireplace and shoved a poker into
the blaze. The logs crackled and sparked, the noise adding to the nearly unbearable tension that already filled the
small room.

"They can't take her from my protection, not with any
spell I know of," the Old One replied. "As long as I'm
alive, she should be safe. Thanks to Jase." He turned and
flashed a smile at the young boy standing in the doorway.

Jase shrugged, ignoring the pain that ripped through his
shoulder. A pink stain spread across the white bandages
covering his wound.

"And what about Jase?" Kyle Darland let go of his
wife's hand to stand and walk to the bay window. Moonlight spilled through the glass. He wore a troubled expression.

"Jase can come with us," Susan chimed in. "Can't he,
Kyle?" She cast a questioning gaze at her husband who

simply shook his head and stared out into the moonlit yard.

"Of course he can," she asserted, ignoring her husband's response. "He saved our Kayla. We can't just let him go back to them. We wouldn't be here—*alive*—if it wasn't for him. Max would have done away with all of us. *All of us,*" she said. "And Kayla would still be in their power. We owe Jase." She stared hard at her husband who remained silent. "Dammit, Kyle," she went on. "The boy took a bullet meant for *you!*"

"I'm well aware of what brave thing Jase did. I just don't see how we can keep him with us. Not with everything that's at stake."

Susan Darland was on her feet, grasping her husband's arm and forcing him to face her. "I can't believe you're seriously considering throwing a twelve-year-old child back to those animals." Her voice was incredulous.

"Need I remind you that you and I lived and practiced with those *animals* for most of our lives," he said through clenched teeth, shrugging off her hand. "Keep a civil tongue, Sue. They can hear..." His sentence trailed off, his attention going back to the moonlit clearing.

"I won't go back," Jase said in a fierce whisper. "Ever!" Tears burned his eyes and he swiped at them with the back of his hand. He hadn't cried through any of it, not the sacrifices, not the rituals, and he hadn't cried when the bullet had ripped into his shoulder. So why did he feel the urge to cry now?

Because it was over. Kayla was safe...and now they had to go their separate ways.

They had to forget the vows, the sharing of blood, the promise.

Jase glanced at Kayla's mother as she entreated, "We can't send him back. He helped us." She turned a bright pleading gaze on the Old One.

"We won't send him back, Susan," the old man replied, pivoting to face her. His gaze was unblinking, his eyes filled with a light that bespoke knowledge and wisdom. The deep timbre of his voice rang clear and true. "Jase will stay here with me. You and Kyle will take Kayla and go as far away as you can. They won't expect me to let any of you leave my protection. I wouldn't, but under the circumstances, I think you will all fare better by leaving, and you must do it soon, while they think I have Kayla hidden here. That will afford you a good head start."

"And go where?" Kyle asked.

"Someplace far from here. Distance weakens them. They can't pinpoint you as long as you stay far enough away from the covendom, at all times."

"What about you and Jase?" Susan asked, concern sparkling in her topaz eyes.

"We'll be fine. Without Kayla, Jase is of no use to them. He has a brother that can easily serve as high priest when the time comes. They'll let Jase go, hopefully, but Kayla is the last of her line." His words hung in the air surrounding them.

Tears trickled down Susan Darland's cheeks as she slumped to the edge of the sofa. "They won't let her go," she whispered. "Damn it, why didn't I stop them? I just stood there while they promised my baby girl. I *knew* the ritual was black, and I let Alexander do it, anyway. I let him take my baby and I didn't say a damn word to the contrary!"

"It's not your fault, Sue." Kyle was beside her, reaching for her hand. "I knew what Alexander was up to, but I never thought he'd go so far. Hell, I never thought any of the others would be fool enough to follow him."

"The both of you, stop blaming yourselves," the Old One said with a wave of his hand. "Kayla was destined to rule. You and Kyle are direct descendants of two very powerful witches. You both would have led the coven once

I grew too old and feeble to serve as high priest. Alexander took that knowledge and used it for his own machinations. He doesn't play fair and he doesn't practice the magic we all know. His power comes from a dark source. The man's no ordinary witch. His soul is as black as that book he covets. Neither of you could have known what was coming, nor could you have stopped him.''

"Can you?" Kyle Darland was on his feet again, pacing in front of the window like a caged lion.

"I can't stop him," the Old One said with a shake of his head. "I don't know the black ways, and I can't combat a magic I know nothing about. But I can protect myself, and those near me. Alexander is young, new… It will take him time to learn the extent of his powers, and to conjure new ones. Time, children—" he held out his hands "—is on our side."

"Then why do you still look so worried?" Kyle countered.

The old man shook his head. "I fear when Alexander comes into full power and knowledge. He'll be far more deadly than either of you can imagine. As long as he has that book."

"There must be some way to get it from him," Susan said.

"Right now he's too cautious," the Old One replied. "And later, destroying the book might not make any difference."

"But you don't know that for sure. Maybe if we can get our hands on it—"

"Stop grasping at straws, Sue," Kyle said. "Even if we did stand a chance of getting the book, we can't risk going back."

"Kyle's right," the Old One said. "It would be far too great a risk. Alexander has tapped a magic I know nothing about. I'm no match for him. Just an old white witch practicing the ancient ways."

"How do we get away from here?" Kyle asked after a silent moment.

"They'll be watching," the Old One replied. "We must figure a diversion so you two can take Kayla and slip away."

"We have to leave tonight," Kyle said. "Something doesn't feel right." He stopped pacing to stare out into the yard, as if he watched something only he could see.

Tonight. Jase's heart protested as loudly as his soul at the one word, but reason, or maybe fear, sounded above all. The darkness was stalking them . . . he felt it. He trembled. "You have to go tonight," he said, his voice drawing three intent gazes. "Father is close."

"Come," the Old One said, motioning to Susan and Kyle. "Let us go and prepare."

"You go on," Susan told her husband. "I'll be there in a minute."

Kyle nodded, then followed the Old One down the hall into one of the bedrooms. Seconds later, the smell of incense drifted through the door cracks. A muffled chant reverberated through the house.

"How close is he?" Susan asked Jase after a tentative moment, her fingers wrapped around her moonstar.

"Too close," he replied.

Susan's eyes went wide. "Oh, no," she mumbled a moment before a brilliant streak of light pierced the bay window.

Glass shattered. The door burst open. Wind whipped through the house, stirring the broken shards in a deadly whirlwind.

Then Jase saw his father—a robed shadow of blackness, two pinpoints of red gleaming in his shrouded face as he stood in the doorway.

When Susan bolted from the sofa, Alexander waved his arm and the wind picked up an end table. The corner crashed into her head, sending her suddenly limp form melting to the floor as if her spine had been plucked out.

"Kyle," Susan said, her voice a pained whisper as she called out to her husband. "Help me."

The shadow moved toward her.

Jase glanced down the hall to the room at the far end. The knob jiggled, muted shouts echoed as the high priest and the witch tried to wrench open the door that an unseen force held firmly shut. They wouldn't be able to get out, not while Alexander was there. *I can't combat a magic I don't understand.* The Old One's words rang through Jase's head. Then his gaze darted to the next room—Kayla's room.

Bracing himself, hands gripping the door frame, Jase called on his own power. Power he'd never dared use, for it frightened him. Jase knew the darkness, the evil, almost as well as his father did and he feared that knowledge. But to protect Kayla, he would use it. He had to.

"You betrayed the Keepers," came the voice, cold and harsh.

"*You* betrayed them," Susan countered, a thin trickle of blood winding a path down the side of her temple. "You'll burn, Alexander Terrell. By all my own powers and that of my ancestors, I'll see you burn!"

"*Powers!*" he scoffed, an eery chuckle filling the room. "Your white ways are nothing. Before I'm finished with you, you'll beg mercy from me. You shouldn't have stolen the child."

"Kayla is mine."

"Kayla is *ours*," he growled. "A coven child. Just as you are."

His father's shadowy figure closed in on Susan. A bloodcurdling scream pierced the night, the sound dying the moment the blackness enfolded her and swept her toward the doorway.

"And you, Jase," the shrouded face turned toward him, the eyes like gleaming coals, burning into Jase's memory to forever haunt him. "You have betrayed me. Do you think your powers are so strong that you can escape destiny? You can't. You and Kayla are mine."

"No! You won't have her, Father. Not ever!" The walls trembled as furiously as Jase's hands. He swept his gaze from side to side, an orange flame sparking on one side of the room, to travel the direction of his stare, until a fiery wall separated father and son. *"Never!"*

"I see you've learned well," Alexander Terrell remarked, his attention riveted on the flaming barrier. "I want the girl."

"Try and take her, then." But Jase knew his father wouldn't. He couldn't. The line of fire was a magical boundary that Alexander couldn't cross, not unless Jase extinguished it or invited him over, neither of which he had any intention of doing. "Try and cross, *if* you think you can," Jase added.

Laughter reverberated through the house and it shook harder. Then the laughter died and Alexander's voice grew as chilling as an arctic wind. "Hone your power, my son. The day will come when we meet again, and I'll not only have her, but you, as well."

A gust of wind ripped through the room, stirring debris and dust. Jase's eyes burned and he turned his head. That's when he saw her.

Kayla—not the wide-eyed child, but the grown woman—standing in the shadows just inside the kitchen doorway. Tears streamed down her cheeks as she watched the shadow of Alexander Terrell vanish into the night with her mother.

"Why didn't you tell me, Jase?" Her words reached out to him. Betrayal glistened in the deep topaz of her gaze. "Why?"

Jase's eyes snapped open and he left the nightmare behind. But it was too late. She knew.

Kayla gripped the edge of the kitchen table, her attention riveted on the pictures scattered across the worn surface. With a trembling hand, she reached for one.

Stunned and sickened, she stared at her own likeness and the shrouded figures that surrounded her. A suffocating sensation tightened her throat and she dropped the picture to the table. She snatched another, and another, each like the one before.

The figures surrounded her, closer every time she looked, relentless in their pursuit. And they would stop at nothing to bring her back to them, just as they'd stopped at nothing to recapture her mother. The Keepers.

The past stirred, rising like a cresting wave to smash over Kayla with blinding force, and she remembered. For the first time, she *really* remembered.

Her mother's smiling face. Reassuring embraces when the nights had been too dark. Kisses for every cut and scrape she'd managed to collect. A mother who had sacrificed everything to save her from the darkness, to see her grow into womanhood with no bitter memories of the rituals, or the midnight Masses, or the Keepers themselves.

They took her, the child's voice replayed in her mind. *Daddy wouldn't tell me, but I saw. I was watching through the crack under the door.*

Kayla realized with a shudder of vivid recollection that the child she'd seen had been a projection of herself. The part of her that was hidden away... the part that remembered... the part she'd left here at the cabin so long ago.

You called me. You wanted to remember.

Kayla squeezed her eyes shut against the scalding tears. Her hand went to her neck, but she felt no comforting silver, no moonstar. Gone like her mother. Like her father and Gramps.

You'll always be able to feel me, Kayla. Her father's words returned to haunt her. *Death can't part us.* But he'd been wrong.

Your old gramps will be with you always. The Old One's raspy voice drifted through her mind. Time had made a liar out of him, as well.

A violent rage erupted inside of her, gripping her entire body, as if to squeeze the life from her. The floor tilted and she grasped the edge of the table to keep from keeling over.

Lies. Her entire life had been an accumulation of lies to hide who she really was, *what* she really was, and keep those few precious memories of her mother from her.

Her father and Gramps—no, he wasn't even her Gramps. More tears burned her eyes at the realization. He was the Old One who'd masqueraded as her grandfather, his entire existence as much a lie as Kayla's had been.

Her father and the Old One had started the lies, and Jase had perpetuated them, refusing to tell her the truth, knowing how important it was to her that she remember.

She stumbled over to the sink and cranked the water pump. Cupping one hand, she splashed ice-cold water on her face. The drain gurgled, sucking at the water, pulling it down into nothingness as another vivid recollection swept over her.

The promise.

Your bodies will join, you will show her our ways, and together you and Kayla will produce a child of the purest blood.

A new anguish seared through her as the significance of what she and Jase had done became frighteningly clear.

Tonight, Jase had come to her, taken her to bed, then pulled her into his nightmare to show her the truth about her past.

Your bodies will join.

You will show her our ways.

Two-thirds of the promise had been fulfilled.

Jase's young voice drifted through her mind, coming from deep within her. From the hidden parts of her soul where she'd locked his image away for safekeeping.

I'll be with you always, moonchild. Watching over you and keeping you safe. Always keeping you safe.

His parting words to her before he'd slipped into the darkness the night her mother was taken. He'd disappeared. Run away. The next day, she and her father and the Old One had left the protection of the house and fled for their lives.

Always keeping you safe. Yes, Jase had been the biggest liar of all.

"Kayla." She heard the deep rumble of his voice behind her, but she couldn't face him.

"Go away," she whispered. "Please, Jase. Just go away."

"Now you know," he said, the words low, void of any remorse or regret. "It was time you finally remembered."

She whirled on him. "And what a way for me to remember! Kind of a front-row seat, right? It saved you the trouble of having to tell me the truth to my face. Instead, you could just let me watch everything, see my mother dragged away while I stood helplessly by." Her voice broke and she put her back to him again.

Staring through the kitchen window, she fixed her tear-filled gaze on the woodshed. Yet, she didn't really see the shed, or the yard, or the fortress of trees swaying in the distance. She saw only her mother's terrified face.

"They took my mother," she breathed, fingers clenching in her chest, making every breath a painful exercise. "They *murdered* her."

"She betrayed them by taking you. You were their future. They couldn't let her get away with that. They wanted your father, too, but Alexander couldn't get to him. Your father was on my side of the power line."

Kayla slumped against the edge of the sink, lost in her own memories, oblivious to his words. "So many scenarios raced through my mind when I opened Gramps's safe-deposit box and found the old photographs," she whispered. "At first, I couldn't believe that my father and Gramps had lied to me about something so important. When the shock wore off, I stared long and hard at those pictures, trying to figure out what had become of the woman I saw. She looked so warm and loving, like she really cared about the child in the picture with her... about *me*."

She stifled a sob with the back of her hand. "I—I couldn't believe someone like that could run off and abandon her child. But that was the only answer that explained why my father had kept the pictures from me. He'd been bitter over her leaving. That's why there were never any mementos, except for the moonstar. It was almost as if she'd never existed. But she didn't leave me." Tears flowed down her face. "She didn't."

"She never would have left you, Kayla. Not willingly. She sacrificed her life for you."

"Damn them," she cried, hugging her arms as a chill ripped through her. Grief iced her blood. "They called her a traitor and killed her." She said the words, more for herself than him, as if saying the words could ease the hurt and help her understand. But no words could do that.

More tears glided down her cheeks, splashing in telltale drops across the front of Jase's T-shirt she'd slipped on when she'd left the bedroom.

Traitor. The word sounded in her head, playing over and over like a scratched record. Only, her mother wasn't the traitor. Jase was.

Forgive me. Now Kayla understood his whispered plea. The desperation she'd sensed in those two simple words.

"Tonight you sold me out, Jase," she said, her voice fueled with all of the hurt and bitterness swirling inside of

her. She turned on him. "You knew about the promise,
and you knew I *didn't* know. You stole my soul and you
didn't even give me a choice in the matter."

"Choice?" He shook his head, his eyes gleaming with
a ruthlessness that reached out and gripped her by the
throat. "There was never any choice, Kayla, for either of
us. I've spent the past twenty-two years trying to forget the
darkness. I thought I could deny it, escape it, but it lives
and breathes within me." His voice held a steely edge. "I
can't change who and what I am. Neither can you. And we
can't change destiny. The Keepers proved that tonight."

Her anger faltered for a split second as she remembered
the blackout at Big Mick's.

"Tonight was a warning, Kayla. A show of power. They
can take you from me in the blink of an eye and there isn't
a thing I can do to stop them."

"No!" she gasped, desperate to deny the truth. "You've
managed to keep me safe and put a stop to the blackouts
these past two weeks. You're stronger than they are."
Words failed her as she fell captive to the raw power radiating from his body.

Gone was the hunted look that usually filled his eyes, the
compassion, the anguish. Rather, he looked like the
hunter, his gaze alight with a silver glow that could hyp-
notize even the boldest animal as he moved in for the kill.

Instantly, her mind conjured his reflection in the mirror
when he'd come to her earlier. She'd seen the same strange
light, felt the same magnetic pull, and she'd fallen victim
to him. A very willing victim.

"I won't let them take you from me," he growled.
"We'll return to the coven together." Moonlight poured
through the window, flowing over the ridges and swells of
his muscular torso and catching the silver moonstar suspended around his neck. "You were meant for me, Kayla.
I can't bear the thought of another man touching you.
You're mine. *Mine!*"

The room fell into silence, which grew more chilling with each moment. Before her stood a man—dark, dangerous, aroused. But his eyes held a hint of softness. He had sold her out, right along with himself, but the decision hadn't been an easy one. In the shimmer of his gaze, she glimpsed his hunger—painful, all-consuming and irresistible—and she couldn't hate him for giving in. He'd held out, fought valiantly. A lesser man would have thrown her to the wolves days ago.

Compassion and warmth welled up inside of her—ironic, considering she wanted, no, needed, to despise him. Her mind flashed back to their lovemaking, to his climax, the tears on his face, and she knew that whatever force had seized hold of him and driven him to betray her, didn't claim him entirely.

"I'm sorry," he whispered, his voice strained. He raked taut fingers through his hair. "I can't believe I finally gave in. After all this time." And as he stared deep into her eyes, she saw the Jase who'd saved her, taken care of her, loved her.

Kayla crossed the room and touched a hand to his shoulder.

Anger and guilt fought a battle on his face, despair fueling the silver depths of his gaze. "What have I done?" Gone was the predator, and instead, before her was the wounded animal, his face that of a man who'd seen too much death. His skin burned beneath her fingertips, a fiery hurt that seared her very soul. For a long, drawn-out moment, she held his gaze and cupped his stubbled jaw, letting herself feel the maelstrom of emotion that whirled within him.

And as she stared at him, she saw the child he'd been, haunted and tormented and lost.

"Where did you go when you left here?" she asked, suddenly needing to know all about him, about his hurt, his struggles, his pain for the past twenty-two years.

Needing, more than anything, to share the burden he'd carried for so long.

He placed his hands over hers, his fingers strong, warm against hers. He closed his eyes, a bittersweet expression on his face, as if he relished the feel of her touching him, yet hated himself for allowing it.

"I wandered around Texas for a while, not staying in any one place for too long. Begging for jobs here and there, for food. I slept outside, mostly. Eventually, I found my way to Houston. I didn't have any money, or anyplace to go. God, I was only twelve..." He faltered then, swallowing as if the words stuck in his throat. Tears shimmered on his thick lashes.

"I ended up in the welfare system," he went on, his voice shaky. "Which wasn't much better than being on my own. I went from family to family, never really fitting in. Never really belonging. I kept to myself, for the most part. I was scared." The last word was a whisper. "So scared, Kayla."

She felt the tears winding down her cheeks, just as she felt his tears on her palms. "I'm the one who's sorry, Jase. For all that you never had. You deserved so much more. You were there when I needed you. You saved me. If only I could have been there for you."

He opened his eyes and stared at her for a long moment, as if he truly wanted to believe her. Still, doubt simmered in his eyes, doubt ingrained in him as a young child who'd never had anything or anyone.

"I thought about you all the time," he murmured. "Every minute, almost. And I stayed as close to you as I could, Kayla. I knew that one day you would need me. I knew they would come. I knew they would come to take the only thing I had left. You." And with the last word, he stiffened, his eyes taking on a strange light.

She sensed the sudden change in him, the tensing of his body, the stirring of emotions, as if he were a stick of dynamite, his fuse just lit. She backed away from him, slowly, her gaze locked with his, watching and waiting for the explosion.

"You've always been mine, Kayla." He moved toward her with a predatory grace that was as unnerving as his voice. "Hate me if you want to, but I can't change what happened between us, and I won't regret even a minute of it. I would sell my soul a thousand times over for a moment with you." He inched closer, until her bottom pressed against the counter and his very prominent arousal nestled against her fluttering stomach.

"N-no." She managed to form the word with trembling lips. "This isn't right." She pushed against his bare chest, his skin blazing hot beneath her palms. "Please..."

"Don't deny me, Kayla. I want you again."

She gave up trying to push him away and twisted in his arms, putting her back to him. "I won't let you doom us to this promise," she said, her voice an urgent whisper. "Nothing more can happen between us, Jase. Not until it's over and your father's dead. We can't give in again!"

His only answer was to lean closer, the hard wall of his chest flush against her back. The silver charm he wore burned through her shirt to singe the skin between her shoulder blades.

"Don't," she breathed when he brushed aside her hair to place a lingering kiss on her neck. She tried to shrug away, but he gripped the counter on either side of her, braced his legs around hers.

"I have to, Kayla. I can't be near you and not touch you. *I can't.*"

"No!" she cried. She pushed against his arms, fought him all the while her heart shattered. "Stop, Jase. Please!" The roar of her own voice seemed to fill the house, her anguish so intense the walls rattled. A flash of wild grief ripped through her. The tears came harder, for her mother and a young boy with haunted moonsilver eyes. Both lost to her forever.

Jase locked one arm around her waist and pulled her full against him, his hardness pressing insistently into her soft buttocks. With his free hand, he touched her bare thigh, leaving a trail of tingling flesh as he pushed the hem of the T-shirt up past her waist, to caress her bare bottom, the insides of her thighs, the damp flesh crying out for him.

We were meant to be together, Kayla. The shadows enveloping her seemed to whisper the words as Jase licked a path from her neck, down the slope of her shoulder.

They were whispering the words, she realized, but she wouldn't surrender to the darkness. She would fight destiny, just as she'd fight Jase, until it was all over and Alexander Terrell was dead. It didn't matter that she and Jase had already become lovers, that she now knew the truth. There was still a third part of the promise—a part she wouldn't fulfill.

"No!" she wailed, despite her body, which sang beneath his touch. The kitchen door burst open, then the window, the process repeated all through the house... wood crashing against wood, hinges ripping at the sudden force, until the entire place stood open to the elements.

The wind howled through, like Death screaming obscenities at them, and Jase released her with a suddenness that had her clutching the counter for support. He took a step back, his attention riveted on the window in back of her.

A bright orange glow lit his features, feeding the deep pools of his eyes until they glittered like hot volcanic rock.

She swung around and stared out the window at the thin wall of fire circling the clearing. "Oh, my God—" Her words fell short as the kitchen curtains burst into flames. Kayla jumped backward, trembling, suddenly terrified of herself. She knew she had nothing to do with the fire outside of the cabin, but the curtains had flamed at her will. *Her* power.

Kayla stumbled backward, then turned to run. But where? She halted in the living-room doorway, all the while knowing she couldn't escape the dormant power now sizzling through her body. She couldn't run from herself, from what she was.

Her gaze flew to the drapes, which sparked and blazed. The wind rushed through the front door, slapping at the flames until they grew more frenzied.

For a moment, she stood entranced as forgotten memories muddied her thoughts. A fiery altar, shrouded figures circling, paying homage.

Sparks flew and the sofa ignited in a swirl of orange and red. Kayla forced the past away and flew down the hall to the bedroom. The curtains flamed at a glance. A shower of sparks cascaded around her as she hurried inside and gathered the quilts from the bed. She wanted to squeeze her eyes shut, but she couldn't. No more than she could control or understand the power that pulsed through her veins and turned the cabin into a searing holocaust.

She found Jase where she'd left him in the kitchen. The flames danced around him, having spread to several of the chairs. Fiery fingers caressed the tabletop, spreading across the worn surface.

"I'm sorry," she whispered. "So sorry! I don't know what's happening to me." She shook her head frantically and clamped her eyes shut, afraid to look at Jase. Afraid he would burst into flames right in front of her. Because of her.

Control, an inner voice whispered. Breathe.

She did, in huge, frantic gulps until her lungs swelled with air and the trembling in her hands ceased. Smoke filled her nostrils and suddenly her fear of herself disintegrated as an all new threat took root. Her eyes flew open. The room was ablaze around them, caging them, closing in. They would both burn to death if she didn't do something. Now!

"Jase, we have to get out of here!" she shouted, daring a look at him. He didn't even flex a muscle, almost as if some invisible hand held him to the spot, his gaze fixed on the window that overlooked the clearing.

"Jase," she cried, grabbing his hand. With all of the strength she could find, she tugged him toward the door. "Please, Jase! Help me, for God's sake. *Help me!*"

Where all of her pulling and shouting had done no good, those two words seemed to reach him. He shook his head. His eyes registered their surroundings and he tightened his fingers around hers. And then he was pulling her outside.

In the yard, Kayla flung one of the quilts at him while she draped one around her own shoulders. "Hurry, we have to get out of—" The words died on her lips.

Eyes wide, she turned in a complete circle, staring at the thin wall of fire that surrounded the clearing and caged them. Her hold on the quilt faltered, the cover slipped to a pile at her feet and reality crashed around her.

They were trapped.

The blaze, which spanned the circumference of the clearing, appeared a blue sheet of shimmering air. Transparent enough for Kayla to see the foliage on the other side. Deadly enough to send ice water racing through her veins. The wind blew with a devil's fury, licking at the fire, making it burn bluer, the shimmers reaching, waving to the starless sky.

"Come on," Jase said, his voice low, guttural, unearthly. He let go of her hand to snatch the quilt and drape it around her. "Hurry, Kayla," he added, grabbing her shoulders and propelling her around. "There isn't much time."

"You—you'll be behind me, right?" She let him steer her toward the blazing woodshed, around to the spot where they'd followed the path out to the highway what seemed like an eternity ago.

"When you get to the other side," he said, turning her to face him, "you'll see the path." His steely gaze caught and held hers. "Follow the path to the road and don't look back. Do you hear me?" He gave her a quick shake, and without waiting for a reply, growled, *"Don't look back!"*

"You'll follow me—" Her words died as he spun her and shoved her into the fire.

Heat enveloped her, sucking the breath from her lungs as though she'd been thrust into a raging oven. She staggered forward, through the inferno, the blanket suddenly ablaze around her.

Once she cleared the flames, she flung the burning cover off. Whirling, she stared with watery eyes at the luminescent blue wall, Jase's silhouette a darker shade of cobalt on the opposite side.

"Jase!" she called. "Come on! Hurry!"

She saw him pull the blanket up over his head. He took a step forward. The material sparked, then flamed. He stumbled backward.

"Nooooooo!" she screamed as the wall flared orange, a brilliant white, then an angry red. The flames rose higher, hotter, like a living, breathing crimson dragon that swallowed the cobalt silhouette.

Jase's voice rang out, the cry of a tortured soul begging redemption. *Run, Kayla! Run and never look back!*

In a split second, she glimpsed him, a vague shadow, a man of flames, melting and blending into the fire that raged between them.

Run! His voice echoed the fierce command that seized hold of her very spirit, it seemed, and she couldn't defy him. *Now!*

She spun and took flight just as a fiery wave rose and crashed. Flames caught the foliage at her back. Blindly she ran, gasping for every breath. She trampled branches and leaves, the blaze in back of her lighting her way. Heat licked at her heels. Jase's image rose in her mind, urging her faster, his arms reaching out to her, coaxing her.

"Jase!" she cried as the toe of her boot caught on a protruding root. She fell forward, her head slamming into a gnarled tree trunk.

Move! a voice screamed, urging her on. She dug her hands into the scorched earth to heave herself forward. Again and again, she inched along, but it was no use. She couldn't escape the fire, the pounding in her skull, not on her own. Collapsing, she gave in to the inevitable.

Oblivion descended—a black angel sent to snatch her from the very bowels of hell, and the heat vanished. Then she felt nothing.

CHAPTER ELEVEN

"Damn traitorous fool," Max Talbot said tightly, then spat on the ground next to Jase's still body. Saliva sizzled against the charred earth, crackling and popping like butter in a frying pan.

"Enough!" Alexander Terrell growled, his attention riveted on the unconscious figure of his son. He knelt and touched death-white fingers to Jase's soot-covered face. The skin of one shoulder had turned a blistering red where the fire had burned him. His once-gleaming ebony hair now hung limp, lifeless, portions burnt. The blanket was a smoldering pile of ashes beside him, also ravaged by the fire. A fire caused by Alexander's own hand.

The high priest closed his eyes for a brief moment, a strange feeling stirring in his breast. He'd acted quickly, retracting the flames from Jase's blanket as soon as he'd sparked them. They'd been meant only to render Jase unconscious. To stop him from getting away, just as he'd tried to stop Kayla. Not to burn him...certainly not to kill him.

"You served us well, my son," Alexander said, a slight tremor in his voice. *Forgive me,* a voice whispered in the dark corners of his soul.

Soul? He had no soul. It had been traded a long time ago—an even exchange for the darkness that inhabited his body. A long, long time ago.

"You did well to stop him. If only we could have stopped her, too," Max said.

"She won't get far. She's alone now. The others will find her," Alexander said. "Have Jase picked up and brought with us."

"He'll do us no good now. Just added baggage. Leave him."

Alexander whirled on Max, his fingers clenched. "You'll be the one staying behind if you don't follow my orders. I'll not leave Jase here to rot. Besides, we need Kayla's co-operation. If we have him..." His words died as he stared at his son once again.

"We can persuade her some other way. Jase is a traitor. He's—"

"Enough!" Alexander snapped. "Do as I say, Max, or suffer the consequences of your foolish actions."

Gazes clashed, dark fury warring with blazing rebellion. But Alexander was older by a few years, wiser, more powerful.

"As you wish," Max conceded, his voice strained. Reluctantly, he signaled to another robed figure standing a few feet away. Then another and another.

In minutes, several Keepers materialized and closed in on Jase.

Alexander grasped the moonstar suspended around Jase's neck. With a quick tug, he ripped the charm loose and stepped back as his son's body was hoisted. Then he turned and walked through the flames, the dizzying heat like a rush. The twinge of regret he'd felt vanished. The moonstar turned ice-cold in his grasp.

No redemption and no forgiveness. His own words roared in his head—a reminder of who he was, what he was, what the future held for him.

Now Alexander's second son would step into Jase's place. Tomorrow night, Kayla would conceive a child. A vessel for Alexander's knowledge and power...for his spirit.

At the exact stroke of midnight...

The renewal of life.

The witching hour...and Alexander's last birthday in this aged and haggard body.

"You'd better hope she wakes up soon, Maggie. I'll not be a party to housing no criminal," a rusty voice pushed its way into Kayla's mind.

"Shh, Hershel. What if she can hear you?" a female voice, as soothing as honey, countered.

"All the better. The sooner she gets up and outa here, the sooner I can go back to restin' easy. I ain't gettin' myself into a heap of trouble over some stranger. Wait—" The static of a radio split the silence, then another voice blared.

"...fire-fighters are still on the scene and local authorities are calling the blaze a result of arson. This is the biggest woods fire Texas has seen in twenty years."

"*Arson*, Mother," the man muttered. "Did you hear that?"

"I'm sure campers started the fire. You know how careless folks can be."

"No," he grumbled. "The police wouldn't be calling it arson if it looked like an accident, Mother. They know their business. They said arson. *Arson.*"

"All right, Hershel. Don't beat it to death."

"For heaven's sake, Maggie, we found that girl sprawled on the side of the road, shirt and hair burned, looking like she done walked through hell, or something."

"Shh. You'll wake her up. Maybe she got caught by the fire rather than started it. Have you thought of that, Hershel?"

"Maybe, and maybe not."

"You always believe the worst," the woman retorted. "In the fifty years I've known you, you've never given anyone the benefit of the doubt."

"And you're always too soft on folks. This ain't a nice world, Mother. You can't deny her hands. Blisters! She had something to do with that fire, all right."

The voices turned into an endless string of syllables that hurt too much for Kayla to try to link together.

Only one word seemed to stick in her thoughts. Echo over and over.

Fire.

Kayla felt the heat again, searing her flesh, her hair, and then she saw it—a flaming silhouette in the blackness of her mind.

"Jase," she croaked, grasping at the bed sheets.

The voices stopped.

"Hear that, Hershel? I think she's coming to."

"It's about time."

"Oh, hush up, you old coot," the female snapped. Then her voice softened. "Honey?" Kayla felt a touch on her shoulder. The blazing heat subsided and reality pushed its way into her conscience. "Can you hear me?"

"Where...?" Kayla tried to open her eyes, but blinding sunlight forced them shut again. Her head pounded. The throbbing in her temples kept time with the steady tick of a clock somewhere in the room. The sound magnified. *Tick, tock, tick, tock,* until Kayla wanted to scream.

Then she felt the soft hands again. At her forehead this time. Soft, soothing, comforting, and she heard the woman's voice croon, "The name's Fletcher, honey, Maggie Fletcher."

"Maggie," Kayla managed to whisper. "I have...to...help...have to..." The words seemed to stick together.

"Here, have some water, sugar."

Kayla felt her head being lifted. Cool drops splashed her parched lips. She struggled up on her elbows and gulped greedily.

"There," Maggie said once Kayla had swallowed the last of the water. "That ought to help you feel a little better."

Kayla slumped back against a fluffy white pillow. She touched the tender area of her forehead, flinching when her fingertips made contact with the sticky bandage. Recollection swept over her and she felt her skull crashing against the tree trunk, the ground slipping away, then the blackness snuffing out everything.

"Move your hand, honey. We don't want you getting an infection." Maggie pushed Kayla's fingers away and settled down on the bed beside her, a first-aid kit in her lap. "Let me see what I did with that peroxide." She rummaged inside the box.

Kayla took several deep breaths and glanced around the room, which seemed to sway ever so slightly. White eyelet curtains framed the windows. A matching eyelet bedspread draped the end of the bed, and a goose-down comforter covered Kayla's legs.

The room was so normal it almost made Kayla believe she'd imagined the past two weeks...the blackouts, Jase's rescue, their lovemaking, the fire. *Fire.*

Kayla closed her eyes against the vicious tap dance at her temples. The Keepers had been responsible for the fiery wall outside, but *she* had set the blaze inside the house. When Jase had touched her, her anger had unleashed a power she'd never known existed.

She took a deep breath, the pain inside of her like a large scalpel carving and slashing at her heart, reminding her of the unreal reality of her life. Reminding her of who—no, *what* she was.

"...tell you, when Hershel and I spotted you on the side of the road, it gave me an awful fright. I let loose a holler and Hershel slammed on the brakes. The dang fool nearly landed us in a ditch."

"Road?" Kayla asked. She tried to think, but the drumming in her head increased.

"...sprawled out so helpless. And then Hershel spotted the smoke rising from the trees." She shook her head.

"We barely got you inside the truck before we heard a whole mess of fire engines, police cars—you name it. The whole thing's still burning."

Burning. Jase's image rose in Kayla's mind. He smiled at her, held out his hands and she reached for him. Only to see him melt, his skin dissolving into a cluster of flames.

"No!" she cried. A pain unlike anything she'd ever felt before slammed into her, doubled her over.

"Honey, are you all right?"

"My God...Jase. *Jase.*" came her desperate plea, as if saying his name would bring him to her. Impossible! He was lost in the fire.

Lost, maybe dead.

Probably dead, a voice corrected.

Surely dead, another insisted.

"There, there, honey. Don't cry." The woman patted Kayla's shoulder awkwardly. "You'll be all right. You need to rest. Things will seem a heap better once you get some sleep—"

"No!" Kayla shook her head. The sun seemed to eclipse for a full second. Then the light clicked back on, more blinding than before. "I can't sleep," she whispered with thick lips, a strange sensation rising in her throat. "I have to go back...have to find Jase. To make sure...please!" The last word came out as a thin wail as Kayla tried to crawl from the bed. The effort proved too much and she gasped against an overwhelming sickness. She leaned over bent knees, her face buried in the comforter, Maggie Fletcher's soothing hand at her back.

"Breathe through your nose, honey. Please. Just a few easy breaths and the nausea will pass."

Kayla turned her head to the side and managed to inhale, the single breath excruciating. Her lungs burned for oxygen, and for a moment she longed to give up the effort and let go—let go of the life that Jase had already left. Or had he? She'd managed to escape. Maybe he had, as well.

Hope flickered. What if he was alive? He could be badly hurt, calling out to her, begging for help. She pressed her hands to her head. If she could just concentrate. Maybe she could *connect* with him.

Jase! her mind cried. *Please answer. Please!* But no voice spoke to her. She heard only the ticktock of the clock.

Panic seized her. "I have to go back!" she shrieked, her head snapping up as she clutched one of Maggie Fletcher's hands. *"I have to!"*

"Get rid of that notion, sugar." Maggie shook her head, sympathy shining in her eyes. "There's nothing to go back to. Those woods are a mess of flames."

"But Jase—"

"I'm sorry, honey, but if this Jase fella got caught in that fire, you probably lost him. The police ain't found a living soul. It's a miracle me and Hershel happened upon you. A few feet and you would have been stuck back in the foliage, hidden from sight, just waiting to burn. And now you're certainly in no shape to go running back." Her voice softened. "And it won't do any good, honey. Nobody could have made it out of that fire. If so, the sheriff and his men would have found him by now."

Nobody, not even Jase with his strength and determination.

Kayla saw the silver sparkle of his eyes go dim, like someone had flicked off a light switch. The truth weighed down on her, crushing her heart into tiny pieces. She would never hear his voice. Never feel his arms again. Never be able to say all the things that she wanted to.

Thank you. I'm sorry. I love you.

The tears came faster, harder, until her entire body shook and the sound of her own anguished sobs rang in her ears.

"There, there, child. Maggie's here."

Kayla found herself pulled into plump arms, her head cradled on a pillowlike bosom. Maggie Fletcher emanated a peaceful warmth—a comforting ordinariness, like the sunlit room, the down comforter, the oversize flannel nightgown Kayla wore.

She wrapped her arms around the woman's pudgy middle and held on for dear life, as if she could draw warmth from the woman to thaw the cold fist where her heart had been. But the fiercer Kayla hugged, the colder she grew. Her chest constricted and she felt pain and misery and grief, the likes of which she'd never known.

"You go ahead and cry, sugar. Just let it all out."

And Kayla did just that. She cried for what seemed like hours. Just when she thought she'd used up every drop of moisture in her body, the tears would start again, springing from the never-ending supply of sorrow that welled up inside of her.

"We need to get in touch with your family, honey," Maggie said when Kayla's sobs started to quiet and her body stilled to a slight quake. "Folks is probably worried about you. Tell me your name, sugar."

"Kayla," she whispered into the curve of the woman's shoulder. "Kayla Darland."

"Well, now, Kayla," Maggie crooned, smoothing the curls from Kayla's face. "I'm sure somebody, somewhere, is mighty anxious to know what happened to you. You give me a name and I'll get in touch with them—let 'em know where you're at and that you're all right."

"Marc," Kayla finally said, the name catching on a hiccup. "Marc Miles."

"Well, now, you just tell me this Marc's phone number and—"

"Mother, your roast is burnin'!" a man grumbled from the hallway.

"Sorry, sugar. You settle back down and I'll be right back. Coming, Hershel!" she called, tucking the blankets around Kayla's legs before hurrying from the room. The door clicked shut.

Kayla wanted to bolt from the bed and race from the room, back to the cabin and Jase, but she could barely tighten her fingers around the comforter. Her body felt bone-weary, her mind weak, her heart so heavy the beat seemed sluggish.

And she hurt with a fierceness unlike anything she'd ever experienced.

She'd lost the man promised to her, the man she'd joined with, the man who'd stolen her heart and betrayed her, all in the name of protection.

The fight for her sanity was over and she was free. Free! She could return to her life, forget about her past.

Only she would never forget. Not again. She'd waited a lifetime to find Jase. And at that moment, Kayla would have gladly sought out the devil himself and traded her soul for Jase Terrell. If only it wasn't already too late.

"Kayla," Marc's familiar voice drew her attention.

She met his gaze as she slipped the last button of the dress into place and shoved her feet into white sandals a size too large.

"It's not exactly the latest fashion, but you do look rather wholesome," he said, giving her one of his full-dimple smiles. He stood in the doorway, his blue eyes catching fragments of sunlight streaming through the bedroom window.

Kayla stared down at the flower-print dress she wore. "This is all Mrs. Fletcher had," she murmured, her voice distant, small. "She said it used to belong to one of her daughters." She rubbed her arms, desperate to ease the cold that had crept into her bones. But she couldn't. No matter how hard or how fast she rubbed. No relief.

"Way back in the fifties, I'd bet. But it's quite fetching, my dear," Marc replied in his best English accent.

Kayla tried to smile, but the effort seemed impossible. Her forehead throbbed. Reaching for the hairbrush Maggie had left her, she sucked in a breath. The room seemed to tilt. She grabbed for the bedpost. Then Marc was beside her, slipping a steadying arm around her waist.

"Take it easy," he said. "I think we need to get you to a doctor."

"No, I'm fine. Just a little dizzy," she replied, her voice a breathless whisper. "I—I'm still a little groggy from my nap. And then trying to stand and get dressed..."

"You can rest in the car," he said, studying her face with a thoroughness that made her want to turn and bury her head in the mound of covers she'd burrowed beneath such a short time ago. "The trip back to Houston will take a couple of hours. Plenty of time for you to sleep."

"I don't want to sleep, Marc." She rubbed her arms again. "I need to ask you a favor."

"Ask away," he replied, his icelike fingers brushing a stray curl from her cheek. It was a meaningless gesture from him, the caress feather-light, friendly, yet the way he looked at her, almost through her, made it seem intimate and very disturbing. Her chills multiplied.

"The fire," she breathed. "I—I was with someone in the woods and we were separated when the fire started. I need to see if the police have found him, or maybe some sign of him." Her voice caught on a sob.

"We'll call the Austin authorities first chance we get. You're going to have to talk to them, anyway. Thankfully, they ruled out arson and declared the fire a camping accident. Of course, since you were one of the campers, they'll want you to fill them in on particulars. But first things first, we'll head home—"

"No," she cut in. "I *need* to know what happened. I need to know for sure that Jase is gone." She tried to pull from Marc's grasp, but his frigid fingers were like clamps around her arms. The ruby ring he wore caught the sunlight and flashed brilliant prisms of red, blinding her for a split second. "If you won't help me, I'll find a way, myself. Just go back to Houston and I'll get some answers on my own." She managed to yank free of him and stumble across the room to the window. She clutched the windowsill and stared out into the afternoon sun. So much light on the outside. But inside of her, there was only darkness . . . emptiness.

"You're stubborn, do you know that?" Marc asked, his voice filled with exasperation.

"I have to know," she repeated. "Please understand, Marc."

He came up behind her and placed a hand on her shoulder. "Let's get out of here and we'll see if we can find out what happened to this Jase guy you're so worried about."

"Thanks," she murmured, glancing at him. "For getting here so fast and being so understanding." It had been barely three hours since she'd poured out her heart in Maggie Fletcher's arms and then fallen unwillingly into an exhausted sleep. She'd awoken about ten minutes ago, with Marc standing in the doorway and Mrs. Fletcher nudging her shoulder, murmuring, "Your friends are here, Kayla."

"You really do look quite fetching in this," he added, fingering one of her sleeves.

"It's better than nothing."

"Now, that's a matter of opinion," he replied, giving her a sly grin. "I would have brought you some of your own clothes had I known you didn't have anything. I won't ask what you were doing on the side of the road wearing only a T-shirt."

"Neither will I." Rickie Morgan appeared in the doorway, hands on her hips, an impatient look on her face.

"Thanks for coming," Kayla said, her cheeks heating beneath Rickie's bold scrutiny.

"You have some nice friends here," Maggie Fletcher said as she strolled past Rickie into the room. She came up to Kayla. Her face was set in a worried frown as she touched Kayla's cheek. "But you really shouldn't be up so soon, honey. You don't have to be taking off. This bed doesn't belong to anybody. You could stay a few days and let that nasty head wound heal."

"I think Kayla would be better off at home," Marc chimed in. "Plus, I would feel better if she saw a doctor, just to make sure she doesn't have a concussion or anything like that."

"Certainly," Maggie agreed, her frown deepening. "Maybe Hershel and I should have taken her to a doctor instead of bringing her here. But this was so much closer."

"You did the right thing," Kayla assured her. "I'm sure it's just a nasty scratch. The offer to stay is very tempting, but I've imposed enough on your hospitality."

"It was no imposition." Maggie's comment received a snort from the hallway and Kayla glimpsed Hershel Fletcher looming behind Rickie.

"Don't mind him, honey," she said, patting Kayla's hand. "He's just a fussy old grouch."

"You were more than kind to help me out." Kayla had a good idea that Hershel was the reason Maggie had called Marc so quickly. The woman must have run to the phone the minute Kayla had dozed off, no doubt with her husband urging her every step of the way. Even then, Marc and Rickie had made excellent time from Houston. Record time, in fact.

Kayla pushed the odd notion away. So they'd shown up fast. That just proved what good friends they were. One phone call and they'd been on their way—

Another thought struck her. Had she given Maggie Fletcher the phone number? Of course, she must have. Marc and Rickie were here, and they were going to help her find out the truth about Jase, good or bad.

"Thank you for everything, Mrs. Fletcher," Kayla said as a bout of fresh tears welled up in her eyes. She dashed the moisture away.

"You're very welcome, sugar. The Lord has a way of looking after those who can't look after themselves, and you certainly needed looking after. Here," she said, handing Kayla the burned and bloodstained T-shirt. Then she hesitated. "Unless you want me to throw it in the trash—"

"No," Kayla said, her voice sharper than she meant. She took the shirt from Maggie and raised it to her cheek. Despite the acrid smell of smoke and the dirt and the blood, she could have sworn she caught a whiff of Jase's familiar scent. The tears squeezed past her lashes to trickle down her cheeks.

"Come on." It was Marc's rich voice. His arm came around her. She let him lead her from the room, outside to the car, the shirt clutched between her fingers.

Marc helped Kayla into the front seat of the black BMW. Then he closed the door and climbed in the back seat behind her. Rickie slid into the driver's seat and started the engine.

Kayla glanced through the tinted glass at Maggie Fletcher. The woman smiled and waved, yet her eyes held a glimmer of worry. Her smile seemed almost forced. An unexplainable sliver of fear crawled down Kayla's spine, only to drown in the grief that swirled inside of her.

She held the T-shirt in her lap and leaned her head against the cushioned headrest. Jase's image filled her mind. Imagined or not, his scent overpowered her, and she didn't feel the loneliness or the pain or the fear anymore.

She felt only him.

I'm coming, Jase. I'll find you.

Kayla opened her eyes a few minutes later as they turned onto the highway. They had driven only a short distance, when a fire truck sped past in the opposite direction. Kayla twisted to see black smoke billowing in the far distance.

"Rickie, wait!" Kayla whipped around to Rickie who wore a solemn expression, her gaze fixed on the road in front of them. "You're going the wrong direction. Marc said we were going back to look for Jase. We're moving *away* from the fire, do you hear—" She reached out, only to snatch her hand away as Rickie flashed her a sharp look, her eyes like chips of onyx.

Rickie flexed her fingers around the wheel, her ruby ring catching the afternoon sunlight that streamed through the windshield. The stone flashed blood-red in the dim interior of the car and the air caught in Kayla's chest.

"You!" The word was a sharp gasp, as if someone had landed a punch to Kayla's middle. "My God, you were the one at Big Mick's. It was *you!* I knew something about you seemed familiar, but I couldn't see your face."

Rickie made no reply, her gaze never straying from the road. But Kayla felt the other woman's full attention—an unnatural force that reached across the expanse of the car. A jolt of panic struck Kayla. She whirled, only to find Marc staring at her with unnerving ice-blue eyes.

In those few seconds, the truth pounded Kayla like hail in an ice storm.

Rickie and Marc were a part of everything. They were *Keepers*. All along, they'd pretended to be her friends, staying close to her, trying to win her confidence. Now they'd come to claim her.

"You're both involved in all of this," she said, her voice an incredulous whisper. Mentally, she rifled through memories for some sign that she'd missed. She'd been so close to both of them and she'd never suspected. "Who else?" she asked, afraid of the answer, yet needing to hear it.

"Just me and Rickie at KCSS. When you were across town at the top-forty station, it was a couple of the jocks and the program director. Back in college, it was a few of your professors, a couple of classmates." At Kayla's sharp intake of breath, he added, "The Keepers are very wealthy and powerful. There was no place for you to hide from us, Kayla. There was always someone watching you. We were always there. Always."

"This can't be real," she whispered, denial hammering within her, as furiously as the pain at her temples.

"Oh, but it is," Marc assured her with a cold exactness that made her tremble. "You know it is. You remember us now, Kayla. But even before the past returned to you, you knew the truth deep down inside when Jase first showed up. An ordinary person would have called him a crazy and fought him every step of the way. Human instinct is to disbelieve, but you're more than human, Kayla. You believed *first*, before rational thought took over and you convinced yourself you shouldn't be so gullible. You're one of us. A Keeper. Like your mother and father—"

"Stop!" she cried. "My mother and father weren't anything like you. They weren't evil and—"

"Now they're dead," he finished. "Turned to dust for their disbelief. They didn't see the darkness was more powerful than the light they'd worshiped for so long. They didn't aspire to be more than healers, soothsayers, their powers limited by their own sense of morality. We are what we are, Kayla. Different, blessed with powers that ordinary humans would kill for. We're witches who—"

"Are forbidden to hurt anyone with the magic we practice," Kayla cut in, the words pouring from her lips from some unknown source inside of her. "The Old Ways are not evil. The power we possess isn't evil. Hurting others is strictly forbidden!"

"I see you remember your lessons." He laughed, the sound cut short when he snapped, "Nothing is forbidden to us anymore. We do what we want, have all that we want.

Our power is stronger because of the evil. We're darker, yes, and invincible."

He leaned forward, his arm shooting over the front seat to grasp her face. His fingers bit into her cheeks as he urged her gaze to meet his. "You *are* one of us, Kayla. The darkness is within you now, Jase saw to that. You'll feel the hunger just as we do, and you'll willingly give all that you are to see that hunger satisfied."

"No!" she wailed, trying to twist away from him.

He loomed closer, an eerie chuckle bursting from his lips. "Yes, you'll feel the hunger. I can see it in your eyes. Smell it." He sniffed. "I can smell Jase, too, sweet Kayla. I can smell his scent on you."

"Stop it," Kayla breathed.

Grabbing a handful of fiery hair, he jerked her head back with a suddenness that blinded her. He touched his lips to her ear, his breath turning her skin to gooseflesh. "I can smell *you,* Kayla . . . your heat . . . your blood."

Kayla clutched Jase's T-shirt in both hands, praying for a salvation she knew would never come. All of her life, she'd been headed for this. Her destiny. Only now, she would face it alone . . . without Jase.

The hell she would!

She grabbed the door handle, only to have Marc's arm snake around her neck. His hold on her hair tightened. He forced her back against the seat, his grip so tight Kayla thought her neck would snap in two.

It would, she realized, with just the tiniest bit more pressure from him. She knew it, and so did he.

"You're smarter than that, Kayla," he whispered, his lips a steady, frightening vibration against her ear. "And in case you're not, we have a friend waiting for you at the end of our journey, just to see that you're as cooperative as possible."

"Who?" she asked, her body going deathly still. She felt the triumphant curve of his lips as he smiled.

"Jase is a stubborn bastard. Not even a damned inferno could kill him."

"He's alive?" Wild hope fired to life.

"Yes, so don't even think about trying to get away. Alexander won't be happy if we're delayed. And Jase will suffer for each minute we're behind schedule."

"If you hurt him, I swear I'll—"

"You'll what?" He sounded amused. "Snap your fingers and turn me into a toad? I'm afraid that old trick is simply media hype. The truth is, you won't do anything, because you can't. You don't even know what powers you have, and they're nothing compared to what Alexander has given us. The demon *Ashtaroth* himself strengthens us, Kayla. You're no match."

"I'll make you sorry if you hurt Jase. I swear it. I don't care what demon gives you your powers. I'll find a way and I'll destroy you!"

"Jase will be left alone, as long as you cooperate. You must fulfill the promise of your own free will. Do it, and Jase might even make it to a doctor. He's hurt pretty bad. Refuse me, and Jase will rot."

"Shut up," Kayla begged. "Please, just shut up. I'll cooperate."

"Good. Now settle down. Uncle Marcky's here and everything's going to be fine." He laughed then, an unnerving sound that pushed its way into Kayla's mind, settled deep in her bones.

"In fact," he went on, "if your performance last night with Jase was a preview of what I can expect, everything will be more than fine. Tonight will be heavenly, if you pardon the expression. I must thank you for keeping my brother so busy. His thoughts were so focused on you, he never noticed me getting closer. He never *felt* any of us."

"Your *brother?*" The truth shook Kayla with a bloodthirsty vengeance. She managed to turn, despite Marc's hold on her neck. She stared into his piercing eyes, their usual blue depths lit with the same unearthly fire she'd seen in Jase's. That was the only similarity between them, she realized as she searched Marc for some resemblance to the man who'd stolen her heart, her soul.

Jase, with his dark good looks, personified all that was forbidden and dangerous. Yet, deep, deep down, he was good. He was still the small boy who'd comforted her, wiped away her tears, fueled her strength.

Marc was the opposite, as different from Jase as fire from water. His fair hair and skin gave the impression of all that was light and wholesome—his appearance an outright mockery to the blackness of his soul. He was a demon in the guise of an angel.

Yes, that's what she faced now. No less than a demon. A whole coven of them, to be exact. Angels turned demons.

Jase's image flashed in her mind and she relaxed against the seat. He was alive! The knowledge filled her with courage, summoned her control. The memory of his deep gaze warmed her. Jase had been there to protect her. He'd been her very own Keeper to see her through the darkness and lead her to the light.

Jase had been her savior. Now she would be his.

"I knew you were smart," Marc murmured, releasing her to lean back into his seat, obviously satisfied that she would fight them no longer.

Kayla felt the gaze he drilled into her back. She sensed the hate and lust brewing within him. *Tonight* came his silent promise, thundering through her head as if he'd screamed the words into her ears.

"Once we reach our destination," Marc continued, "you'll see there's nothing to fear as long as you cooperate. You'll have everything...all that you should have had long ago if those damn-fool idiots hadn't kidnapped you. It's too bad it took so long before Alexander could do away with your father and the Old One. We could have brought you back long before now."

The words drew her around to face him, tears stinging her eyes. "My father died in a car accident, and Gramps of a heart attack," she said, as if saying the words could deny the truth she already knew in her heart.

"Haven't you figured out anything?" He shook his head. "They died at *our* hands . . . for their betrayal. Your father was very powerful. It took us a while to get to him, but we did. And the Old One . . . well, he was a high priest. He took even longer. He was smart. He could have taken you far away, to another country if he wanted, but he knew we would come. He knew in order to protect you completely, he had to be close to the coven, to call on our powers even though we were the very ones pursuing you."

"You killed them both," she said in a choked voice, her throat suddenly tight. "You killed them."

"The Old One knew it was coming." Marc went on as if he were relating a typical day's events rather than the murders of two of her loved ones. "It was your father who was surprised when we came for him. Stupid bastard thought the Old One could protect him like he was protecting you. But your father was a mature witch, under no one's protection but his own. He learned his lesson for thinking otherwise."

Marc's voice faded as the car sped along, winding and curving down the deserted road. Soon, they left behind the brown stretch of prairie land for a thick forest. The road grew more narrow. The army of surrounding trees seemed to reach out, their stark, twisted branches hanging low, the remaining leaves brittle and brown and shriveled.

A vague recollection swept over Kayla, the scene similar to the one she now lived. Only it was nighttime. She sat in the back seat on her mother's lap, speeding away from her fate, rather than to it, as now.

Other memories swirled in her mind—the fire, the blood, the sacrilegious rituals in the darkness, the robed figures who'd been her family, some in the literal sense and others merely regarded as such because of the powers they shared.

Suddenly, the significance of what lay ahead of her crystallized. She was going home.

Home. The word hammered in her skull, an abomination to the true meaning in every sense. She was returning to darkness rather than the light she'd been born to. A darkness ready to devour her soul. And in the midst of the darkness, Jase waited, hurt and wounded and crying out for her.

Indeed, she was going home. But only for Jase.

As if Marc had read her thoughts, he leaned forward and stroked one wayward curl near her cheek. "Welcome home, Kayla."

And with his touch came a cold numbness that worked its way through her body. A cold that obliterated Jase's image, sucked away her will and her sanity, until she could do nothing but slump back against the seat.

Welcome home.

CHAPTER TWELVE

"I knew you weren't completely done for." The familiar voice cut through the thick silence of the room.

Jase tried to open his eyes, but the onslaught of light forced them shut again. Still, he felt the presence—cold and intense like an ice statue suspended above him.

"We should have left you at the cabin to burn." The voice came closer and Jase felt the brush of a robe against his bare shoulder. He flinched as a searing pain ripped through his body. Waves of heat slammed over him to stir his blood to a frenzy and jar him from oblivion.

"Oh, do forgive me, dear boy. I forgot the sad shape you're in." A chilling laugh erupted. Fingers followed the motion of the robe, grazed Jase's shoulder, then lingered to poke and prod the raw flesh.

Jase clenched his teeth against the pain, sucking in a sharp breath, clamping down on his bottom lip until he tasted a salty sweetness.

"Yes, very sad shape. But then, that's why I'm here. I thought I would put you out of your misery, out of the goodness of my heart, of course." More laughter, thundering through Jase's head, making his skin turn to gooseflesh despite the flame that ate away at half of his body.

Jase's eyes snapped open the moment the blade touched his throat. He felt only a slight pressure, just enough to draw a thin line of blood, which slid down his heated flesh like a trickle of boiling oil.

"Would you look at what I've done?" Max Talbot asked, a malicious gleam in his black eyes as he stared down at Jase. The flicker of the candles cast writhing shadows across his pale face. His eyes seemed deeper, more sunken, his features severe. "Didn't mean to nick you, dear boy. Merely plotting the path I'm going to cut."

He smiled then and traced a trail straight down the center of Jase's bare chest with the tip of the gleaming knife. A thin line of fire marked his path. Jase drew in a ragged breath and grappled for his last bit of strength. But he had none. He was frozen, a slab of meat on the concrete altar, awaiting the butchering he knew would come.

Jase closed his eyes, resigned to his fate. He'd spilled blood in this very room, the crimson symbols that covered the black walls evidence of the countless sacrifices made. In a way, it seemed poetic justice that his life should end as all the others before him. Now he would know the helplessness, the agony as the life drained from his body. He would pay for what he'd done, and the nightmares would end.

"You should have given up long before now, Jase. You would have saved us so much trouble. We would have had Kayla with us long ago, ready and willing to take her place among us."

Kayla. Her name came like a rush of arctic wind, numbing him to the pain, fueling his strength. He managed to open his eyes.

"Surprised?" Max lifted a dark eyebrow and held the knife in front of him. "You shouldn't be. You knew we would prevail. That's why you gave in and bedded her. Tell me, Jase," Max murmured, running a pale finger along the blade and gathering the crimson drops, "was the real thing as good as your dreams?"

"Hurt her and I'll kill you," Jase said from between clenched teeth.

"Oh, really? That, indeed, would be a miracle and I stopped believing in those many years ago."

"Where's Kayla?" Jase managed to ask, despite his raw throat, which screamed in protest.

"Getting ready for the ceremony. Our Kayla is quite a busy girl." He smiled, staring at the knife in crazed fascination. "Two lovers in one day. And to think, your body won't even be cold when she joins with Miles. I wonder if she'll like him more? I must admit, you'll be a tough act to follow after last night."

Always watching... listening... knowing.

Jase balled his fingers into a fist, desperate to concentrate on something other than the pain and Max's taunting voice. Something other than the damned vision of Kayla and Miles that filled his head.

"Don't worry yourself. I'm sure Miles will please her. He's been looking forward to this. We all have. We'd hoped the two of them would have become intimate by now. That's why we sent him to the radio station—to give him time to seduce her. It would have made tonight so much easier. But, alas, we didn't know we would have you to contend with." He leaned closer. "Neither did Kayla, I'm sure. You might have spoiled her, Jase. I wonder if she'll think of you when Miles is inside of her, spilling his seed?"

Max's words formed a vivid picture in Jase's mind. He heard Kayla's screams, saw her tears as his brother hovered above her.

Jase reached up and grasped Max's wrist. The knife clattered to the floor. Surprise flickered across the other man's features. Briefly. Then it was gone, hidden beneath the fury twisting his face.

"You're strong, Jase. You always have been. But you've got one weakness—you don't have a stomach for the killing. That's why you didn't finish me off twenty-two years ago. Your mistake, I must say."

"I should have gutted you like the animal you are," Jase growled.

"You should have...but you didn't. Your biggest mistake yet. Now look at us—back here where we started." Max dipped his head a fraction, his putrid breath fanning Jase's face. "One of us *will* die this time. I promise you that."

"You—" Jase's fingers dug into Max's wrist.

"No, dear boy. This time, I'll have the last laugh. Your father was a fool to think you could be trusted again. It would have served him right to lose Kayla and his last chance at immortality. In fact, I might have intervened to see that happen, but if your father dies, the power dies. And I've become quite fond of what I am." He let out a deep sigh. "But that doesn't change the fact that your father's a weak, old fool."

"A weak, old fool who'll cut out your heart," Jase rasped, "and laugh the entire time if he hears your traitorous words."

"Maybe he would have—once, a long time ago. No more. He's weaker now. Dying. Tonight, he'll be reborn, the past forgotten, the future a promise of power and darkness for another lifetime. With his new life, he'll leave behind the old. Immortality will erase his memory. He'll know only the darkness. You'll be forgotten—a bad dream that vanishes once the sun rises. That's all you've ever been, Jase. A bad dream. One about to end."

Max reached down and scooped up the knife, oblivious to Jase's hold on his wrist.

Jase stared up at the *athame* as Max lifted it overhead, the blade a dazzling flash of brilliance against the pitch black of the sanctuary. The silver streaked above him, like a shimmering rainbow trailing down.

A white-hot pain wrenched through Jase's chest and he drew a breath through his teeth. The moment of blinding sensation fed his consciousness and brought every nerve in his body alive.

Waves of heat jolted through him as his blood spilled and spread across the altar where he lay. He smelled the pungent odor of life, death and the in-between, that half-life where time seems suspended, the pain gripping, excruciating, as precious oxygen drains and the spirit slips away.

Through glazed eyes, Jase watched the progress of the knife. Back up through the air, raised high once again. The blade dripped red. Max laughed, the sound a muffled intrusion into Jase's mind that mingled with the thunder of his heartbeat—the only reminder he still lived and breathed. But not for long.

Once again, the blade flashed a blinding silver, like silver tears...tears of the moon...shed for two lost children now separated. Each lost in the darkness. Alone. Scared.

Kayla's image materialized before him, so close he could touch her, smell her. She hovered within arm's reach, her pale cheeks streaked with tears. Then he saw her lips move, call to him, her voice an urgent cry that rattled his soul, stirred his strength and fed the restless beast within him.

The knife arced down, in slow motion, it seemed, as rage boiled, overflowed and Jase's body fired to life. His arms shot up to meet the challenge that Death was dealing him.

And even Max Talbot, a man with his own powers and his own ties to the darkness, was little match for the devil himself.

"It's time, Kayla."

Kayla blinked her eyes, her gaze darting around the spacious bedroom where she stood, from the antique four-poster bed to the cherrywood armoire against the far wall. She gazed down at the black robe she wore, her bare toes peeking out from beneath the edges, and searched her mind for the past few hours. How had she come to be here? And where was here?

She remembered Marc…his chilling fingers stroking her hair, her temples…then the blackness.

Home.

"They're waiting for us," Rickie murmured, tucking her brown braid beneath the collar of her robe. Her ruby ring caught shafts of light from the fire warming the hearth. Prisms of red flashed against the walls like demons gyrating to some silent melody. The woman extended her hand, the red demons streaking across the wall to Kayla. "Come," she said, the word more in invitation than command. Still, Kayla heard the unmistakable threat just below the surface.

"Where is Jase?" she asked, his image vivid in her mind. Calling to her. Begging help.

"You'll see him after the ceremony, *if* you cooperate," Rickie said, a thread of steel in her voice. "Otherwise…"

Her words trailed off and Kayla's mind filled in the rest. Frightening images assaulted her—Jase's lifeless eyes staring into the blackness. Blood gushing across a stained altar. Flames rising, consuming. The black demon *Ashtaroth,* like a giant billow of smoke, claiming Jase's soul.

"His fate rests in your hands, Kayla," Rickie said.

Without a moment's hesitation, Kayla stepped forward.

Rickie led her from the room, down a long hallway to a spiral staircase. They descended. Kayla counted the steps as she counted her breaths, desperate to stay calm. To feel nothing, no panic, no dread, no terror, no fear. Only the fierce instinct to protect.

They entered a summerhouse. Shimmering beams of light poured through the clear roof. The luster of the moon, waxing full and silver above, lent an unearthly glow to the white tulips that lined the walkway.

Kayla continued to count her steps, focusing on the chilly stone path beneath her feet. The air was warm, like that of a fresh spring night so as to keep the garden in full bloom, yet cold drafts snaked around her ankles with each step, each slight shift of her robe. She shivered, only to curse herself silently.

A door opened in front of her, then closed behind, and the garden disappeared. The smell of life became a faint memory as she walked on, past an ivy-covered wall to the clearing beyond.

In the clearing, there was no familiar sound of night insects like the ones she'd heard on the other side of the wall. The air was still. Expectant. Kayla found herself surrounded by what she could only call Death—a living, breathing death that circled her, creeping steadily upon her like a night stalker. Death's only intent was to devour her until she stood as lifeless as the dozens of Keepers lining the perimeter of the clearing. They appeared an army of silent shadows, standing at attention, waiting for orders to close in and pounce.

Kayla's attention riveted on the center of the circle where a black marble altar had been erected. The smooth planes gleamed dark perfection in the moonlight. The architecture was superb, the edges carved into serpent heads, eyes inlaid with gleaming red rubies. The entire creation seemed so out of place in such a desolate place. Such a *dead* place.

Large piles of kindling stood at each end of the altar, the wood stacked high in obvious anticipation of the ceremony. The blaze would burn with the fury of the demon it conjured as Marc and Kayla came together.

Her thoughts skidded to a halt as she watched a single robed figure approach the center of the circle, a torch in his hand. With a sweep of his arm, he set each pile of wood ablaze. The flames rose, writhing and dancing with frenzied zeal.

Kayla stopped in midstride. Fear jolted through her. No, not fear. Pure terror as she stared deep into the fire.

She saw the shimmering blue wall.

Jase's cobalt image on the opposite side.

Run, Kayla! His voice sang through her head and she closed her eyes, her heart crying out for him, pleading for help she knew he couldn't give. She was on her own.

"No!" she gasped, panicked when Rickie tried to pull her forward. "I—I can't."

Then Marc materialized from the shadows, his grip on her arm viselike, refusing to give. "You can," he said, voice as cold as the night air which turned her cheeks to ice. "And you will, or Jase will die." Marc stared down at her, eyes intense, compelling, hood pulled back to reveal his pale blond mane, which gleamed like angel's hair in the dim light.

Not an angel. A demon. She longed to turn and bolt for freedom. But she couldn't. They had Jase.

Jase... His name echoed. Memories swamped her and she saw his face, mouth hinting at a smile, eyes so deep and mesmerizing she wanted to drown in them.

"Come, Kayla," Marc beckoned to her again, his voice low, firm, refusing to be denied. But it wasn't Marc who drew her forward. It was Jase.

"I knew you were smart, love. Smart and very beautiful." They stopped just short of the altar and he turned to face her, their bodies a fraction apart. Marc gazed down at her with eyes that glittered, pitch-black and ominous now, with no trace of blue. "Very beautiful." He trailed cold fingers across her cheek. Her stomach churned.

Kayla held his gaze, her breathing slow, easy. Calm. Controlled. Relaxed.

"It's time," another voice declared.

Kayla swung around as far as Marc's hold permitted, to see where the circle parted. Another robed figure seemed to float toward her. He wore no hood, his hair a silvery white, his eyes chips of ebony ice. He cradled a tattered black book in his arms. A purposeful expression etched his weathered features.

She stared at the other faces surrounding her. Some she recognized from her childhood. They seemed older, their features harsher. Others were strangers.

Her gaze came to a jolting halt when she spotted a familiar pile of red hair, the heavily made-up features. Gracie, the security guard from her building, stared back at her, eyes dark, glittering, and Kayla felt betrayal knife through her yet again. Indeed, what Marc had said was true. The Keepers had been everywhere. Always watching. Always.

Alexander dropped to his knees at the altar. "The hour draws nigh. Let us begin." He closed his eyes and placed the book on the marble slab next to his other tools—the chalice, the ebony serpent's wand, the charred pentagram. He opened the book's cover and paged through until he found his place. He flung his head back. A string of incoherent syllables poured from his lips. The wind stirred to life within the circle.

Next, when Alexander leveled a stare at her, his eyes were like gleaming coals. She felt invisible fingers caress her cheeks, her jawline, turning her skin to gooseflesh. Despite the heat in his eyes, Kayla felt only cold. A cold intensity that slowed her heartbeat and chilled her blood.

His gaze dropped, and she felt the same touch at her breasts. Wind licked at the ends of her robe, to dip beneath and do all that its master bid. The touch moved lower, down her belly—a damp cold that slithered across her bare flesh, to wrap around her like a serpent.

Wide-eyed, Kayla held her breath, afraid to move, terrified the sensation wasn't just an invisible force, but a *real* snake. Again, the damp cold circled her, winding, constricting.

"Now," Alexander whispered, closing his eyes, his palms flat on the pages of the black book. The kindling blazed, sparked, then burned with renewed frenzy, lighting the smooth surface of the marble.

Voices joined and an eerie chant filled the night, taunting, coaxing. The hypnotic melody slid into Kayla's ears, filtered through her body and drowned out her spirit's violent protests.

Marc released her to remove his robe. His eyes locked with hers, his stare probing, drilling into her. The robe pooled at his feet, his body an ivory carving—hard, cold, reflecting orange brilliance in the firelight. The hands that reached out to Kayla were firm, purposeful, and so very chilling. And she wanted to pull away, to run screaming from the horrible nightmare unfolding in front of her eyes.

Strength. The word whispered through her mind, the voice familiar, stirring her grief and making her eyes sting.

"No," the word slipped from her lips even though she'd vowed to endure whatever she had to. The small protest was inconsequential, considering the fact that she couldn't force herself to pull away. She wanted to. God, how she wanted to! But she couldn't move lest the cold tighten around her and shut off her air for good.

Marc's hands went to the closure of her robe and then she was naked, as well. The frigid wind gripped her, shook her until she caught her bottom lip to stop its trembling. If only she could lift her arm, shove him away.

Her gaze darted wildly, searching for an escape.

But the Keepers surrounded her.

Watching, listening.

Their chant grew louder as they tried to seduce her with their voices. Then Marc touched her, and Kayla felt a black chill sweep her insides, close around her heart, and slowly, painfully, rip her soul away.

"Come, Kayla," he whispered, his touch purposeful, his gaze all-consuming.

And then she felt the cold marble slab at her back and Marc moved over her, blocking out the moon and the stars and the watchful stares. She saw only him poised above her. His rough hands urged her legs apart.

"...we call upon your power," Alexander Terrell's voice pushed its way past the frantic beat of Kayla's heart. "In return we offer devotion, the blood of innocents...a new spirit to do your bidding, perpetuate your knowledge..." His words became a distant drone as Kayla's heart hammered faster, louder, threatening to burst from her chest.

Marc's icelike touch moved up the inside of one thigh, his legs pinning hers, holding her prisoner. "Beautiful," he murmured. The word seemed to come from *inside* her head, as if he'd invaded her thoughts as he was about to invade her body. "And you'll be mine...soon."

"Jase!" she managed to cry. Anger and fear reeled into a whirlwind of emotion that funnelled through her. She stared up into Marc's crazed eyes, and she knew, even before she heard his next words, that fulfilling the promise wouldn't save Jase.

"He's as good as dead, Kayla," Marc hissed, as he positioned himself to thrust into her. "Dead."

"No!" Kayla screamed, legs kicking, arms pushing.

Marc drew back. Only enough to jam his knee between the legs she tried to clamp together, his thighs holding her prisoner. "This is meant to be," he growled, gripping her wrists and pinning her arms above her head. "Cooperate, or I'll have Jase's body dragged out here."

Helplessness fed her fear. Fear fed her rage. And fury rose like a tidal wave gathering momentum.

Kayla, the voice whispered through her mind. Jase's voice, so deep and strong and reassuring. *Resist! Remember who you are, moonchild. What you are. A Keeper, like your ancestors, with powers and a will to battle any enemy, seen or unseen.*

Kayla's mind returned to the cabin, to the burst of flames in the kitchen when Jase had tried to overpower her. Fire had sparked at her glance. Fire that had blazed as hot as her anger. Fire. Power.

And the tidal wave broke, smashing inside of her and forcing a tormented wail from her lips. She wrenched her wrists from Marc's grasp and shoved at his chest.

He looked stunned for a moment—long enough for Kayla to twist onto her side before he clamped his hands around her and tried to fling her onto her back.

"Hold her down!" Alexander shouted, his face a mass of wrinkles and creases, as if he'd aged a hundred years in the past five minutes. His life was slipping away. From the desperate rage glowing in his eyes, it was clear he didn't intend to let it go peacefully. Silver glinted as he unsheathed a huge knife.

Kayla struggled, grasping at the golden chalice that sat at the edge of the altar. Twisting, she slammed it into Marc's temple. He swayed, shock on his face. A rivulet of blood snaked a ruby path down his cheek.

A string of curses erupted and Marc's hands became almost clawlike, biting into her shoulder, sending pain screaming through her body.

Strength. Jase's voice whispered through her mind again, steadying her heart, feeding her courage. She reached for the ebony wand.

And Marc's fist crashed into her face, sending her spinning into a world of pain.

"Kayla!" Jase's voice was real this time, pulling her back to reality, forcing her eyes open.

Marc and Alexander stared at the break in the circle of Keepers where Jase, wounded and bloody and barely standing, had pushed his way through.

The chanting stopped.

"Seize him!" Alexander commanded and a mob of Keepers turned on Jase.

"Noooooo!" Kayla wailed, making a mad grab for Alexander's black book. "Leave him alone!" she cried, whipping the book up in front of her.

"Never!" Alexander snapped. He whirled on her, knife poised and ready. "Give the book to me!"

"Never!" she echoed, thrusting the book of shadows into the fire near her head.

Then all hell broke loose.

The fire flared higher, sparks showered and Alexander reeled backward, bursting into a mass of flames. His tormented shriek pierced her ears.

The sparks arced over her, like a brilliant orange rainbow, leading to their next target.

Marc screamed as his hair caught fire, flamed, spread until the blaze swallowed him up and he fell away from her.

Kayla scrambled from the altar, away from the fire and the blazing figures of Marc and Alexander Terrell.

Anguished wails split the night and Kayla whipped around. The fire had risen to reach out with fiery tentacles toward the surrounding Keepers. Robes flared, hair ignited and the stench of burning flesh and something much more rotten—evil incarnate—rushed at Kayla in a furl of smoke. She swung around toward the spot where she'd seen Jase, now a blaze of dead bodies.

A crippling loss swept through her and she sank to her knees. The fire burned hotter, brighter. The flames joined at the center of the circle to form a huge ball of orange fury that lived and breathed and consumed the Keepers. And Jase...

Dead. Marc's voice replayed in her mind. Now it was true. Jase was lost forever. *Forever.*

"Kayla!"

She turned at the sound of her name, to see Gracie, the only other person not being devoured by flames. The woman moved toward her, arms outstretched, eyes wide

with fear and concern and something else—an emotion
Kayla felt deep inside. A completeness, like the lost piece
of a puzzle finally fit into place. In a crystalline moment,
Kayla realized the final truth.

Mother.

Questions whirled through Kayla's mind. Endless questions as she stared into eyes so similar to her own. Eyes
filled with knowledge and love. Her *mother's* eyes.

"I was close by all those years, baby," Gracie cried,
dropping to her knees to wrap her arms around Kayla.
"Always watching you. I wanted to do more, to protect
you, but Alexander was too powerful. He forced me back
to the coven and tried to make me into what he and the
others were." She shook her head. "I fought him, fooled
him. Inside, I never changed. Never!" She pulled away,
shrugged off her robe to reveal a plain black gown, then
draped the cloak around Kayla's bare shoulders.

"You're alive," Kayla said, the words singing through
her head. Shock holding her stiff. *"Alive."*

"I was there, baby," her mother went on, touching
warm hands to Kayla's face. "Even when you didn't know
it, I was looking after you."

"I know," Kayla murmured, marveling at how familiar her mother's voice was. The same voice that had sung
lullabies, told bedtime stories. The same voice she'd heard
the past year when she'd left her job at the station every
morning. She'd never made the connection, never seen the
truth right in front of her. Not consciously, anyway, but
she'd known. Deep in her heart, she'd always known.

"I felt you," Kayla whispered into her mother's embrace. "All along I felt you."

A strange high-pitched wail split open the night. Kayla
pulled away from her mother, and froze.

"Oh, my God!" she gasped. Her gaze riveted on the
apparitions rising from the steadily burning flames. She
saw the sea of faces, eyes wide, spirits screaming of inno-

cence and vulnerability. They ascended into the black night, to blend and vanish into the silver glow of the moon.

Nameless faces. Innocent people. Years of sacrifices to the demon that Alexander Terrell and the other Keepers had made pacts with to secure their power. Now the souls of their victims were free.

She was free.

Jase would have been free...

"Kayla." His voice came to her, clear, distinct. He seemed to materialize from the smoke and flames, staggering toward her as if he might collapse at any moment.

"Jase! Oh, my God, Jase!" She lunged to her feet and rushed toward him.

He stumbled just as she reached him. Wrapping her arms around his waist, she tried to hold him, but he slipped from her grasp. He fell to his knees, the force of his weight bringing her down with him.

"I thought you were dead!" she cried, touching his soot-covered face. "I thought—"

"No," he cut in. "I told you I wouldn't leave you." His voice was a pained whisper as he doubled over, arms wrapped around his middle. "I promised you, moon-child."

She glanced down to see the blood on his hands. So much blood. "You're hurt—" Her words stopped as she noted two more wounds on his chest. His entire body shuddered with each frantic breath. He slumped forward. Hot tears spilled down Kayla's cheeks.

She gathered him in her arms and cradled his head on her lap. He still held his middle, as if he could hold in the precious life seeping from his wounds. A thin line of blood trickled from the corner of his mouth as his lips parted.

"Kayla," he rasped, forcing his eyes open. "You're alive..." His smile was nothing more than the faint crook of his lip, but it dazzled nonetheless. Kayla drank in the sight.

"Yes. Thanks to you. You came into my life and saved me, Jase. My savior."

His upper body quaked as he tried to breathe. Kayla's tears came faster.

"That's all...I ever wanted," he panted. "Ever..." His face twisted in pain—a pain that flowed through Kayla's fingertips to knife through her until she hurt as much as he did. "Now it's done. Over."

"No. No, it's not over, Jase," she said, her voice filled with desperation. Frantically, she balled the ends of her robe and pressed the material to his wounds. If she could just stop the bleeding. "We'll get you to a hospital," she rushed on, unwilling to accept that he was slipping away from her. They'd fought too hard, been through too much. "My mother's here. She'll help us. This isn't over! It *isn't!* Just hold on!"

"It hurts..."

"I know—" The words caught on a sob. She shook her head, denying the truth that was staring her in the face. Death waited to snatch him away and she knew she had to do something. *Anything.* "I can feel your pain, Jase. Concentrate. Let me take all the pain from you so you don't have to feel it. Maybe that'll buy us time and we can get some help—"

"No!" He gasped for a breath. "It's too late."

"Then just let me feel *for* you. Please! I can't stand to see you hurt, Jase. I can't stand it! *Please!* I'll take the pain—all of it."

"The pain is good." A shudder went through him and she held him tighter, absorbing what he felt the way a sponge soaks up water. Her chest burned, her throat caught fire and she wanted nothing more than to sink to the ground and close her eyes.

She didn't. She forced a breath and held him closer. "There's nothing good about pain."

"For me, it is. Penance, Kayla." He swallowed, the sound choked. "These hands...have been soiled...too many times."

"The sacrifices weren't your fault. Nothing was. You were a victim, Jase. Their *victim!*"

"A willing victim...at the end. I had given up...did you know?" He closed his eyes, as if he couldn't bear to look her in the eyes. "Too weak to resist them, to resist you...couldn't help myself."

"It's okay—"

"The worst part is...I don't regret it..." Words failed him as he winced, gasped, winced again. "The evil took control...but...it was still me. *I* held you, touched you." Pain twisted his mouth again as he sucked for another breath.

"Don't talk," she whispered. Tears blinded her. His pain blurred her vision. Then she felt his fingers close around hers.

Slowly, he came into focus. His eyes were open. Silver fused with topaz and he squeezed her hand tighter as if he never meant to let go. "Thank you," he whispered, the sound full of pain and desperation. In that moment, he seemed to find his voice, all his effort fixed on saying the words that burned within him. "You gave me the only peace I've ever known. I'll meet you on the other side one day, and I'll love you then, as much as I do right now."

And his eyes closed.

And there was no more moon, no more stars. Nothing.

"Nooooooo!" Kayla wailed, her anguished voice carrying on the wind. She tilted her face to the sky and raised her arms in surrender, begging for Jase's life with all of her own.

Palms high, hands trembling, she stared into the moon, holding its silver gaze, drinking in the heavenly light.

The tingling started in her hands, washed through her body until she felt radiant and more alive than ever. Life itself fired through her and she gathered Jase in her arms and held him.

"Please!" she begged, sobbing, holding him close, willing and praying for the soft echo of his heart, the slight movement of his chest. "I love you, Jase. I love you."

The clear, black velvet sky rumbled above and Kayla felt the soft splash of rain on her face. The drops came like a rejuvenating shower, extinguishing the flames around her and washing away the evil and the death and the destruction.

Tears of the moon cleansing two of its lost children.

Two children who'd braved the darkness and found each other.

The rain stopped. The moon disappeared behind a wall of shadows. And the night closed in.

And Kayla heard the faint thump of a heartbeat.

EPILOGUE

"It's half-past midnight on a warm Dallas night and you're listening to KPZX, the hottest rock-and-roll spot on your FM dial. I'm the night child, Kayla Terrell, and I'll be kicking off a long-play compact-disc weekend where you'll hear your favorite CDs uninterrupted. Let's get things rolling with some Pink Floyd."

Kayla slid the mixing level up and the sizzle of an electric guitar filled her ears.

Leaning back in her chair, she swept a glance around the dim control room. A single overhead lamp poured light across the mixing console. Windows spanned the length of one wall, affording her a spectacular view of the Dallas skyline. The moon waxed full, bathing the city in a pale celestial light.

But Kayla no longer needed the light. The darkness didn't hold any more secrets. No more stalking shadows, no more fear and no more loneliness. The Keepers were gone ... Alexander, Marc, Rickie ... the evil extinguished, once and for all.

With a deep sigh, she put her headset on, adjusted the volume to a moderate level and reached for the latest issue of *Dallas Metropolitan*. Thumbing through the pages, she flipped the magazine open to the center layout—a photo spread on several valuable pieces of art currently being displayed at a prestigious Dallas museum. Jase's byline stared back at her, bold and black at the bottom of the page, in its usual spot since he'd signed an exclusive contract with the magazine.

She smiled, then put the magazine aside to reach for a stack of CDs scheduled for the next hour.

She sang the words to the melody drifting over her headset, her thoughts going to Jase. He'd shown her the difference between heaven and hell, love and lust, good and evil. Her life was now filled with more joy than she'd ever imagined. For someone who'd walked in the dark for so long, she now stood in the light, and she relished every minute of it.

"You have a very lovely voice," the deep male rumble cut through the music on her headset, the voice sliding into her ears, spiraling through her.

Kayla closed her eyes as a smile tugged at her lips. "You think so?" she murmured. "I'll give you a live performance sometime."

"Tonight?"

"Maybe," she replied. "If I'm not too tired. I still have three hours left on my shift. I'll probably be half asleep by the time I get home."

"I'll wait up for you," he offered, the underlying sensuality of his words holding her prisoner. "And then I'll wake you up."

"I just bet you will."

"Since I have to wait, why don't you give me a little preview of coming attractions," the words were a low, seductive whisper, filled with promise and unchecked desire.

"But I'm all alone—"

"No," he interrupted, the word followed by a tap on the window.

She glanced up to see him in the hallway outside the control booth, a silhouette of a man, a dark shadow blending into the surrounding darkness as if he were a part of it.

"Open the door," he said, his voice husky, sending a tingle of anticipation sizzling down her spine.

Kayla was opening the door as she took her next breath—a breath that caught in her chest the moment Jase moved through the doorway and pulled her flush against him. He backed her into the room, closing the door behind them before capturing her lips in a kiss that sapped the strength from her body.

"How long before your assistant comes back?" he murmured, his lips moving against hers with hungry persuasion.

"Thirty—" But she didn't get a chance to finish. He was kissing her again. With little effort, he lifted her onto the counter next to the control board. His hands drifted from her thighs to her breasts where he molded the soft knit of her blouse to nipples that throbbed and begged for him.

Jase caught her moan, trailing his tongue across her bottom lip. He sucked and nibbled and stroked until Kayla thought she would surely scream with the ache gripping her body.

An ache that six months with him hadn't begun to ease. Kayla knew in her heart that six years, or even sixty, wouldn't quell her need for Jase Terrell. He was a fever that burned her clear to the bone. A sweet malady that had no cure, for she had a fatal case of love for this man—her savior, friend, lover.

"We're not really going to do this here, are we?" she managed to ask when he pulled away to lick a path down the side of her neck. "Mickey might come back early."

"The security light will come on if he does."

"You've been doing your homework," she murmured as she glanced at the lifeless red bulb above the door. "I completely forgot about the security light."

"I wouldn't let my wife spend her nights here if I didn't think she was safe, and I don't expect you to think straight right now. In fact, I'm trying very hard to keep you from thinking at all. Just feel . . ."

With a seductive smile, Kayla wrapped her arms around his neck, only to have him pull away from her as if a thought had just struck him.

"You're feeling all right, aren't you?" He eyed her with a thoroughness that made her smile. His eyes blazed with worry and barely checked hunger. "Your mother told me some women get more tired than others—"

"I'm fine," she assured him. She trailed a finger over his bottom lip, catching her breath when he sucked the tip inside to nibble the sensitive flesh near her knuckle. "Both of you need to stop worrying about me."

He moved her hand from his mouth. "If you're feeling queasy or tired or—"

"Fine," she cut in, shrugging free and placing her fingers over his lips again. "Better, in fact, because you're here."

"I'll always be here," he said, placing a kiss on her palm. Then his hands went to her slightly rounded abdomen and he stroked her with a reverence that made her eyes sting. "And a part of me will always be here. At least for the next four months, anyway."

"That part of you kicked the devil out of me earlier."

He gave her a wicked smile. "And I thought I was the one responsible for that."

Laughter bubbled from her lips. "Your son is carrying on the tradition."

"Son?"

"Let's just say I have this feeling, and Dixie desperately wants a little boy. Since Wanda found out her new baby's going to be a girl, Dixie sees our baby as her chance to have a little brother, as well as a new sister." She smiled. "I'm so glad things are going well for Wanda and Floyd. She deserved a good man in her life after all her struggles. And Dixie adores her new daddy. As much as this baby is going to adore his daddy."

Jase smiled, then his expression grew serious, his shadowed jaw set, his eyes drilling into her. "I want you, but I can wait, Kayla. It won't be easy. Just looking at you makes me ache all over, but I can—I *will* wait. Are you sure you feel all right?"

"Almost."

Worry creased his handsome features. "What's wrong?"

"Maybe you can wait, but I can't. You've wasted five of my thirty minutes, and I'm not a patient woman." With those words, she slipped her arms around his neck and pulled him to her.

"I love you," he said, his voice low, fierce.

"And I love you, Jase Terrell," she murmured, parting her lips to meet his.

For the next twenty-five minutes, with the music beating the same frenzied rhythm as her heart, Kayla gave herself to Jase, her body transformed by sensations as wild and potent as the man who held her. Loved her.

And, through the windows, the moon beamed silver brilliance, keeping watch over two of its own.

* * * * *

Welcome To The
Dark Side Of Love...

COMING NEXT MONTH

#66 FOREST OF THE NIGHT—Evelyn Vaughn
The Circle

The Witch: Something wicked had come to Stagwater, Louisiana, and Cypress Bernard was directly in its path. She had to fight it, but she couldn't do it alone. Only one man had the power to save her, but Drake Benedict refused to put himself on the line.

The Guardian: Within Drake's blood coursed the magic of light and darkness—a power that both frightened and tempted him. Because to protect Cypress, he would have to expose his very soul to evil...and risk the love they'd found.

This July, watch for the delivery of...

An exciting new miniseries that appears in a different Silhouette series each month. It's about love, marriage—and Daddy's unexpected need for a baby carriage!

Daddy Knows Last unites five of your favorite authors as they weave five connected stories about baby fever in New Hope, Texas.

- **THE BABY NOTION** by Dixie Browning
  (SD#1011, 7/96)

- **BABY IN A BASKET** by Helen R. Myers
  (SR#1169, 8/96)

- **MARRIED...WITH TWINS!**
  by Jennifer Mikels
  (SSE#1054, 9/96)

- **HOW TO HOOK A HUSBAND (AND A BABY)**
  by Carolyn Zane
  (YT#29, 10/96)

- **DISCOVERED: DADDY** by Marilyn Pappano
  (IM#746, 11/96)

Daddy Knows Last arrives in July...only from

TM

DKLT

BEGINNING IN APRIL
FROM

SILHOUETTE®

Desire®

The Wedding Night

Three passion-filled stories about what happens when the wedding ring goes on...and the lights go out!

In April—A kidnapped bride is returned to her husband in
FORGOTTEN VOWS by Modean Moon

In May—A marriage of convenience turns into so much more in
INSTANT HUSBAND by Judith McWilliams

In June—A once-reluctant groom discovers he's a father in
THE PRODIGAL GROOM by Karen Leabo

THE WEDDING NIGHT: The excitement began when they said, "I do."

Alicia Scott's

Elizabeth, Mitch, Cagney, Garret and Jake:

Four brothers and a sister—though miles separated
them, they would always be a family.

Don't miss a single, suspenseful—sexy—tale in
Alicia Scott's family-based series, which features four
rugged, untamable brothers and their spitfire sister:

THE QUIET ONE...IM #701, March 1996

THE ONE WORTH WAITING FOR...IM #713, May 1996

THE ONE WHO ALMOST GOT AWAY...IM #723, July 1996

"The Guiness Gang," found only in—

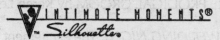

Silhouette's recipe for a sizzling summer:

* Take the best-looking cowboy in South Dakota
* Mix in a brilliant bachelor
* Add a sexy, mysterious sheikh
* Combine their stories into one collection and you've got one sensational super-hot read!

Summer Sizzlers

MEN OF Summer

Three short stories by these favorite authors:

Kathleen Eagle
Joan Hohl
Barbara Faith

Available this July wherever
Silhouette books are sold.

Look us up on-line at: http://www.romance.net

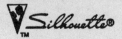

Silhouette®